Other Books by Edward D. Hoch

The Shattered Raven
The Judges of Hades
The Transvection Machine
The Spy and the Thief
City of Brass
Dear Dead Days (editor)
The Fellowship of the Hand
The Frankenstein Factory
Best Detective Stories of the Year 1976 (editor)
Best Detective Stories of the Year 1977 (editor)
Best Detective Stories of the Year 1978 (editor)
The Thefts of Nick Velvet
The Monkey's Clue & The Stolen Sapphire (juvenile)
Best Detective Stories of the Year 1979 (editor)
Best Detective Stories of the Year 1980 (editor)
Best Detective Stories of the Year 1981 (editor)
All But Impossible! (editor)
The Year's Best Mystery and Suspense Stories 1982 (editor)
The Year's Best Mystery and Suspense Stories 1983 (editor)
The Year's Best Mystery and Suspense Stories 1984 (editor)
The Quests of Simon Ark
Leopold's Way
The Year's Best Mystery and Suspense Stories 1985 (editor)
The Year's Best Mystery and Suspense Stories 1986 (editor)
The Year's Best Mystery and Suspense Stories 1987 (editor)
Great British Detectives (coeditor)
Women Write Murder (coeditor)
The Year's Best Mystery and Suspense Stories 1988 (editor)
Murder Most Sacred (coeditor)
The Year's Best Mystery and Suspense Stories 1989 (editor)
The Year's Best Mystery and Suspense Stories 1990 (editor)

THE YEAR'S BEST

MYSTERY AND SUSPENSE STORIES

1991

THE YEAR'S BEST
MYSTERY AND SUSPENSE STORIES
1991

Edited by Edward D. Hoch

WALKER AND COMPANY
NEW YORK

All the characters and events portrayed in this work are fictitious.

First published in the United States of America in 1991
by Walker Publishing Company, Inc.

Published simultaneously in Canada by Thomas Allen & Son
Canada, Limited, Markham, Ontario

Library of Congress Cataloging-in-Publication Card Number
83-646567

Printed in the United States of America

2 4 6 8 10 9 7 5 3 1

CONTENTS

Introduction

The previous year's trend toward fewer mystery magazines and more anthologies of original stories continued during 1990. Despite promises of new magazines both here and in England, the only two widely distributed publications remained *Ellery Queen's Mystery Magazine* and *Alfred Hitchcock's Mystery Magazine.*

There were a few bright spots in the magazine field, however. Women's periodicals like *Cosmopolitan, Woman's Day* and *Woman's World* continued to use mystery and suspense stories to varying degrees, and in the men's field *Playboy* published three crime-suspense stories during the year, not counting excerpts from novels. The longtime fan publication *The Armchair Detective* began running three short stories in each quarterly issue. Although the initial reaction of its subscribers was mixed, the quality of the stories was quite high. There were also occasional literary magazines like *Crosscurrents* that devoted an entire issue to mystery fiction.

Mostly, though, the mystery market of the 1990s seemed to be original anthologies, often in a continuing series. From England last year we had *Winter's Crimes 22* and *New Crimes 2.* Canada brought us the aptly titled *Cold Blood III,* and the United States offered *Sisters in Crime 2* and *Sisters in Crime 3,* as well as the fourth volume of new stories from the Private Eye Writers of America.

The number of such anthologies presented a special problem for the anthologist attempting to choose the year's best, since several of them appeared late in the year, aimed at the Christmas book buyer. In a few cases Canadian and British anthologies that did not arrive in this country until after the first of the year had to be held for consideration during 1991.

The selections this year are especially strong, including for the first time in this series all five Edgar-nominated stories, by Lynne Barrett, Lawrence Block, Ed Gorman, Sue Grafton, and Clark Howard. It's interesting to note, too, that the series detective is still very much with us, represented here by Sue

Grafton's Kinsey Millhone, Bill Pronzini's Nameless, Ruth Rendell's Inspector Wexford, Donald E. Westlake's Dortmunder (both thief and occasional sleuth), and Carolyn Wheat's Cass Jameson.

I hope reading these stories will be as enjoyable as choosing them has been. My special thanks this year to Daniel Stashower, Eleanor Sullivan, and my wife, Patricia, who spotted some things I might have otherwise missed.

Edward D. Hoch

THE YEAR'S BEST

MYSTERY AND SUSPENSE STORIES

1991

LYNNE BARRETT

ELVIS LIVES

Although Lynne Barrett has published short fiction in various magazines and in a 1988 collection, The Land of Go, *from Carnegie Mellon University Press, her name is new to the mystery field. We hope the success of this story, which won the Mystery Writers of America Edgar award as the best of the year, will encourage her to give us more.*

"Vegas ahead—see that glow?" said Mr. Page. "That's the glow of money, babes."

Lee looked up. All the way from Phoenix he'd ignored the others in the car and watched the desert as it turned purple and disappeared, left them rolling through big nothingness. Now lights filled his eyes as they drove into town. Lights zipped and jiggled in the night. Ain't it just like humans, he thought, to set up all this neon, like waving fire in the dark to scare away the beasts, to get rid of your own fear. Lights ascended, filling in a tremendous pink flamingo. There was something silly about Las Vegas—he laughed out loud. "What's so funny, man?" the kid, Jango, asked with that flicker in the upper lip he'd been hired for, that perfect snarl.

Lee shrugged and leaned his cheek against the car window, studying the lights.

"He's just happy 'cause we're finally here," said Baxter. "Here where the big bucks grow and we can pick some, right?" Baxter was a good sort, always carrying Lee and the kid. A pro.

"Just you remember, babes, we're here to collect the bucks, not throw 'em down the slots." Mr. Page pulled into the parking lot of the Golden Pyramid Hotel and Casino. On a huge marquee, yellow on purple spelled out E L V I S, then the letters danced around till they said L I V E S. The lights switched to a display of Elvis's face. "They do that with a computer," said Mr. Page.

Lee, Baxter, and Jango were silent, staring up. The same look came over them, a look that spoke of steamy dreams and sadness women wanted to console. The face—they all three had it. Three Elvises.

It was surely a strange way to make a living, imitating another man. Sometimes Lee thought he was the only one of them who felt its full weirdness. As they moved their gear into the suite of the hotel provided for Talent, the others seemed to take it all for granted. Of course, Baxter had been doing Elvis for ten years. And the kid thought this was just a temporary gig that would bankroll a new band, a new album, where he'd be his punk-rock self, Jango. But Lee had never been in show business before. Maybe that was why it kept striking him as something horrifying, bringing the dead to life.

He threw his suitcase on a bed and went out to the living room, where the bar was stocked for Talent. He poured himself a whiskey and carried it back to sip while he unpacked. Or maybe, Lee thought, he was just getting into the role, like Mr. Page said to, understanding Elvis Presley's own hollow feeling. He played the sad, sick Elvis, after all. Maybe his horror was something the man had had himself in his later years as he echoed his own fame.

Lee snapped open his old leather suitcase, the same valise his mamma had forty years ago when she was on her honeymoon and getting pregnant with him. "Why buy something new?" he'd said when Cherry pestered him before their trip to New York that started all the trouble. "This is leather, the real thing—you can't get that any more."

Cherry admired fresh vinyl, though. Her wish for new things was so strong it tore her up, he could see. Game shows made her cry. She entered sweepstakes, stayed up late at night thinking of new ways to say why she should win in twenty-five words or less. There was so little he could give her, he *had* to let her enter him in the contest the Bragg *Vindicator* ran. New York wanted, as part of its Statue of Liberty extravanganza, dozens of Elvis Presley imitators, and Bragg, Tennessee, was going to send one. Cherry had always fancied he resembled Elvis—she used to roll around with delight when he'd sing "hunka hunka burnin' love" to her in bed. She borrowed a cassette deck and sent a tape of him in, along with a Polaroid taken once at a Halloween party.

When he won, Lee said he didn't have the voice for it, that great voice, but they said no one would notice, there'd be so many others up there, he could mouth the words. He could too sing, Cherry said—oh, she still loved him then—he sang just beautifully in church. There was little enough Cherry was proud of him for any more. They still lived in the trailer on his mamma's land, and now that he'd put it on a cement foundation and built on a porch it seemed all the more permanently true that they were never going to have it any better. He was picking up what jobs he could as an electrician since the profit went out of farming and their part of the country got depressed. A free trip to the Big Apple was maybe what they needed.

And it was fun. Lee liked the pure-dee craziness of the celebration, a whole city in love with itself. Cherry bought one of those Lady Liberty crowns and wore it with a sexy white dress she'd made with just one shoulder to it. When they were riding on the ferry he heard a man say, looking at them, "Duplication is America's fondest dream," and the man's friend laughed and answered, "Such is identity in a manufacturing nation." Lee glared at them, I ain't a duplicate, and anyway, he noticed, they both had the same fifties sunglasses and wrinkled jackets as everyone in soda-pop commercials. But when he got to rehearsal with all the other Elvises, he knew that, yes, it was hard to see them as real men instead of poor copies.

Because he had some age and gut on him, they put him toward the back, which was just fine. He didn't even feel too embarrassed during the show. After, he and Cherry were partying away when a white-haired man, very sharp in his western-tailored suit, came up and said Lee was just what he needed. Lee laughed loudly and said, "Oh, go on," but Cherry put Mr. Page's card inside her one-strap bra.

And when they were back home and Cherry sighing worse than ever over the slimy thin blond people on *Knots Landing*, Mr. Page showed up, standing on their porch with a big smile. Cherry had called him, but Lee couldn't be mad—it meant she thought he was good for something.

Mr. Page's plan was a show like a biography of Elvis in songs. And he wanted three impersonators. For the kid Elvis, who drove truck and struggled and did those first Sun sessions and Ed Sullivan, he'd found Jango, a California boy with the right hips and snarl. He had Baxter, who had experience doing Elvis at his peak, the movie star, the sixties Elvis. And he wanted Lee to be late Elvis, Elvis in gargantuan glittery costumes, Elvis on the road, Elvis taking drugs, Elvis strange, Elvis dying. "It's a great part, a tragic role," said Mr. Page. "The King—unable to trust anyone, losing Priscilla, trapped by his own fame—lonely, yes, tormented, yes, but always singing."

"Have you heard me sing?" Lee asked. He was leaning against the fridge in the trailer, drinking a beer.

Mr. Page beamed at his pose, at his belly. "Why, yes," he said. "I listened to the tape your lovely wife sent. You have a fine voice, big whatchacallit, baritone. So you break up a bit now and then or miss a note—that's great, babes, don't you see, it's his emotion, it's his ruin. You'll be beautiful."

And Cherry's eyes were shining and Mr. Page signed Lee up.

"Check, check, one two three," Baxter said into the mike. His dark Presley tones filled the Pharaoh's Lounge, where they'd spent the morning setting up.

"Man, what a system," Jango said to Lee. "If they'd let me do my stuff, my real stuff, on a system like this, I'd be starsville in a minute."

Lee looked over at the kid, who was leaning against an amp in the black-leather suit he'd had made after they played Indianapolis. Jango wasn't saving a penny, really—he kept buying star gear.

"Yeah, one of these nights," Jango said, "when I'm in the middle of a number—'All Shook Up,' I think—I'm just gonna switch right into my own material. You remember that song I played you, 'Love's a Tumor'?"

Lee grinned and finished his can of beer. Worst song he'd ever heard in his life.

"Yeah, they'd be shook up then, all right," said Jango.

Mr. Page came over to them. "Go hit some high notes on

there, kid," he said, "let's check out the treble." While Jango went over to the mike, Mr. Page said to Lee, "How you doing?"

Lee squatted down by the Styrofoam cooler they always stashed behind the drummer's platform, fished out a Coors, popped it open, stood drinking.

"You seem a little down, babes. Can I do something?"

"You can let me out of the contract so I can go on home," Lee said.

"Now, why should I do that? I could never find somebody else as good as you are. Why, you're the bleakest, saddest Elvis I've ever seen. Anyway, what home? But let me fix you up with a little something—some instant cheer, you know?" Mr. Page leaned over and put some capsules into the pocket of Lee's western shirt.

"What home" is right, Lee thought. He dug out one of the pills and washed it down with beer. Why not?

"Yeah, babes," said Mr. Page, "party. Here." He gave Lee a twenty. "After you get through here, go take a shot at the slot machines. But don't bet any more than that, right? We don't want you to lose anything serious."

"Oh, right," said Lee. He moved downstage to where Jango and Baxter were hacking around, singing "Check, Baby, Check" and dancing obscenely.

"My turn," said Lee and they went off so he could do his sound check.

He looked out into the theater filled with little tables set up in semicircles. Looks like a wedding reception, he thought, and laughed and then jumped back—we was always startled when he first heard his voice coming out through the speakers, it sounded so swollen and separate from him. It made him feel shy. He'd been so shy and frightened, he'd had to get drunk as hell the first time they did the show, and he'd been more or less drunk ever since. He started sweating as the men up on the catwalk aimed spots at him. They always had different lighting for him because he was bigger than the others. He squinted and went through his poses, singing lines for the sound check. The band took their places and swung in with him for a few bars of "Suspicious Minds," and then he was done and they started working on the band's levels.

He toured around the theater a bit, nodding to the technicians. Everywhere they went, Mr. Page hired local crews and Lee had found they were the only people he felt comfortable with. He'd always been good at electronics, ever since they trained him in the service, and hanging out with those crews the last few months he'd learned a lot. The Golden Pyramid had the most complicated system he'd seen. Up in the control booth, a fellow showed him the setup, talking about presets and digital display. The show always had the backdrop with pictures suggesting what was happening in Elvis's life. Up until now they'd done this with slide projections, but here it would be computerized, same as the sign outside. Lee looked out at the stage and the fellow tapped into a keyboard and showed him Graceland all made of bits of light and then the blazing THE KING LIVES! that would come on with his finale.

He said thanks and made his way back down behind the set. Might be computers that were the brains of it, but there was a whole lot of juice powering the thing back here. Usually, he could stand behind the scrim backstage and follow what was going on, but now he faced a humming wall of wires. He knelt down by a metal box with power cables running out of it and held out his hands. Seemed like he could feel the electricity buzzing right through the air. Or Mr. Page's party pills, maybe.

Lee went through the backstage door and found his way into the casino. Bright? The place made his head whirl. He changed his twenty and the cashier gave him a chit. If he stayed in the casino an hour, he got a free three-minute call anywhere in the country.

He got a waitress to bring him a drink and started feeding quarters into a slot machine. He had a hard time focusing on the figures as they spun. He was buzzed, all right. He tried to go slow. If he made his money last an hour, who would he call?

When they began rehearsing in Nashville, he called Cherry every Saturday. Cherry would put on the egg timer so they'd keep track of the long distance. Mr. Page was giving a stipend, but he said the real bucks would have to wait till they were on the road. Lee, Baxter, and Jango shared a room, twin beds with a pull-out cot, in a motel. Mr. Page drilled them every minute, made them walk and dance and smile like Elvis. They practiced their numbers all day and studied Elvis footage at night. To Lee, it was a lot like the service, being apart from Cherry and having all his time accounted for. In '68, when Lee was drafted, Cherry was still in high school—too young, her daddy said, to be engaged. He remembered calling her from boot camp, yearning for the sound of her but terrified when they did talk because she seemed so quiet and far away. Just like she sounded now.

They'd barely started on the road, trying out in Arkansas and Missouri, when Cherry gave him the axe. She'd filed papers, she said when she called. She was charging him with desertion—gone four months now, she said.

"I'll come right back tonight," said Lee.

"I won't be here. You can send the support money through my lawyer." She said she'd hired Shep Stanwix, a fellow Lee knew in high school and never did like. He'd grown up to play golf and politics.

Cherry was still talking about money, how they wanted compensatory damages. "I gave up my career for you, Lee Whitney," she said.

She'd gotten her cosmetology license when they were first married, but she'd never gone past shampoo girl. She always said it was hopeless building up a clientele out there in the country, anyway—everybody already had their regular. Only hair she ever cut was his. She said she liked its darkness and the way it waved up in the front, like Elvis's.

"You can come along with us," Lee said, his voice breaking. "I'll get Mr. Page to hire you on as our hairdresser—he's spending money on that, anyway, dyeing us all blue-black and training our sideburns."

"There's no use talking. It's desertion and that's that."

"But, Cherry, this was all your idea."

"Oops, there's the timer," Cherry said. "Gotta go now."

"Wait—we can keep talking, can't we?"

"Save your money," Cherry said. "I need it." She hung up.

When he called back, he got no answer, then or all night. In the morning he called his mamma and she said Cherry'd been going into town till all hours since the day he left and now she'd taken everything out of the trailer that wasn't attached and moved into Bragg.

Lee went to Mr. Page—they were playing the Holiday House in Joplin, Missouri—and said he quit. That was when Mr. Page explained that Lee'd signed a personal-service contract for two years with options to renew and no way out. "Anyway," said Mr. Page, "what's one woman more or less? There's plenty of them interested in you—didn't you hear the sobbing over you last night? You were sad, babes, you were moving."

"Ain't the right woman," said Lee.

The women who came to the show only depressed him. Every night, die-hard Elvis Presley fans, women with their hair permed big and their clothes too girlish, were out there sighing, screeching, whimpering over Jango and Baxter and him. They'd come back after the show and flirt—hoping to get back their young dreams, it seemed to Lee, trying to revive what was in truth as lost as Elvis. Baxter took a pretty one to bed now and then—he considered it a right after so much time in the role. But then sometimes Lee wasn't sure Baxter fully realized he wasn't Elvis. Jango confided he found these women "too country." He waited for the big towns and went out in his punk clothes to find teenage girls who'd want him as himself. Lee slept alone, when he could get drunk enough to sleep.

When they were in Oklahoma, he got the forms from Shep Stanwix. He sent Cherry monthly checks. He had more money now than ever in his life and less to spend it on that mattered. Now and then he bought things he thought were pretty—a lapis lazuli pin, a silver bracelet made by Indians—and sent them to Cherry, care of Shep. No message—no words he could think of would change her mind.

One night in Abilene Jango said he was going crazy so far from civilization and good radio and tried to quit. When he understood his contract, he went for Mr. Page in the hotel bar but Lee and Baxter pulled him off. Why? Lee wondered now. They dragged Jango up to his room and Baxter produced some marijuana and the three of them smoked it and discussed their situation.

"It's two years' steady work," Baxter said. "That's hard enough to find."

Lee nodded. He lay back across the bed. The dope made him feel like he was floating.

"Two years!" Jango stood looking at himself in the big mirror. "When two years are up I'll be twenty-three. Man, I'll be *old*."

Lee and Baxter had to laugh at him.

"Thing is," Lee said, "he tricked us."

"Not me," said Baxter. "I read the contract. Why didn't you?"

Lee remembered Cherry's hand on his shoulder as he signed. Remembered Mr. Page saying what a sweet Miss Liberty she made. And he felt Bax was right, a man's got to take responsibility for his mistakes.

Baxter passed the joint to Jango, who sucked on it and squinted at himself in the mirror.

"Mr. Page is building something up here," Baxter said. "What if we were quitting on him all the time and he had to keep training replacements? As it is—do you know he's hiring on a steady band? They'll travel in a van with the equipment while we go in the car. And he's upgrading the costumes. Not long, he says, till we'll be ready for Vegas. It's like what Colonel Parker did for Elvis."

Jango swiveled his hips slow motion in front of the mirror. " 'Colonel Tom Parker was a show-biz wizard,' " he quoted from his part of the show. He laughed. "Page wrote that. 'He guided me. And I' "—Jango's voice deepened into Memphis throb—" 'I came to look upon him as a second father.' Shit. Isn't one enough?"

"My daddy died when I was a boy," said Lee dreamily.

"Mine's a money-grubbing creep," said Jango. "Just like Page."

" 'Course, Elvis should have broken with him in the sixties," Baxter said. "That was his big mistake—he kept doing all those movies exactly alike because the Colonel was afraid to change the formula. No, at the right moment, you've got to make your break."

Jango snarled at the mirror. "I'm gonna save every dollar, and when I've got enough I'm going to rent the best recording studio in L.A. and sing till I get Elvis out of my throat forever."

Lee circled quarters through the machine till they were gone. He hailed a waitress and while buying a drink asked her the time. Four o'clock here. It would be suppertime in Tennessee and darkness falling. Darkness never reached inside the casino, though—there were no windows, no natural light. Could you spend your life here and never feel it? He went and turned in his chit and they let him into a golden mummy case that was a phone booth.

He dialed his mamma. When she heard it was him, she went to turn down the pots on the stove and he was filled with longing for her kitchen. So far off. She exclaimed all right when he told her he was calling from a Las Vegas casino where he was to perform that night, but he could tell it didn't mean much to her, it was too strange.

The telephone glittered with gold spray paint.

"I only have a minute here, Mamma," he said, "so tell me straight—how's Cherry?"

"She was out here the other day. Kind of surprised me. Listen, Lee, you coming back soon?"

"I don't see how I can. Is something wrong?"

"It's Cherry. I know you're legally separate and all, but I don't think she's as hot on this divorce as she was. I was talking to my friend at the grocery, Maylene, she said to say hey to you—"

"Thirty seconds," said the casino operator.

"Mamma—" Lee's heart was pounding.

"Well, I mentioned Cherry stopping by for no good reason and Maylene said it's all over Bragg that Shep Stanwix dropped her to chase some country club girl and—not that she deserves you, honey, after how she's acted—but maybe if you get back here right now, before she takes up with anyone else—"

Lee fell into a night with stars in it. When he came to, he was slumped in the golden mummy case and the line was dead. A lady from the casino leaned over him. "I'm fine," he said, "I just forgot my medicine." And he took a pill out of his pocket and washed it down with the last of his whiskey.

The lady was tall and half naked and concerned. "Is it heart trouble?"

"That's right, ma'am," said Lee. "My heart."

They ate dinner in their suite, at a table that rolled into the living room. The hotel sent up champagne in a bucket, for

Talent on Opening Night. After they knocked it off, they ordered up some more to have while they got into costume in the mirrored dressing room off Jango's bedroom. Jango was ready first, in black jeans and a silky red shirt.

"Uhwelluh it's one fo the moneyuh," he sang into the mirror, warming up. "Uhwelluh it's one," he sipped champagne, "one fo the moneehah." He looked sulkier every day, Lee thought.

Baxter leaned into the mirror opposite, turning his head to check the length of his sideburns, which weren't quite even. He plucked out a single hair with tweezers. Beside him on the dressing table was a tabloid he'd picked up that had a cover story about how the ghost of Elvis got into a cab and had himself driven out past Graceland, then disappeared. Baxter read all this stuff for research.

"Uhwelluh it's two fo the show, damn it, fo the showowhuh," sang Jango.

Lee, who was drunk but not yet drunk enough to perform, confronted his costume. Hung up on wooden hangers, it looked like a man he didn't want to be—the vast bell-bottoms, the jacket with shoulders padded like a linebacker's, the belt five inches wide and jewel-encrusted. The whole deal heavy as sin. Lee sighed, took off his shirt and jeans, and stepped into the pants. The satin chilled his legs. He wrapped a dozen scarves around his neck to toss out during the show. He held out his arms and the others lifted the jacket onto him. The top of the sequined collar scratched his ears. He sucked in his stomach so they could fasten the belt on him, but just then Mr. Page breezed in, all snappy and excited.

"You know who we got in the audience tonight, babes? You know who?"

They all just looked at him.

"Alan Spahr!" he crowed. "I'm telling you, Alan *Spahr*. The Dealmaker!"

Baxter said, "What kind of deals?"

"Hollywood deals, babes. Hollywood. The Emerald City. We're talking moolah, we're talking fame, we're talking TV movie. What's this, champagne? Yeah, let's have a toast here." He filled their glasses. "Las Vegas to Hollywood—westward ho, babes, westward ho!"

"The Emerald City," said Lee.

The champagne was cool and sour. He poured some more and flexed his shoulders.

"Listen, man," Jango said. He still held Lee's belt in his hands. It flashed in all the mirrors. "I am not going to Hollywood. There's no way I'm going to play Elvis where anyone I know might see me."

"You won't be playing *in* Hollywood," said Mr. Page. "In fact, if we make this deal I'm going to see to it that the script is expanded—you know, do the whole life, filmed on location. Might even find a child, you know, to play Elvis at six, seven."

The poor kid, thought Lee.

"But a TV movie is on everywhere," said Jango.

"You betcha." Page drank champagne.

"I won't do it," Jango sneered. "Sue me—I don't have anything to lose."

Page leaned close to him. "Oh, no? A lawsuit lasts a long, long time, babes, and I would own all your future work if you quit me. Any albums, any concert tours, I would own your damn poster sales, babes, get it?"

"Mr. Page," Lee said, "you don't need me and Jango for a TV movie. Baxter is the real talent here. On film they can do everything with light and makeup—Baxter can go from twenty to forty, can't you, Bax?"

Baxter looked up from his tabloid and said, "I know I could do it. It'd be my big break, sir."

"Babes, I can see you wouldn't be anywhere without me," said Mr. Page. "That there's three of you"—and he gestured at the mirrors where, small in his white suit, he was surrounded by ominous Elvises—"that's the whole gimmick. The three stages of the King. And with a TV movie behind us, babes, this show could run forever."

The show was on downstairs. Lee had finished the champagne and switched to whiskey. He had to find the right drunk place to be. The place without thought. Like in the army. Which he never thought about. Stay stoned, don't think. He checked the clock—lots of time yet. He was in full costume, ready to go. Lee avoided the mirrors. He knew he looked bad. When he was young, he was dark and slim—like an Indian, Cherry used to say. Cherry had loved him. Cherry—better not think about Cherry. Where were his pills? In his shirt, on the floor of the dressing room. He tried to bend, but the belt cut into him, stopped him. He had to kneel, carefully, and then, as he threw back his head to wash down the pill, he saw. Who was that? Down on one knee, huge and glittery, his hair dark blue, his chest pale and puffy, his nose and eyes lost in the weight of his face. He looked like nothing human.

He had to get away. He took the service elevator down. It was smothering in there, but cold in the corridor, cold backstage. Sweat froze on his chest. Jango was on, near the end of his act. Offstage left, Lee saw Baxter talking to Mr. Page. He started toward them, then stopped.

Baxter had Mr. Page by his bolo tie. He pulled him close, shook him, then shoved him onto the floor. Baxter moved through the curtains, going on just as Jango came off with a leap, all hyped with performing and sparkling with sweat. Mr. Page was on his hands and knees, groggy. Jango did a swiveling dance step behind him and kicked out, sending him sprawling again. Then Jango saw Lee, shrugged, snarled, and flashed past.

Lee came forward and Mr. Page grabbed onto him and helped himself up. The old man was flushed—his red scalp glowed through his puffed white hair. He pulled at the big turquoise clasp of his tie and squawked. Baxter was singing "Love Me Tender." Lee shushed Mr. Page and led him behind the back wall, where the music was muffled. Page kept shaking his head and squinting. He looked dizzy and mean.

"I got contracts," he said. "There's nothing they can do." He started brushing his suit—dust smeared the white cloth.

Lee held out his shaking hands. "Look—I can't go on."

"Oh, babes, you're a young man still," said Page. "You just gotta cut down on the booze some. Listen, I'll get you something that'll make you feel like a newborn child."

"When I get too old and sick to do this, will you let me free?"

"At that point Baxter'll be ready for your job. And Jango for Baxter's." Page patted his hair.

"And you'll find a new kid."

"That's the way this business goes, babes. You can always find a new kid."

Lee's heart was pounding, pounding. He had to look away from Mr. Page, at the wall of wires, lights, power.

"Yeah, kids are a dime a dozen. But I'll tell you what, babes," said Mr. Page, "you were my greatest find. A magnificent Elvis. So courtly and screwed-up. A dead ringer."

Lee looked away, listening to the noise of his punished heart. "A dead ringer?" He remembered the first pills Mr. Page handed him, just after Cherry—don't think about Cherry—and Lee knew he would die, would die as Elvis had and never again see his wife, his mother, Tennessee.

"Magnificent," said Mr. Page, "we gotta get that look on film! It's gorgeous, it's ruinous—I tell you, babes, it's practically tragic."

And Lee struck him, with all his weight and rage. Mr. Page fell onto the metal box where the power cables met. Lee bent over him, working fast. Green sparks sizzled around them.

Onstage, Lee was doing the talk section of his last song, "Are You Lonesome Tonight?" He was supposed to get lost, say what he liked, then come back into the lyric with a roar. "Tell me, dear—" he murmured into the mike and remembered Cherry when she was just out of high school. "You were so lovely." Wrapping a towel around him with a hug before she cut his hair. "And I know, I know you cared—but the—" Oh, what went wrong? "What went wrong? You sent me away—"

He stood still and looked out at the people sitting at little tables like they were in a nightclub. Well, it is a nightclub, he rememberd, a hot spot. And he laughed. "Watch out." He shook his head. "Gotta get straight," he muttered and, looking out, saw tears on faces. "Don't cry for me," he said, "she's waiting." And then the song came back to him as it always returned, the band caught it up, and behind him the wall of light blazed and then ripped open with a force that cast him out into the screaming audience.

Breakfast was cheap here. Even in the diners they had slot machines. Lee drank black coffee and scanned the newspaper.

He read how Liberace's ex-chauffeur had plastic surgery to look more like Liberace and about the tragic accident backstage at the Golden Pyramid. The manager of the ELVIS LIVES show had been caught in the electrical fire caused by the new computer system. Now, days after the accident, the newspaper was running follow-up stories about past casino fires.

The first day or so, there had been investigators around, in and out of their suite, but they mostly left Lee alone. He'd been onstage during the fire, when the finale display overburdened the wires, causing a short and an explosion. And there'd been so much emphasis on how complex the system was, digital this and that, no one imagined a hick like Lee could understand it. Even to him, his own quick work seemed now beyond himself, like something done by someone else. Lee supposed the other two thought they'd contributed to Page's death—left him woozy so he passed out backstage and got caught in the fire. But they accepted the explosion as the dazzling act of some god of electricity looking out for them. The second night, when Baxter came in with their contracts, they ripped them up without a word.

A new three-Elvis act was opening soon—Mr. Page had owned *them*, but anyone could use his gimmick. Baxter was staying on in Vegas—he'd pitched himself to Alan Spahr and they were talking about cable. This morning Jango was heading west, Lee east. Wasn't everyone better off? Except Page—better not think about Page. Already he seemed far back in time, almost as far back as things Lee'd done in the army. Anyway, Lee blamed the pills. He'd sweated himself straight in the hotel sauna and meant to stay that way.

Lee paid for breakfast, picked up his old leather valise, and went outside. This early, you could smell the desert. The sun showed up the smallness of the buildings, their ordinariness squatted beneath their flamboyant signs. Lee stuck out his thumb and began walking backward.

The trucker who picked him up was heading for Albuquerque. At the truck stop there, Lee drank some beers and hung around till he found a ride through to Memphis. He had resolved to cut back to beer only until he saw Cherry again, but in the middle of the night in Texas he felt so good, heading home,

home, home, he wanted to stay up the whole way and bought some speed for himself and the guys who were driving him, and knocked it back with some whiskey the driver had. Home, home, home, they tore along Route 40, through the darkness, listening to the radio. When Elvis came on, they all sang along.

"Hey, Lee, you sound like Elvis. Look a little like him, too," the driver said. He nudged his buddy. "What do you think? Have we picked up Presley's ghost?"

"Naw," said Lee. "He's dead and I'm alive and going home." Sipping whiskey through the night, song after song, he felt so happy he just sang his heart out.

LAWRENCE BLOCK

ANSWERS TO SOLDIER

Lawrence Block is one of the most dependable of today's crime writers, delivering literate, memorable suspense with every novel and short story. Even when not writing about Matt Scudder or one of his other series characters, there is a compelling quality about his work that keeps one reading to the very end. This fine story of a hit man far from home is a perfect example. It might well become a favorite with anthologists, and was one of the nominees for this year's MWA Edgar award.

Keller flew United to Portland. He read a magazine on the leg from J.F.K. to O'Hare, ate lunch on the ground and watched the movie on the nonstop flight from Chicago to Portland. It was a quarter to three, local time, when he carried his hand luggage off the plane, and then he had only an hour's wait before his connecting flight to Roseburg.

But when he got a look at the size of the plane, he walked over to the Hertz desk and told them he wanted a car for a few days. He showed them a driver's license and a credit card and they let him have a Ford Taurus with 3,200 miles on the clock. He didn't bother trying to refund his Portland-to-Roseburg ticket.

The Hertz clerk showed him how to get on I-5. Keller pointed the Taurus in the right direction and set the cruise control three miles over the posted speed limit. Everybody else was going a few miles an hour faster than that, but he was in no hurry, and he didn't want to invite a close look at his driver's license. It was probably all right, but why ask for trouble?

It was still light out when he took the off ramp for the second Roseburg exit. He had a reservation at the Douglas Inn, a Best Western on Stephens Street. He found it without any trouble. They had him in a ground-floor room in the front, and he had them change it to one in the rear and a flight up.

He unpacked, showered. The phone book had a street map of downtown Roseburg and he studied it, getting his bearings, then tore it out and took it with him when he went out for a walk. The little print shop was only a few blocks away on Jackson, two doors in from the corner, between a tobacconist and a photographer with his window full of wedding pictures. A sign in Quik Print's window offered a special on wedding invitations, perhaps to catch the eye of bridal couples making arrangements with the photographer.

Quik Print was closed, of course, as were the tobacconist and the photographer and the credit jeweler next door to the photographer and, as far as Keller could tell, everybody else in the neighborhood. He didn't stick around long. Two blocks away, he found a Mexican restaurant that looked dingy enough to be authentic. He bought a local paper from the coin box out front and read it while he ate his chicken enchiladas. The food was good and ridiculously inexpensive. If the place were in New York, he thought, everything would be three of four times as much and there'd be a line in front.

The waitress was a slender blonde, not Mexican at all. She had short hair and granny glasses and an overbite, and she sported an engagement ring on the appropriate finger, a diamond solitaire with a tiny stone. Maybe she and her fiancé had picked it out at the credit jeweler's, Keller thought. Maybe the photographer next door would take their wedding pictures. Maybe they'd get Burt Engleman to print their wedding invitations. Quality printing, reasonable rates, service you can count on.

In the morning, he returned to Quik Print and looked in the window. A woman with brown hair was sitting at a gray metal desk, talking on the telephone. A man in shirt sleeves stood at a copying machine. He wore horn-rimmed glasses with round lenses and his hair was cropped short on his egg-shaped head. He was balding, and that made him look older, but Keller knew he was only thirty-eight.

Keller stood in front of the jeweler's and pictured the waitress and her fiancé picking out rings. They'd have a double-ring ceremony, of course, and there would be something engraved on the inside of each of their wedding bands, something no one else would ever see. Would they live in an apartment? For a while, he decided, until they saved the down payment for a starter home. That was the phrase you saw in real-estate ads and Keller liked it. A starter home, something to practice on until you got the hang of it.

At a drugstore on the next block, he bought an unlined paper tablet and a black felt-tipped pen. He used four sheets of paper before he was pleased with the result. Back at Quik Print, he showed his work to the brown-haired woman.

"My dog ran off," he explained. "I thought I'd get some fliers printed, post them around town."

LOST DOG, he'd printed. PART GER. SHEPHERD. ANSWERS TO SOLDIER. CALL 555-1904.

"I hope you get him back," the woman said. "Is it a him? Soldier sounds like a male dog, but it doesn't say."

"It's a male," Keller said. "Maybe I should have specified."

"It's probably not important. Did you want to offer a reward? People usually do, though I don't know if it makes any difference. If I found somebody's dog, I wouldn't care about a reward; I'd just want to get him back with his owner."

"Everybody's not as decent as you are," Keller said. "Maybe I should say something about a reward. I didn't even think of that." He put his palms on the desk and leaned forward, looking down at the sheet of paper. "I don't know," he said. "It looks kind of homemade, doesn't it? Maybe I should have you set it in type, do it right. What do you think?"

"I don't know," she said. "Ed? Would you come and take a look at this, please?"

The man in the horn-rims came over and said he thought a hand-lettered look was best for a lost-dog notice. "It makes it more personal," he said. "I could do it in type for you, but I think people would respond to it better as it is. Assuming somebody finds the dog, that is."

"I don't suppose it's a matter of national importance, anyway," Keller said. "My wife's attached to the animal and I'd like to recover him if it's possible, but I've a feeling he's not to be found. My name's Gordon, by the way. Al Gordon."

"Ed Vandermeer," the man said. "And this is my wife, Betty."

"A pleasure," Keller said. "I guess fifty of these ought to be enough. More than enough, but I'll take fifty. Will it take you long to run them?"

"I'll do it right now. Take about three minutes, cost you three-fifty."

"Can't beat that," Keller said. He uncapped the felt-tipped pen. "Just let me put in something about a reward."

Back in his motel room, he put through a call to a number in White Plains. When a woman answered, he said, "Dot, let me speak to him, will you?" It took a few minutes, and then he said, "Yeah, I got here. It's him, all right. He's calling himself Vandermeer now. His wife's still going by Betty."

The man in White Plains asked when he'd be back.

"What's today, Tuesday? I've got a flight booked Friday, but I might take a little longer. No point rushing things. I found a good place to eat. Mexican joint, and the motel set gets HBO. I figure I'll take my time, do it right. Engleman's not going anywhere."

He had lunch at the Mexican café. This time, he ordered the combination plate. The waitress asked if he wanted the red or green chili.

"Whichever's hotter," he said.

Maybe a mobile home, he thought. You could buy one cheap, a nice double-wide, make a nice starter home for her and her fellow. Or maybe the best thing for them was to buy a duplex and rent out half, then rent out the other half when they were ready for something nicer for themselves. No time at all, you're in real estate, making a nice return, watching your holdings appreciate. No more waiting on tables for her, and pretty soon, her husband could quit slaving at the lumber mill, quit worrying about layoffs when the industry hit one of its slumps.

How you do go on, he thought.

He spent the afternoon walking around town. In a gun shop, the proprietor, a man named McLarendon, took some rifles and shotguns off the wall and let him get the feel of them. A sign on the wall read, GUNS DON'T KILL PEOPLE UNLESS YOU AIM REAL GOOD.

Keller talked politics with McLarendon, and socioeconomics. It wasn't that tricky to figure out his position and to adopt it as one's own.

"What I really been meaning to buy," Keller said, "is a handgun."

"You want to protect yourself and your property," McLarendon said.

"That's the idea."

"And your loved ones."

"Sure."

He let the man sell him a gun. There was, locally, a cooling-off period. You picked out your gun, filled out a form, and four days later, you could come back and pick it up.

"You a hothead?" McLarendon asked him. "You fixing to lean out the car window, shoot a state trooper on your way home?"

"It doesn't seem likely."

"Then I'll show you a trick. We just backdate this form and you've already had your cooling-off period. I'd say you look cool enough to me."

"You're a good judge of character."

The man grinned. "This business," he said, "a man's got to be."

It was nice, a town that size. You got into your car and drove for ten minutes and you were way out in the country.

Keller stopped the Taurus at the side of the road, cut the ignition, rolled down the window. He took the gun from one pocket and the box of shells from the other. The gun—McLarendon had kept calling it a weapon—was a .38 caliber revolver with a two-inch barrel. McLarendon would have liked to sell him something heavier and more powerful. If Keller had wanted, he probably would have been thrilled to sell him a bazooka.

Keller loaded the gun and got out of the car. There was a beer can lying on its side perhaps twenty yards off. He aimed at it, holding the gun in one hand. A few years ago, they started firing two-handed in cop shows on TV, and nowadays, that was all you saw, television cops leaping through doorways and spinning around corners, gun gripped rigidly in both hands, held out in front of their bodies like a fire hose. Keller thought it looked silly. He'd feel so self-conscious, holding a gun like that.

He squeezed the trigger. The gun bucked in his hand, and he missed the beer can by several feet. The report of the gunshot echoed for a long time.

He took aim at other things—at a tree, at a flower, at a white rock the size of a clenched fist. But he couldn't bring himself to fire the gun again, to break the stillness with another gunshot. What was the point, anyway? If he used the gun, he'd be too close to miss. You got in close, you pointed, you fired. It wasn't rocket science, for God's sake. It wasn't neurosurgery. Anyone could do it.

He replaced the spent cartridge and put the loaded gun in the car's glove compartment. He spilled the rest of the shells into his hand and walked a few yards from the road's edge, then hurled them with a sweeping sidearm motion. He gave the box a toss and got back into the car.

Traveling light, he thought.

Back in town, he drove past Quik Print to make sure it was still open. Then, following the route he'd traced on the map, he found his way to 1411 Cowslip Lane, a Dutch-colonial house on the north edge of town. The lawn was neatly trimmed and fiercely green, and there was a bed of rosebushes on either side of the path leading from the sidewalk to the front door.

One of the leaflets at the motel told how roses were a local specialty. But the town had been named not for the flower but for Aaron Rose, a local settler.

He wondered if Engleman knew that.

He circled the block, parked two doors away on the other side of the street from the Engleman residence. VANDERMEER, EDWARD, the white-pages listing had read. It struck Keller as an unusual alias. He wondered if Engleman had picked it out himself, or if the Feds had selected it for him. Probably the latter, he decided. "Here's your new name," they would tell you, "and here's where you're going to live and who you're going to be." There was an arbitrariness about it that somehow appealed to Keller, as if they relieved you of the burden of decision. Here's your new name, and here's your new driver's license with your new name already on it. You like scalloped potatoes in your new life, and you're allergic to bee stings, and your favorite color is blue.

Betty Engleman was now Betty Vandermeer. Keller wondered why her first name hadn't changed. Didn't they trust Engleman to get it right? Did they figure him for a bumbler, apt to blurt out "Betty" at an inopportune moment? Or was it sheer coincidence or sloppiness on their part?

Around six-thirty, the Englemans came home from work. They rode in a Honda Civic hatchback with local plates. They had evidently stopped to shop for groceries on the way home. Engleman parked in the driveway while his wife got a bag of groceries from the back. Then he put the car in the garage and followed her into the house.

Keller watched lights go on inside the house. He stayed where he was. It was starting to get dark by the time he drove back to the Douglas Inn.

On HBO, Keller watched a movie about a gang of criminals who have come to a town in Texas to rob the bank. One of the criminals is a woman, married to one of the other gang members and having an affair with another. Keller thought that was a pretty good recipe for disaster. There was a prolonged shootout at the end, with everybody dying in slow motion.

When the movie ended, he went over to switch off the set. His eye was caught by the stack of fliers Engleman had run off for him. LOST DOG. PART GER. SHEPHERD. ANSWERS TO SOLDIER. CALL 555-1904. REWARD.

Excellent watchdog, he thought. Good with children.

He didn't get up until almost noon. He went to the Mexican place and ordered huevos rancheros and put a lot of hot sauce on them.

He watched the waitress's hands as she served the food and again when she took his empty plate away. Light glinted off the little diamond. Maybe she and her husband would wind up on Cowslip Lane, he thought. Not right away, of course; they'd have to start out in the duplex, but that's what they could aspire to. A Dutch colonial with that odd kind of pitched roof.

What did they call it, anyway? Was that a mansard roof or did that word describe something else? Was it a gambrel, maybe?

He thought he ought to learn these things. You saw the words and didn't know what they meant, saw the houses and couldn't describe them properly.

He had bought a paper on his way into the café, and now he turned to the classified ads and read through the real-estate listings. Houses seemed very inexpensive. You could actually buy a low-priced home here for twice what he would be paid for the week's work.

There was a safe-deposit box no one knew about rented under a name he'd never used for another purpose, and in it, he had enough cash to buy a nice home here for cash. Assuming you could still do that. People were funny about cash these days, leery of letting themselves be used to launder drug money.

Anyway, what difference did it make? He wasn't going to live here. The waitress could live here, in a nice little house with mansards and gambrels.

Engleman was leaning over his wife's desk when Keller walked into Quik Print. "Why, hello," he said. "Have you had any luck finding Soldier?"

He remembered the name, Keller noticed.

"As a matter of fact," he said, "the dog came back on his own. I guess he wanted the reward."

Betty Engleman laughed.

"You see how fast your fliers worked," he went on. "They brought the dog back before I got the chance to post them. I'll get some use out of them eventually, though. Old Soldier's got itchy feet; he'll take off again one of these days."

"Just so he keeps coming back," she said.

"Reason I stopped by," Keller said, "I'm new in town, as you might have gathered, and I've got a business venture I'm getting ready to kick into gear. I'm going to need a printer, and I thought maybe we could sit down and talk. You got time for a cup of coffee?"

Engleman's eyes were hard to read behind the glasses. "Sure," he said. "Why not?"

They walked down to the corner, Keller talking about what a nice afternoon it was, Engleman saying little beyond agreeing with him. At the corner, Keller said, "Well, Burt, where should we go for coffee?"

Engleman just froze. Then he said, "I knew."

"I know you did; I could tell the minute I walked in there. How?"

"The phone number on the flier. I tried it last night. They never heard of a Mr. Gordon."

"So you knew last night. Of course, you could have made a mistake on the number."

Engleman shook his head. "I wasn't going on memory. I ran an extra flier and dialed the number right off it. No Mr. Gordon and no lost dog. Anyway, I think I knew before then. I think I knew the minute you walked in the door."

"Let's get that coffee," Keller said.

They went into a place called the Rainbow Diner and had coffee at a table on the side. Engleman added artificial sweetener to his and stirred it long enough to dissolve marble chips. He had been an accountant back East, working for the man Keller had called in White Plains. When the Feds were trying to make a RICO case against Engleman's boss, Engleman was a logical place to apply pressure. He wasn't really a criminal, he hadn't done much of anything, and they told him he was going to prison unless he rolled over and testified. If he did what they said, they'd give him a new name and move him someplace safe. If not, he could talk to his wife once a month through a wire screen and have ten years to get used to it.

"How did you find me?" he wanted to know. "Somebody leaked it in Washington?"

Keller shook his head. "Freak thing," he said. "Somebody saw you on the street, recognized you, followed you home."

"Here in Roseburg?"

"I don't think so. Were you out of town a week or so ago?"

"Oh, God," Engleman said. "We went down to San Francisco for the weekend."

"That sounds right."

"I thought it was safe. I don't even know anybody in San

Francisco; I was never there in my life. It was her birthday; we figured nothing could be safer. I don't know a soul there."

"Somebody knew you."

"And followed me back here?"

"I don't even know. Maybe they got your plate and had somebody run it. Maybe they checked your registration at the hotel. What's the difference?"

"No difference."

Engleman picked up his coffee and stared into the cup. Keller said, "You knew last night. Did you call someone?"

"There's somebody I can call," Engleman said. He put his cup down. "It's not that great a program," he said. "It's great when they're telling you about it, but the execution leaves a lot to be desired."

"You hear things," Keller said.

"Anyway, I didn't call anybody. What are they going to do? Say they stake my place out, the house and the print shop, and they pick you up. Even if they make something stick against you, what good does it do me? We'll have to move again because the guy'll just send somebody else, right?"

"I suppose so."

"Well, I'm not moving anymore. They moved us three times and I don't even know why. I think it's automatic, part of the program; they move you a few times during the first year or two. This is the first place we've really settled into since we left, and we're starting to make money at Quik Print, and I like it. I like the town and I like the business. I don't want to move."

"The town seems nice."

"It is," Engleman said. "It's better than I thought it would be."

"And you didn't want to develop an accounting practice?"

"Never," Engleman said. "I had enough of that, believe me. Look what it got me."

"You wouldn't necessarily have to work for crooks."

"How do you know who's a crook and who isn't? Anyway, I don't want any kind of work where I'm always looking at the inside of somebody else's business. I'd rather have my own little business, work there side by side with my wife; we're right there on the street and you can look in the front window and see us. You need stationery, you need business cards, you need invoice forms, I'll print 'em for you."

"How did you learn the business?"

"It's a franchise kind of thing, a turn-key operation. Anybody could learn it in twenty minutes."

"No kidding?" Keller said.

"Oh, yeah. Anybody."

Keller drank some of his coffee. He asked if Engleman had said anything to his wife and learned that he hadn't. "That's good," he said. "Don't say anything. I'm this guy, weighing some business ventures, needs a printer, has to have, you know, arrangements so there's no cash-flow problem. And I'm shy talking business in front of women, so the two of us go off and have coffee from time to time."

"Whatever you say," Engleman said.

Poor scared bastard, Keller thought. He said, "See, I don't want to hurt you, Burt. I wanted to, we wouldn't be having this conversation. I'd put a gun to your head, do what I'm supposed to do. You see a gun?"

"No."

"The thing is, I don't do it, they send somebody else. I come back empty, they want to know why. What I have to do, I have to figure something out. You don't want to run."

"No. The hell with running."

"Well, I'll figure something out," Keller said. "I've got a few days. I'll think of something."

After breakfast the next morning, Keller drove to the office of one of the realtors whose ads he'd been reading. A woman about the same age as Betty Engleman took him around and showed him three houses. They were modest homes but decent and comfortable, and they ranged between $40,000 and $60,000.

He could buy any of them out of his safe-deposit box.

"Here's your kitchen," the woman said. "Here's your half bath. Here's your fenced yard."

"I'll be in touch," he told her, taking her card. "I have a business deal pending and a lot depends on the outcome."

He and Engleman had lunch the next day. They went to the Mexican place and Engleman wanted everything very mild. "Remember," he told Keller, "I used to be an accountant."

"You're a printer now," Keller said. "Printers can handle hot food."

"Not this printer. Not this printer's stomach."

They each drank a bottle of Carta Blanca with the meal. Keller had another bottle afterward. Engleman had a cup of coffee.

"If I had a house with a fenced yard," Keller said, "I could have a dog and not worry about him running off."

"I guess you could," Engleman said.

"I had a dog when I was a kid," Keller said. "Just the once. I had him for about two years when I was eleven, twelve years old. His name was Soldier."

"I was wondering about that."

"He wasn't part shepherd. He was a little thing; I suppose he was some kind of terrier cross."

"Did he run off?"

"No, he got hit by a car. He was stupid about cars; he just ran out in the street. The driver couldn't help it."

"How did you happen to call him Soldier?"

"I forget. Then, when I did the flier, I don't know, I had to put answers to something. All I could think of were names like Fido and Rover and Spot. Like signing John Smith on a hotel register, you know? Then it came to me—Soldier. Been years since I thought about that dog."

After lunch, Engleman went back to the shop and Keller returned to the motel for his car. He drove out of town on the same road he'd taken the day he bought the gun. This time, he drove a few miles farther before pulling over and cutting the engine.

He got the gun from the glove box and opened the cylinder, spilling the shells into his palm. He tossed them underhand, then weighed the gun in his hand for a moment before hurling it into a patch of brush.

McLarendon would be horrified, he thought. Mistreating a

weapon in that fashion. Showed what a judge of character the man was. He got back into his car and drove back to town.

He called White Plains. When the woman answered, he said, "You don't have to disturb him, Dot. Just tell him I didn't make my flight today. I changed the reservation; I moved it ahead to Tuesday. Tell him everything's OK, only it's taking a little longer, like I thought it might." She asked how the weather was. "It's real nice," he said. "Very pleasant. Listen, don't you think that's part of it? If it was raining, I'd probably have it taken care of, I'd be home by now."

Quik Print was closed Saturdays and Sundays. Saturday afternoon, Keller called Engleman at home and asked him if he felt like going for a ride. "I'll pick you up," he offered.

When he got there, Engleman was waiting out in front. He got in and fastened his seat belt. "Nice car," he said.

"It's a rental."

"I didn't figure you drove your own car all the way out here. You know, it gave me a turn. When you said, 'How about going for a ride?' You know, going for a ride. Like there's a connotation."

"Actually," Keller said, "we probably should have taken your car. I figured you could show me the area."

"You like it here, huh?"

"Very much," Keller said. "I've been thinking. Suppose I just stayed here."

"Wouldn't he send somebody?"

"You think he would? I don't know. He wasn't killing himself trying to find you. At first, sure, but then he forgot about it. Then some eager beaver in San Francisco happens to spot you and, sure, he tells me to go out and handle it. But if I just don't come back—"

"Caught up in the lure of Roseburg," Engleman said.

"I don't know, Burt, it's not a bad place. You know, I'm going to stop that."

"What?"

"Calling you Burt. Your name's Ed now, so why don't I call

you Ed? What do you think, Ed? That sound good to you, Ed, old buddy?"

"And what do I call you?"

"Al's fine. What should I do, take a left here?"

"No, go another block or two," Engleman said. "There's a nice road, leads through some very pretty scenery."

A while later, Keller said. "You miss it much, Ed?"

"Working for him, you mean?"

"No, not that. The city."

"New York? I never lived in the city, not really. We were up in Westchester."

"Still, the whole area. You miss it?"

"No."

"I wonder if I would." They fell silent, and after perhaps five minutes, Keller said, "My father was a soldier; he was killed in the war when I was just a baby. That's why I named the dog Soldier."

Engleman didn't say anything.

"Except I think my mother was lying," he went on. "I don't think she was married, and I have a feeling she didn't know who my father was. But I didn't know that when I named the dog. When you think about it, it's a stupid name, anyway, for a dog, Soldier. It's probably stupid to name a dog after your father, as far as that goes."

Sunday, he stayed in the room and watched sports on television. The Mexican place was closed; he had lunch at Wendy's and dinner at a Pizza Hut. Monday at noon, he was back at the Mexican café. He had the newspaper with him, and he ordered the same thing he'd ordered the first time, the chicken enchiladas.

When the waitress brought coffee afterward, he asked her, "When's the wedding?"

She looked utterly blank. "The wedding," he repeated, and pointed at the ring on her finger.

"Oh," she said. "Oh, I'm not engaged or anything. The ring was my mom's from her first marriage. She never wears it, so I asked could I wear it, and she said it was all right. I used to wear it on the other hand, but it fits better here."

He felt curiously angry, as though she'd betrayed the fantasy he'd spun out about her. He left the same tip he always left and took a long walk around town, gazing in windows, wandering up one street and down the next.

He thought, Well, you could marry her. She's already got the engagement ring. Ed'll print you wedding invitations, except who would you invite?

And the two of you could get a house with a fenced yard and buy a dog.

Ridiculous, he thought. The whole thing was ridiculous.

At dinnertime, he didn't know what to do. He didn't want to go back to the Mexican café, but he felt perversely disinclined to go anywhere else. One more Mexican meal, he thought, and I'll wish I had that gun back so I could kill myself.

He called Engleman at home. "Look," he said, "this is important. Could you meet me at your shop?"

"When?"

"As soon as you can."

"We just sat down to dinner."

"Well, don't ruin your meal," Keller said. "What is it, seven-thirty? How about if you meet me in an hour?"

He was waiting in the photographer's doorway when Engleman parked the Honda in front of his shop. "I didn't want to disturb you," he said, "but I had an idea. Can you open up? I want to see something inside."

Engleman unlocked the door and they went in. Keller kept talking to him, saying how he'd figured out a way he could stay in Roseburg and not worry about the man in White Plains. "This machine you've got," he said, pointing to one of the copiers. "How does this work?"

"How does it work?"

"What does that switch do?"

"This one?"

Engleman leaned forward, and Keller got the loop of wire out of his pocket and dropped it around the other man's neck. The garrote was fast, silent, deadly. Keller made sure Engleman's body was where it couldn't be seen from the street, made sure to wipe his prints off any surfaces he may have touched. He turned off the lights, closed the door behind him.

He had already checked out of the Douglas Inn, and now he drove straight to Portland, with the Ford's cruise control set just below the speed limit. He drove half an hour in silence, then turned on the radio and tried to find a station he could stand. Nothing pleased him and he gave up and switched it off.

Somewhere north of Eugene, he said, "Jesus, Ed, what else was I going to do?"

He drove straight through to Portland and got a room at the ExecUlodge near the airport. In the morning, he turned in the Hertz car and dawdled over coffee until his flight was called.

He called White Plains as soon as he was on the ground at J.F.K. "It's all taken care of," he said. "I'll come by sometime tomorrow. Right now, I just want to get home, get some sleep."

The following afternoon in White Plains, Dot asked him how he had liked Roseburg.

"Really nice," he said. "Pretty town, nice people. I wanted to stay there."

"Oh, Keller," she said. "What did you do, look at houses?"

"Not exactly."

"Every place you go," she said, "you want to live there."

"It's nice," he insisted. "And living's cheap compared to here. A person could have a decent life."

"For a week," she said. "Then you'd go nuts."

"You really think so?"

"Come *on*," she said. "Roseburg, Oregon? Come on."

"I guess you're right," he said. "I guess a week's about as much as I could handle."

A few days later, he was going through his pockets before taking some clothes to the cleaner's. He found the Roseburg street map and went over it, remembering where everything was. Quik Print, the Douglas Inn, the house on Cowslip. The Mexican café, the other places he'd eaten. The houses he'd looked at.

He folded the map and put it in his dresser drawer. A week later, he came across it and laughed. And tore it in half, and in half again, and dropped it into the wastebasket.

STANLEY COHEN

HELLO! MY NAME IS IRVING WASSERMAN

Stanley Cohen is the talented author of just four novels and a handful of short stories over the past two decades. While we await his next novel here's a small sample of the sort of thing he does best—crime that still manages to convey a certain amount of charm.

Morty Kaplan was definitely excited about something as he arrived home from his office on a perfect summer day. When he entered the co-op building on East Sixty-seventh at Third, even Tony the doorman noticed it while pulling the door open for him.

"You just swallow the canary, or what?" Tony quipped.

"Mostly what, Tony. I gave up on canaries years ago. Nothing but feathers and bones."

"Yeah? What about that feather on your necktie?"

Morty grinned. "You're quick, kid. I'll give you that. See you later."

Morty took the elevator to the seventeenth floor, unlocked the door, and went inside. He threw his jacket across a chair and walked into the kitchen where Evelyn was at the sink, rinsing lettuce for the salad.

"And how's the world's most lovable endodontist?" she asked, not looking up from her work. "You root a few hot canals, today?"

Morty walked over to her and gave her fanny a little caress, his usual way of letting her know he was home. Then he gave her a pleasing little kiss behind her ear, an action that was maybe a little less routine, but not out of character. "I just might have a pleasant little surprise for you, today."

She whirled around to face him, a bright expectant smile on her face. "What?" She was into pleasant little surprises.

"You know the rug you've been wishing we could find for the den?"

"What about it?"

"You know, something authentically Navajo, or even quasi-Hopi, something that looks like it had been made by real, honest-to-goodness American Indians?"

"Oh, cut the crap and get to the point, Morty."

"I may, and listen closely, I'm saying, I may, I may have found you the rug you want."

Evelyn was all smiles. "Where? I've been shopping for months and I'm convinced there's not one in this city that's even close. At any price."

"Well, I may have found one. In fact, when you see this rug, you're not going to believe what you're looking at."

"Is it going to cost a fortune? You're always saying that you're not willing to spend a fortune for it. . . . Wait a minute. Where would you be seeing any rugs today?"

Morty's eyes gleamed. "I saw one. And we could have it for nothing."

"What are you talking about?"

"Are you ready for this? As I was walking home from the office just now, I saw this rug that somebody had thrown out on top of a pile of stuff left for pickup, and I took a look at the corner of it, and it really does look like just what we want."

"All you saw was a corner of it?"

"It was tightly rolled up and taped with heavy tape."

"Well, if somebody threw it out, it's probably a mess."

"Not necessarily. Not in that neighborhood. East Sixty-second between Second and Third? That block is all million-dollar town houses. Latching onto a discarded anything in that block can be very promising. Very promising. Nothing about throwaways in that block would surprise me."

"Well, why didn't you just pick it up and bring it then?"

Morty smiled at her and then shifted into a poor excuse for a bodybuilder's stance. He was slight in build, with a paunch, a receding hairline, glasses, and delicate hands. "I know you think I can lift the world," he said, "but that thing was heavy. I could tell just from pushing at it. And it was bulky and lumpy. Whoever threw it out must have gotten rid of a lot of other junk, heavy junk, by rolling it up inside before they taped it up. Admittedly, after we get it up here and get a look at it, we may decide we don't want it, but considering how long we've been shopping for this thing, I certainly think it's worth a look."

"It'll probably be gone before you can get back. This is New York, you know."

Morty smiled. "I thought of that when I looked at it. So, I sort of rearranged the pile a little. I put some other stuff on top of it."

"Get our neighbor down the hall to help you. The big Swede. Lars. He'd be more than glad to, and he could probably carry you *and* the rug. And go *now*. Before somebody else gets it."

"Why don't you give him a call?" Morty said. "He likes you."

The rolled-up rug was definitely heavy. Very heavy. But Lars, their big Swedish neighbor from down the hall, was up to the task. And they were something to look at as they moved along, carrying it. Lars, a giant of a man, had the bulk of the load on his shoulder. Morty walked with his considerably less powerful shoulder under the front end of the thing, where he provided little more than balancc. If that.

When they reached the building, Tony the doorman pulled the door open for them. "A new rug, huh? What? D'you find that somewhere?"

"Does it suprise you?" Morty asked.

"Surprise me? Nothing surpriscs me in this city." Then he grinned at Morty. "What? You couldn't carry it yourself? You had to get Mr. Swenson to help you?"

"You want to try carrying it, Tony? Go ahead. Take it upstairs for us. Lars and I will watch the door for you."

Tony grinned. "I gotta stay here."

It took some negotiating for Morty and Lars to get their burden into the elevator, but they managed. When they reached the door to the apartment, Evelyn opened the door for them. She took one look at the rolled-up rug and had trouble containing her excitement. Since it was a hand-woven Indian rug, its design was the same on both sides.

"Blacks and grays and whites," she said in a controlled manner. "Morty? Do you happen to know what this might be?"

He smiled and nodded. "I think so," he said with certainty, sensing that she didn't want to discuss too much in front of Lars. He and Lars continued struggling with the rug, placing it finally in the den, in position to be unrolled.

"Well," she said, looking at Lars and then at Morty, "I've got to get the fish out of the oven or it'll be spoiled. So I guess we'll have to leave this till after we eat. Lars, would you like to stay and have a bite with us?"

"Oh, thanks, no," he answered, "but you call me if you need any more help. Any time. Okay?" And he meant it. A gentle giant. And a friend among friends.

"Another time," Evelyn said warmly, trying not to let her sense of relief be too obvious. She wanted to get him the hell out of there so she could look at the rug.

After she'd seen him to the door and closed it, she turned to Morty. "Are you thinking what I'm thinking?"

"I sure am." He loved when she got really excited about something.

"That rug looks like an authentic Two Gray Hills. And an early one, at that. If it's in any kind of good condition, do you have any idea what it's worth? That size rug?"

"A lot of money, I'm sure."

"I saw a tiny throw rug that was supposedly a Two Gray Hills at that Indian Museum on upper Broadway, and it cost nearly a thousand dollars. I don't think you can even order them in room size anymore. Morty, this rug could be a real collector's item."

"Believe me. I've been thinking about it."

"Let's go look at it," she said.

"I thought you wanted to eat first."

"The fish's not going anywhere. I've got to look at that rug."

They went into the den to examine their prize, or confirm that it was in fact a prize. Morty very meticulously cut the duct tape wrapped around the rug in four places, and they began unrolling it.

Evelyn liked what she saw as they unrolled it slowly along the floor. The colors! The design! Based on all her research and endless shopping, it was just what she'd pictured in her mind's eye. And it wasn't stained, or even soiled. It was in beautiful condition. Almost like new. Why would anyone throw it away? A piece of art, no less. . . . Only in New York. And especially an area like that block of East Sixty-second. Someone was redecorating? Out it went. . . . But why was the rolled-up rug so bulky and misshapen? What bunch of junk was inside it?

When they reached the end of the rug, she found out. And she fainted dead away. Inside the rug was the body of a middle-aged man, dressed in a fine dark suit with an expensive silk tie. And affixed to the lapel of his jacket was one of those familiar sticky labels which read:

Hello! My Name Is
Irving Wasserman

Morty revived her with a cold, wet towel.

She sat bolt upright and looked around. "Where is he? Or was I dreaming?"

"I dragged him into the bedroom."

"Not our bedroom!"

"The *other* bedroom."

She reached for the towel that was soaking wet at one end and patted her face with the dry end. Then she began to examine the rug with a decorator's eye. She got to her feet and walked around it. "I like this rug. I LIKE this rug. I'll bet the Museum of the American Indian would like to have this baby. And it's in perfect condition. Perfect."

"Well, almost perfect."

"What about it is not perfect?"

"It's missing one of the corner fringes. See, down there at the other end? at the corner?"

"I'd hardly have noticed it. Even *I'm* not that fussy."

"Well, don't get too excited about it. What makes you so sure the police'll let us keep it?"

Evelyn looked at him with alarm. "Have you called the police?"

"No, but I'm getting ready to, right now."

"No!"

"What do you mean, no?"

"I mean, no, don't call the police. I want this rug. If you call the police, you know as well as I do that they'll take it. It's evidence. Morty, I want this rug. Do you know how long I've been looking for exactly this rug? Exactly this rug?"

Morty threw up his hands and looked skyward, his usual gesture when faced with one of Evelyn's absolutely immovable sudden positions. Maybe *this* time he could get some help from above. "Evelyn, listen to me."

"Forget it," she snapped. "I want this rug."

"Will you listen a minute?"

"No. I don't want to hear it."

"Okay, you don't want to hear it. But what are we going to do with Irving in there?"

"I don't know. We'll have to think of something."

"Evelyn, if we call the police now and tell them exactly what happened, and with Lars Swenson as our witness, everything'll be fine. And after the smoke clears, and the excitement is over, I'm sure they'll let us have the rug."

"You're sure? How sure? Can you call them and ask them? No. And I want this rug. Morty, I want this rug. I don't want it leaving this room."

"Then what do we do with Irving? Shall we put him in the bathtub and start buying ice?"

"We'll have to think of something. All we need is some way to get him out of here. I don't have any guilty conscience, Morty. We didn't kill him. We're not responsible for his being dead."

"Well, whoever was sure knew what he . . . or she, but presumably he, was doing." He smiled a little smile of respect. "A real professional, whoever did that. A really neat job."

"What are you talking about?"

"I've read about cases like this one," he said, reflectively. "They take a small calibre gun like a twenty-two short that shoots with a fairly low muzzle velocity and they stick it under the chin, pointed sort of up and toward the back of the head, and they fire. It's instant and painless. And neat. Because with the low muzzle velocity, the bullet doesn't come out. It just enters the cranial cavity and ricochets around, making scrambled eggs out of the brain. But from the outside, neat. The victim looks normal. Just a tiny clean hole where the bullet enters."

"How do you know so much about muzzle velocity? You've never touched a gun in your life."

"I've read about it. I think it was an article in the *Times* magazine about professional hit men and their techniques. . . . Evelyn, what do you propose doing with Mr. Wasserman?"

"I'll think of something."

Morty took the garbage out to the disposal chute, which was located in a utility closet off the corridor. The closet was completely at the other end of the corridor from their door. And there were eleven other co-op apartments on the floor. What were the odds, say, in the middle of the night . . . ? And if somebody did see them? What then?

He opened the port to the chute and dropped in the bag, and as he listened to its descent, he studied the opening. It was a close fit for the small garbage bag. for a man the size of Irving? Who was also a mite paunchy? He thought about Irving getting stuck between floors. But that presumed getting Irving into the chute at all, which wasn't possible. Forget it. The garbage chute was definitely not a viable solution.

When he reentered the apartment, he found Evelyn tugging at a window. "Evelyn. You don't just throw bodies out of windows."

She turned to face him. "Then we'll have to think of something else. Right?"

"Listen to me. We've got to call the police, and quick. Lars is our alibi for having him here, and the longer we wait, the more questionable out story's going to be. Lars won't lie about *anything*. Am I right?"

"We're *not* calling the police."

"Well, if we wanted to call one, we wouldn't have to go far. There's one on duty right across the street from this building at all times. . . . God, I'm sure glad it's Friday, at least. I don't expect to get much sleep while Irving is with us."

"We'll have to come up with a plan for getting him out of here. That's all. Because we're keeping the rug."

"Evelyn, listen to me. Number one, we live next door to our

temple. Next door. But that's nothing. Forget that. As long as we don't try to carry him out while services are letting out, we're okay there. Now for number two. Number two, we live across the street from the Russian Embassy. The Russian Embassy! And directly across from our front door is a guard shack that just happens to be occupied twenty-four hours a day by two of New York's Finest, because the embassy is there. That's number two. And it's not bad enough that they're *there*, they even come across to *this* building to use that bathroom down in the basement. And if that wasn't enough, now for number three. Number three, we have our own doormen on duty, also twenty-four hours a day."

"Morty, we didn't kill this man. Someone else killed him. Someone murdered this poor man and left him out there on the street. We brought him in here by mistake, and all we have to do is figure out some way to get him back outside without anybody noticing. And without calling the police. Because we're keeping the rug."

"Evelyn, you're repeating yourself." Then he stopped, and started wondering if he would ever be able to make himself believable when he began explaining what he was doing with the corpse of Irving Wasserman. Surely some of the prisoners in Attica, or wherever, would need root canal work.

And with that notion, and unable to think rationally because of the feverish state of his mind, he went into the living room and dropped himself into his big chair and flipped on the tube. The Mets were two behind going into the sixth. Couldn't they have been winning big this one time?

During the bottom of the ninth, with the Mets still two behind, but with two on and nobody out, Evelyn came and stood between Morty and the television. "I have a plan," she said. "It's not a wonderful, grandiose plan, but its a plan, and I think it'll work. And I frankly can't think of any other way to do it."

Behind her, on the tube, there was a lot of excitement and a lot of cheering, but he wasn't quite sure what had happened. He'd set the volume low. And it was always her practice, when he was watching and she wanted to talk to him, to stand between him and the screen to be sure she had his attention.

So, under the circumstances, about the best response he could manage was a rather annoyed, "Tell me about it."

Saturday. Morty entered the surgical supply store and looked around. He made a point of going to a store other than the one he used for his own office needs because, as he ruminated about the situation, when you've got a house guest like Irving, it tends to make you a little self-conscious. He certainly didn't want to have to discuss with people who knew him what a dentist needed with a wheelchair.

The night before had been bad, but perhaps not quite as bad as he'd anticipated. The Mets had managed to tie the score in the ninth and then win it in the fourteenth, and staying with this had helped him fall asleep, for a couple of hours, anyway, before he work up, starkly awake, thinking about Irving in the next room.

He paid for the chair in cash, of course, reflecting on the fact as he did that he was thinking like a criminal, leaving no written records or receipts. Then he asked the clerk if the rather large carton could be wrapped.

"Wrapped? You want this wrapped?"

"It's . . . it's going to be a gift." And as he said it, he flushed with guilt, realizing that although he might have paid with cash, he was certainly leaving an indelible impression on the clerk's mind.

"You want it gift wrapped? A wheelchair?"

"It doesn't have to be exactly gift wrapped. Just wrapped. In plain paper is okay. With a rope around it so I can handle it." Things were going from bad to worse. That clerk would never forget him. But he wanted to get the carton past Tony, and into his building without its contents being obvious. Problems. Nothing but problems. At least the store wasn't close to home. It was a ten-dollar cab ride there. And it would be another ten-dollar cab ride back. But worth it.

He helped the clerk, and another clerk, finally get the carton covered with plain brown paper and a few dozen yards of tape, then a rope for carrying. Before walking out, he rather sheepishly asked, "Uh, if this is not exactly right, it can be returned, can't it?"

The two clerks looked at him in disbelief. After a moment, one of them said, "In the carton. And keep the cash receipt." And the other said with a grin, "Don't let it get messed up."

Morty lugged the carton to the street and hailed a cab.

Tony pulled the door open for him when he arrived, and he dragged the carton inside.

"You need a hand with that?"

"Thanks, Tony, but I can handle it okay."

"Hey, we won last night. In the fourteenth."

"I stayed up and watched it. Till the end."

"It's about time Strawberry did something, huh?"

"Yeah."

He carried it into the elevator and pressed seventeen. Another hurdle passed. Tony did as he was supposed to do for a change. Just open the door and not ask a lot of questions. When he reached the seventeenth floor, he started to lift the carton and the rope came loose. He pushed the carton along the carpeted hallway to their door, unlocked it, and then shoved the carton inside.

"You're awfully quiet, tonight, Morty. You, too, Evelyn. Everything okay?" Arnie Perlman, a dentist and close friend, and one of Morty's best sources of referrals, kept looking, first at Morty, then at Evelyn.

"We're fine, Arnie. I stayed up a little late is all. I got hooked on the Mets game."

"The Straw-man really hit that thing," Arnie said. "When he connects, he can give it a ride."

"You watched it, too."

"What else?" Arnie said.

And in a separate conversation between the women, Phyllis asked Evelyn, "What'd you do, today?"

"I spent most of the day shopping. I felt like getting out today."

"Speaking of shopping, did you ever find that rug you were looking for? You know, for your den?"

Evelyn flushed and looked at Morty, who'd heard the question. Then she looked back at Phyllis.

"Did I say something wrong?" Phyllis asked. Then she smiled.

"Oh, God, don't tell me I brought up a sore subject or something."

"No, of course not." Evelyn answered. She glanced at Morty again, and then, "As a matter of fact, we may have spotted one that we're going to consider."

"Really? Where'd you find it? I figured you'd probably have to go to New Mexico or somewhere."

"Oh, at a little shop over on . . ." Evelyn looked at Morty. "Morty, where was that little shop we found?"

"I don't remember, exactly. Somewhere down in the Village. I have it written down at home."

They finished dinner and walked outside.

"Why don't you guys come back to our place for a nightcap?" Arnie asked.

Morty and Evelyn quickly begged off. And Morty looked nervously at his watch. They didn't have a lot of time left to get back home, according to their plan. Service in the restaurant had been slower than usual. The doormen at their building changed shifts at eleven, and they had to be back before Tony left. They hoped the old man, Manolo, who worked nights, wouldn't show up early and see them come in alone. If that happened, they'd have to postpone their plan another night, and that could be disastrous. Would Irving keep that long? Morty pictured himself going into the Food Emporium and trying to look casual when he checked out with thirty or forty five-pound bags of ice.

But they'd elected not to cancel their date with the Perlmans. It might provoke some questions. Besides, they could use the evening out. And Irving certainly wasn't going anywhere.

They made it back in time. Tony greeted them, and the old man was nowhere in sight. There was a bit of activity, however, around the guard shack across the street. The cops changed shifts at eleven, as well. They watched for a moment as the blue and white police van drove away, and then went inside. They entered the elevator and both exhaled.

Waiting time. One, one-thirty, two. They sat and stared numbly at the tube.

"I think we should start getting him into the chair and ready to go," Evelyn said.

Morty nodded. "I think you're right."

"You know what I was thinking," Evelyn said. "I was thinking that he really needs to be wearing a turtleneck so that the hole won't show. You know. Just in case."

"You're probably right."

"I think a white one, to be dressy enough to go with that dark suit he's wearing."

"My new white turtleneck. Right?"

"I'll buy you another one. Besides, you'll get to keep his tie. You said you liked his tie. . . . And maybe we should stick a Band-Aid over the hole."

Morty, with his most resigned sigh, breathed, "Okay, why don't we go do it? Come on."

"We? You'll have to do it. I'm not touching him. Oh, and another thing, why don't you put some of my makeup on him so he doesn't look so pasty-faced? A little rouge, maybe."

"What do I know about applying makeup? Can't you do that one thing?"

"I told you, I'm not touching him. You'll do it fine. Just a little rouge so he has some color . . ." She smiled. "My husband, the undertaker."

Not at all amused, Morty got slowly out of his big chair and moved toward the bedroom.

Four-thirty A.M. That moment of darkest night and deepest sleep. That moment when, even in New York, the pace of life slows to a crawl. A crawl, maybe. But in New York, one can never count on the pace of life grinding to a complete halt. Not at any hour. There is always a reasonable likelihood of activity on the Streets of Manhattan.

Irving was in the chair, ready to go. And getting him there had been no easy task for Morty. He'd struggled with the clothes while Irving was still on the floor. First the jacket, then the shirt and tie, the Band-Aid, and then Morty's new white turtleneck. And a struggle it had been. Especially the turtleneck. Finally, the jacket, once again. The sticky tag was still on the lapel. Morty was beginning to get into the macabre humor of the whole business as he smoothed out the tag, making sure it was on there securely.

Hello! My Name Is
Irving Wasserman

After he'd finished dressing Irving, he'd dealt with the makeup. Like a real pro, he'd covered the crisp white turtleneck with a towel. The more he fussed with the stuff, the worse things seemed to get. But by this time, he was really amused by what they were doing. Almost giddy. To the point of giggling as he put on too much rouge, then tried to wipe some off, then tried a little powder, then more wiping and rubbing and smearing. He thought about using a little mascara, or adding a touch of lipstick, and this made him whisper aloud, "I am from Transylvania." The final effect was one of Irving looking not just healthy, but ruddy, in fact, even more than ruddy. Flushed. And that was perfect.

Then came the job of getting Irving into the chair. And Morty was almost not up to it. With his physique, he was not used to lifting people. Having his hands in their mouths, yes, but not lifting them. In the process of straining and struggling, he was face-to-face, no, cheek-to-cheek with Irving, and as he puffed and sweated, the lyric strains of "Dancing Cheek to Cheek" tripped lightly through his head. Once Irving was into the chair, he went into the bathroom and wiped the makeup off his cheek, deciding finally that nothing less than a shower would do. And with time to burn, he'd taken a nice long one.

They rolled Irving to the door, and Evelyn opened it and peered out. No one in sight. As it should be. She could think of no one on their floor that she'd expect to be up and around at that hour. They moved soundlessly to the elevator, pressed the button, and waited. It arrived, they pushed Irving into it, and pressed LOBBY. As the car began its less than reckless descent, Morty held Irving's collar with one hand to keep him from pitching forward.

The car stopped at the ninth floor, and they looked at each other, panic-stricken. The door opened and a rather nice-looking young man, perhaps in his late twenties, entered the car. He looked at Irving curiously and then at the two of them. Then he looked away, not wanting to appear intrusive or judgmental. Morty sized him up as probably leaving some young woman's apartment. At four-thirty in the A.M.? Morty felt a twinge of jealousy.

When the young man glanced again at Irving, Morty, feeling obliged to comment, said, "Demon rum."

And the young man, feeling obliged to respond, said, "It can do it."

"We're taking him back to his place," Morty said. "It's not the first time."

"But it's going to be the last," Evelyn said, suddenly. "He's disgusting," she added. "He does this every time he comes over, and the next time, I'm not giving him anything to drink. I'm sick and tired of his passing out like this."

The young man nodded and looked relieved when the car stopped. The door moved slowly open and the young man hurried across the lobby.

They rolled Irving out of the car, and as they had hoped, Manolo, the old night man, was dozing on a sofa in the lobby. Manolo woke up when he heard the young man press the inside release and exit to the street. Manolo glanced around and saw them coming toward the door, pushing Irving.

As Manolo started to get to his feet, Morty said quickly, "It's okay, Manolo, we can let ourselves out. Thanks."

Manolo nodded, smiled, and made a thank you gesture with a nod and a wave of his hand. Then he dropped back on the couch and got comfortable again.

When they reached the sidewalk, certainly the tensest moment in the plan, Morty said, "Get back with the car as quick as you can."

And Evelyn promptly responded, "Would you expect me to drive around for a while, first?"

"Just be as quick as you can. Okay?"

Evelyn headed across Third and east on Sixty-seventh to the all-night garage a block away where they kept their car. Morty pushed the chair into what he hoped was the least illuminated spot in front of the building. He looked across the street at the little police shack, but could not tell if the cops inside were watching him. Realizing Evelyn would not be able to bring the car right to the door of their building because of a couple of POLICE LINE sawhorses, he moved a short distance toward the corner of Third Avenue, gripping Irving's collar tightly, and trying to appear as relaxed and casual as possible.

Suddenly a cop emerged from the shack and started across the street toward the building. Morty watched in horror, his heart pounding so furiously he could hear it. Was the cop coming toward him? The cop glanced in his direction and went to the door of the building, where he tapped on the glass. Manolo scrambled to his feet and opened the door, and the cop disappeared down the stairs, heading for the lavatory in the basement.

After what seemed an interminable few minutes, he finally saw Evelyn coming. She pulled the car up, and he quickly opened the back door. He began struggling with Irving and was near collapse from fright. What if the cop returned and happened to be one of the "good-guys"? He'd probably stroll over and offer to lend a hand. And the cop would surely know a stiff when he saw one. How would he explain Irving? . . . Uh, well, you see, Officer, we found him on East Sixty-second Street, rolled up in a rug. . . . And you didn't call the police? . . . Uh, my wife was afraid you'd take the rug.

Somehow he managed to get Irving into the backseat of the car and into an upright position. He collapsed the wheelchair and placed it in the trunk. Then he ran around to the driver's seat and climbed in as Evelyn moved over. As they drove by the guard shack, Morty looked but could see no activity in the little structure. Had they been watching him? Maybe it was only the one cop. Or maybe, if there was another one, and if God was with them, the other cop was cooping, taking a little snooze for himself. Morty drove to the corner of Lexington Avenue and stopped a bit abruptly for the light, and as he did, Irving heaved forward, slipping down, out of sight.

"Where are we taking him?" Evelyn asked. "You said you had a place all picked out."

"It's a fitting place for so special an occasion. A high and significant place." Morty was gradually calming down as he drove, and his sense of macabre amusement with the whole business was returning. "It's a place with a marvelous view," he added.

"A view? Morty, where are we taking him?"

"Wait and see."

A light rain began to fall as they cut back to the East Side, headed north on FDR Drive, onto the Harlem River Drive, and up to the George Washington Bridge. They crossed the bridge into Jersey, went immediately north on the virtually deserted Palisades Parkway, then pulled off at the first overlook, the Rockefeller Overlook, which provided an inspiring view of the Hudson, the opposite shore, the bridge, and beyond it, the skyline of Manhattan. He knew the spot well from having grown up in Jersey, and as he expected, there were no cars in sight. Who comes to an overlook at five in the morning? Especially when it has started raining.

"Is this perfect?" Morty breathed, feeling pleased with himself. "We'll leave him here to be the master of all he surveys." To which he added, "He can watch the dawn come up like thunder over Yonkers 'cross the way."

He pulled the car over parallel to the row of large rocks that provided a barrier to the bluff overlooking the river, and then, out of nowhere, lights flashing, a highway patrol car pulled quickly over next to him. Morty let out a tiny moan of dismay. His life, as he knew it, was over. All because of a lousy rug. He was ready to collapse into tears.

But Evelyn prodded him. "Morty! For God's sake, be cool. He fell down, in back. He's out of sight."

The trooper rolled down his window and shined a flashlight in Morty's face, signaling to Morty to roll his window down. Morty slowly did as he was told. The trooper studied Morty and Evelyn for a moment, and his expression changed. It softened, as if he couldn't possibly suspect this innocuous-looking couple of anything illegal. "Are you two all right?" he asked.

"We're fine, Officer, fine," Morty managed to get out.

"It seemed an odd time for anyone, like yourselves, that is, to be coming in here."

"It's our anniversary, Officer," Evelyn said. Morty turned and looked at her.

"Anniversary?" the officer asked. An amused smile.

"Fifteen years ago we got engaged on this spot. And at just about this time, believe it or not."

The officer looked as if, with that bit of information, he'd finally heard it all. "Well, congratulations. You two take care, hear? I wouldn't hang around this spot too long at this hour."

"Thank you, Officer," Morty said. And they watched as the patrol car roared away toward the exit and disappeared.

"Did he check our license plate?" Morty asked.

"He didn't check anything," she answered. "He didn't look at anything but our innocent faces."

"Good. You know something? You've got the makings of a great criminal mind."

Morty got out of the car and hurried around to the other side. He opened the back door and dragged Irving out, pulling him between two of the large rocks that formed the barrier to the high, steep bluff. Then he propped Irving up against one of the rocks, facing the river, in position to enjoy the view. "Stay loose, old friend," he muttered to Irving. He hurried back into the car and headed for the exit, and home.

The rain grew heavier, and it pelted Irving's face, but Irving did not flinch. The ink on the sticky tag on his lapel was not waterproof, and the rain caused his name to streak, and finally to wash completely away.

Monday morning. In an elegantly appointed town house in Boston's Back Bay area, Mrs. Ira Waterman answered the phone. "No, I don't know where Mr. Waterman is . . . no, I don't know how to get in touch with him . . . no, I, please let me explain. Mr. Waterman and I are separated. We are not in touch and have not been for quite some time, and I frankly have no idea as to his whereabouts, nor do I wish to have . . . yes, he could be in New York, I suppose. We did live there at one time when we were still together, and I think he still has business there. But he could also be most anywhere, and I assure you, I haven't the faintest notion where . . . you're very welcome."

Monday afternoon. Jack Sandifer entered the plane for his flight back to Chicago, went to his seat, and got comfortable. He was a tall man, lean, blond, athletic, striking in appearance.

After completing the project for which he'd flown east, he'd enjoyed a pleasant weekend in the Big Apple. A stay at the Pierre, a meal at Le Cirque, a couple of tough-ticket shows, *Les Miz* and *Phantom*. And this was in addition to the satisfaction of having been paid for a job properly done. The fifty thousand in bearer bonds was in his luggage. He always specified bearer bonds. Asking for cash always seemed a little lacking in class.

As the plane-loading process continued, he riffled through the *Post* he'd bought in the terminal. He studied the article about an unidentified man being found at an overlook off some parkway in New Jersey. A parkway in Jersey? And wearing a white turtleneck? "How in hell?" he said to himself. He glanced at the young woman who had taken the seat next to him. She was beautiful. She could easily be a model.

He reached into his shirt pocket and took out the little tuft of carpet fringe, examining it briefly and then putting it back. This business of keeping mementos of each of his projects was definitely a dangerous one, but it gave his work a quality, an edge of excitement, actually, that pleased him.

He'd liked his client. A very feisty lady for being so educated and polished. He smiled as he thought about her emphatic instructions. "I want you to remove all identification from him, and then label him in some way with his name before he changed it twenty years ago. And then deliver him back to our old address. That should do it for me."

And then she'd added the part about the rug. "Oh. And could you get that horrid Navajo rug of his out of the library? I've hated it since the day he bought it. Maybe you can think of some way to use it on this assignment. That would indeed be a nice touch."

The flight attendant came around to take drink orders. He asked for a couple of Scotches and then asked the woman next to him if she'd like a drink.

"Sure," she said with a disarming smile. "Thanks." And as their continuing conversation established that they were both returning to Chicago, where they both lived, she asked, "What sort of work do you do?"

"I'm a paid assassin."

"Gimme a break. Seriously, what do you do?"

"Actually, I deal in unusual antiques, specifically in primitive art. For example, I just delivered an authentic hand-woven, one-of-a-kind, antique Navajo rug to the City for a client. For which I was extremely well paid, I might add."

"Extremely? May I ask how extremely?"

"How's fifty thousand? And to help me celebrate, have dinner with me when we get to Chicago."

Again that marvelous smile. "I'd love it," she said.

ED GORMAN

PRISONERS

(For Gail Cross)

Perhaps no new writer had a wider impact on American mysteries in the 1980s than Ed Gorman. He wrote novels and short stories, edited anthologies, and even published a successful magazine for fans and professionals, Mystery Scene. *In a way it's fitting that his second appearance in this series is from the hard-hitting British anthology series* New Crimes, *launched by London editor and bookman Maxim Jakubowski. Though they've never met, Gorman and Jakubowski represent a new wave of mystery and suspense that we'll be watching and reading in the coming decade. Now here's "Prisoners," a memorable story and another of the year's Edgar nominees.*

I am in my sister's small room with its posters of Madonna and Tiffany. Sis is fourteen. Already tall, already pretty. Dressed in jeans and a blue T-shirt. Boys call and come over constantly. She wants nothing to do with boys.

Her back is to me. She will not turn around. I sit on the edge of her bed, touching my hand to her shoulder. She smells warm, of sleep. I say, "Sis, listen to me."

She says nothing. She almost always says nothing.

"He wants to see you, Sis."

Nothing.

"When he called last weekend—you were all he talked about. He even started crying when you wouldn't come to the phone Sis. He really did."

Nothing.

"Please, Sis. Please put on some good clothes and get ready 'cause we've got to leave in ten minutes. We've got to get there on time and you know it." I lean over so I can see her face.

She tucks her face into her pillow.

She doesn't want me to see that she is crying.

"Now you go and get ready, Sis. You go and get ready, all right?"

"I don't know who she thinks she is," Ma says when I go downstairs. "Too good to go and see her own father."

As she talks Ma is packing a big brown grocery sack. Into it go a cornucopia of goodies—three cartons of Lucky Strike filters, three packages of Hershey bars, two bottles of Ban roll-on deodorant, three Louis L'Amour paperbacks as well as all the stuff that's in there already.

Ma looks up at me. I've seen pictures of her when she was a young woman. She was a beauty. But that was before she started putting on weight and her hair started thinning and she stopped caring about how she dressed and all. "She going to go with us?"

"She says not."

"Just who does she think she is?"

"Calm down, Ma. If she doesn't want to go, we'll just go ahead without her."

"What do we tell your Dad?"

"Tell him she's got the flu."

"The way she had the flu the last six times?"

"She's gone a few times."

"Yeah twice out of the whole year he's been there."

"Well."

"How do you think he feels? He gets all excited thinking he's going to see her and then she doesn't show up. How do you think he feels? She's his own flesh and blood."

I sigh. Ma's none too healthy and getting worked up this way doesn't do her any good. "I better go and call Riley."

"That's it. Go call Riley. Leave me here alone to worry about what we're going to tell your Dad."

"You know how Riley is. He appreciates a call."

"You don't care about me no more than your selfish sister does."

I go out to the living room where the phone sits on the end table I picked up at Goodwill last Christmastime. A lot of people don't like to shop at Goodwill, embarrassed about going in there and all. The only thing I don't like is the smell. All those old clothes hanging. Sometimes I wonder if you opened up a grave if it wouldn't smell like Goodwill.

I call K-Mart, which is where I work as a manager trainee while I'm finishing off my retail degree at the junior college. My girlfriend, Karen, works at K-Mart, too. "Riley?"

"Hey, Tom."

"How're things going in my department?" A couple months ago Riley, who is the assistant manager over the whole store, put me in charge of the automotive department.

"Good, great."

"Good. I was worried." Karen always says she's proud 'cause I worry so much about my job. Karen says it proves I'm responsible. Karen says one of the reasons she loves me so much is 'cause I'm responsible. I guess I'd rather have her love me for my blue eyes or something but of course I don't say anything because Karen can get crabby about strange things sometimes.

"You go and see your old man today, huh?" Riley says.

"Yeah."

"Hell of a way to spend your day off."

"It's not so bad. You get used to it."

"Any word on when he gets out?"

"Be a year or so yet. Being his second time in and all."

"You're a hell of a kid, Tom, I ever tell you that before?"

"Yeah you did Riley and I appreciate it." Riley is a year older than me but sometimes he likes to pretend he's my uncle or something. But he means well and, like I told him, I appreciate it. Like when Dad's name was in the paper for the burglary and everything. The people at K-Mart all saw it and started treating me funny. But not Tom. He'd walk up and down the aisles with me and even put his arm on my shoulder like we were the best buddies in the whole world or something. In the coffee room this fat woman made a crack about it and Tom got mad and said "Why don't you shut your fucking fat mouth, Shirley?" Nobody said anything more about my Dad after that. Of course poor Sis had it a lot worse than me at Catholic school. She had it real bad. Some of those kids really got vicious. A lot of nights I'd lay awake thinking of all the things I wanted to do to those kids. I'd do it with my hands too, wouldn't even use weapons.

"Well say hi to your mom."

"Thanks, Riley. I'll be sure to."

"She's a hell of a nice lady." Riley and his girl came over one night when Ma'd had about three beers and was in a really good mood. They got along really well. He had her laughing at his jokes all night. Riley knows a lot of jokes. A lot of them.

"I sure hope we make our goal today."

"You just relax, Tom, and forget about the store. OK?"

"I'll try."

"Don't try, Tom. Do it." He laughs, being my uncle again. "That's an order."

In the kitchen, done with packing her paper bag, Ma says, "I shouldn't have said that."

"Said what?" I say.

"About you being like your sister."

"Aw, Ma. I didn't take that seriously."

"We couldn't've afforded to stay in this house if you hadn't been promoted to assistant manager. Not many boys would turn over their whole paychecks to their ma." She doesn't mention her sister who is married to a banker who is what bankers aren't supposed to be, generous. I help but he helps a lot.

She starts crying.

I take her to me, hold her. Ma needs to cry a lot. Like she fills up with tears and will drown if she can't get rid of them. When I hold her I always think of the pictures of her as a young woman, of all the terrible things that have cost her her beauty.

When she's settled down some I say, "I'll go talk to Sis."

But just as I say that I hear the old boards of the house creak and there in the doorway, dressed in a white blouse and a blue skirt and blue hose and the blue flats I bought her for her last birthday, is Sis.

Ma sees her too and starts crying all over again. "Oh God hon thanks so much for changing your mind."

Then Ma puts her arms out wide and she goes over to Sis and

throws her arms around her and gets her locked inside this big hug.

I can see Sis's blue eyes staring at me over Ma's shoulder.

In the soft fog of the April morning I see watercolor brown cows on the curve of the green hills and red barns faint in the rain. I used to want to be a farmer till I took a two-week job summer of junior year where I cleaned out dairy barns and it took me weeks to get the odor of wet hay and cowshit and hot pissy milk from my nostrils and then I didn't want to be a farmer ever again.

"You all right hon?" Ma asks Sis.

But Sis doesn't answer. Just stares out the window at the watercolor brown cows.

"Ungrateful little brat," Ma says under her breath.

If Sis hears this she doesn't let on. She just stares out the window.

"Hon slow down," Ma says to me. "This road'z got a lot of curves in it."

And so it does.

Twenty-three curves—I've counted them many times—and you're on top of a hill looking down into a valley where the prison lies.

Curious, I once went to the library and read up on the prison. According to the historical society it's the oldest prison still standing in the Midwest, built of limestone dragged by prisoners from a nearby quarry. In 1948 the west wing had a fire that killed eighteen blacks (they were segregated in those days), and in 1957 there was a riot that got a guard castrated with a busted pop bottle and two inmates shot dead in the back by other guards who were never brought to trial.

From the two-lane asphalt road that winds into the prison you see the steep limestone walls and the towers where uniformed guards toting riot guns look down at you as you sweep west to park in the visitors' parking lot.

As we walk through the rain to the prison, hurrying as the fat drops splatter on our heads, Ma says "I forgot. Don't say anything about your cousin Bessie."

"Oh. Right."

"Stuff about cancer always makes your dad depressed. You know it runs in his family a lot."

She glances over her shoulder at Sis shambling along. Sis had not worn a coat. The rain doesn't seem to bother her. She is staring out at something still as if her face was nothing more than a mask that hides her real self. "You hear me?" Ma asks Sis.

If Sis hears she doesn't say anything.

"How're you doing this morning, Jimmy?" Ma asks the fat guard who lets us into the waiting room.

His stomach wriggles beneath his threadbare uniform shirt like something troubled struggling to be born.

He grunts something none of us can understand. He obviously doesn't believe in being nice to Ma no matter how nice Ma is to him. Would break prison decorum apparently the sonofabitch. But if you think he's cold to us—and most people in the prison are—you should see how they are to the families of queers or with men who did things with children.

The cold is in my bones already. Except for July and August prison is always cold to me. The bars are cold. The walls are cold. When you go into the bathroom and run the water your fingers tingle. The prisoners are always sneezing and coughing. Ma always brings Dad lots of Contac and Listerine even though I told her about this article that said Listerine isn't anything except a mouthwash.

In the waiting room—which is nothing more than the yellow-painted room with battered old wooden chairs—a turnkey named Stan comes in and leads you right up to the visiting room, the only problem being that separating you from the visiting room is a set of bars. Stan turns the key that raises these bars and then you get inside and he lowers the bars behind you. For a minute or so you're locked in between two walls and two sets of bars. You get a sense of what it's like to be in a cell. The first couple times this happened I got scared. My chest started heaving and I couldn't catch my breath, sort of like the nightmares I have sometimes.

Stan then raises the second set of bars and you're one room away from the visiting room, or VR as the prisoners call it. In prison you always lower the first set of bars before you raise the next one. That way nobody escapes.

In this second room, not much bigger than a closet with a stand-up clumsy metal detector near the door leading to the VR, Stan asks Ma and Sis for their purses and me for my wallet. He asks if any of us have got any open packs of cigarettes and if so to hand them over. Prisoners and visitors alike can carry only full packs of cigarettes into the VR. Open packs are easy to hide stuff in.

You pass through the metal detector and straight into the VR.

The first thing you notice is how all the furniture is in color-coded sets—loungers and vinyl molded chairs makes up a set—orange green blue or red. Like that. This is so Mona the guard in here can tell you where to sit just by saying a color such as "Blue" which means you go sit in the blue set. Mona makes Stan look like a real friendly guy. She's fat with hair cut man short and a voice man deep. She wears her holster and gun with real obvious pleasure. One time Ma didn't understand what color she said and Mona's hand dropped to her service revolver like she was going to whip it out or something. Mona doesn't like to repeat herself. Mona is the one the black prisoner knocked unconscious a year ago. The black guy is married to this white girl which right away you can imagine Mona not liking at all so she's looking for any excuse to hassle him so the black guy one time gets down on his hands and knees to play with his little baby and Mona comes over and says you can only play with kids in the Toy Room (TR) and he says can't you make an exception and Mona slylike bumps him hard on the shoulder and he just flashes the way prisoners sometimes do and jumps up from the floor and not caring that she's a woman or not just drops her with a right hand and the way the story is told now anyway by prisoners and their families, everybody in VR instead of rushing to help her break out into applause just like it's a movie or something. Standing ovation. The black guy was in the hole for six months but was quoted afterward as saying it was worth it.

Most of the time it's not like that at all. Nothing exciting I mean. Most of the time it's just depressing.

Mostly it's women here to see husbands. They usually bring

their kids so there's a lot of noise. Crying laughing chasing around. You can tell if there's trouble with a parole—the guy not getting out when he's supposed to—because that's when the arguments always start, the wife having built her hopes up and then the husband saying there's nothing he can do I'm sorry honey nothing I can do and sometimes the woman will really start crying or arguing, I even saw a woman slap her husband once, the worst being of course when some little kid starts crying and says, "Daddy I want you to come home!" That's usually when the prisoner himself starts crying.

As for touching or fondling, there's none of it. You can kiss your husband for thirty seconds and most guards will hassle you even before your time's up if you try it open mouth or anything. Mona in particular is a real bitch about something like this. Apparently Mona doesn't like the idea of men and women kissing.

Another story you hear a lot up here is how this one prisoner cut a hole in his pocket so he could stand by the Coke machine and have his wife put her hand down his pocket and jack him off while they just appeared to be innocently standing there, though that may be one of those stories the prisoners just like to tell.

The people who really have it worst are those who are in the hole or some other kind of solitary. On the west wall there's this long screen for them. They have to sit behind the screen the whole time. They can't touch their kids or anything. All they can do is look.

I can hear Ma's breath take up sharp when they bring Dad in.

He's still a handsome man—thin, dark curly hair with no gray, and more solid than ever since he works out in the prison weight room all the time. He always walks jaunty, as if to say that wearing a gray uniform and living in an interlocking set of cages has not yet broken him. But you can see in his blue eyes that they broke him a long long time ago.

"Hiya everybody" he says trying to sound real happy.

Ma throws her arms around him and they hold each other. Sis and I sit down on the two chairs. I look at Sis. She stares at the floor.

Dad comes over then and says, "You two sure look great."

"So do you," I say. "You must be still lifting those weights."

"Bench pressed two-twenty-five this week."

"Man," I say and look at Sis again. I nudge her with my elbow. She won't look up.

Dad stares at her. You can see how sad he is about her not looking up. Soft he says, "It's all right."

Ma and Dad sit down then and we go through the usual stuff, how things are going at home and at my job and in junior college, and how things are going in prison. When he first got here, they put Dad in with this colored guy—he was Jamaican—but then they found out he had AIDS so they moved Dad out right away. Now the guy he's with is this guy who was in Vietnam and got one side of his face burned. Dad says once you get used to looking at him he's a nice guy with two kids of his own and not queer in any way or into drugs at all. In prison the drugs get pretty bad.

We talk a half hour before Dad looks at Sis again. "So how's my little girl."

She still won't look up.

"Ellen," Ma says, "you talk to your Dad and right now."

Sis raises her head. She looks right at Dad but doesn't seem to see him at all. Ellen can do that. It's real spooky.

Dad puts his hand out and touches her.

Sis jerks her hand away. It's the most animated I've seen her in weeks.

"You give your Dad a hug and you give him a hug right now," Ma says to Sis.

Sis, still staring at Dad, shakes her head.

"It's all right," Dad says. "It's all right. She just doesn't like to come up here and I don't blame her at all. This isn't a nice place to visit at all." He smiles. "Believe me I wouldn't be here if they didn't make me."

Ma asks "Any word on your parole?"

"My lawyer says two years away. Maybe three, 'cause it's a second offense and all." Dad sighs and takes Ma's hand. "I know it's hard for you to believe hon—I mean practically every guy in here says the same thing—but I didn't break into that store that night. I really didn't. I was just walkin' along the river."

"I do believe you, hon," Ma says, "and so does Tom and so does Sis. Right kids?"

I nod. Sis has gone back to staring at the floor.

" 'Cause I served time before for breaking and entering the cops just automatically assumed it was me," Dad says. He shakes his head. The sadness is back in his eyes. "I don't have no idea how my billfold got on the floor of that place." He sounds miserable and now he doesn't look jaunty or young. He looks old and gray.

He looks back at Sis. "You still gettin' straight As hon?"

She looks up at him. But doesn't nod or anything.

"She sure is," Ma says. "Sister Rosemary says Ellen is the best student she's got. Imagine that."

Dad starts to reach out to Sis again but then takes his hand back.

Over in the red section this couple start arguing. The woman is crying and this little girl maybe six is holding real tight to her Dad, who looks like he's going to start crying too. That bitch Mona has put on her mirror sunglasses again so you can't tell what she's thinking, but you can see from the angle of her face that she's watching the three of them in the red section. Probably enjoying herself.

"Your lawyer sure it'll be two years?" Ma says.

"Or three."

"I sure do miss you hon" Ma says.

"I sure do miss you too hon."

"Don't know what I'd do without Tom to lean on." She makes a point of not mentioning Sis, who she's obviously still mad at because Sis won't speak to Dad.

"He's sure a fine young man," Dad says. "Wish I woulda been that responsible when I was his age. Wouldn't be in here today if I'da been."

Sis gets up and leaves the room. Says nothing. Doesn't even look at anybody exactly. Just leaves. Mona directs her to the ladies room.

"I'm sorry, hon, she treats you this way," Ma says. "She thinks she's too good to come see her Dad in prison."

"It's all right," Dad says looking sad again. He watches Sis leave the visiting room.

"I'm gonna have a good talk with her when we leave here, hon," Ma says.

"Oh, don't be too hard on her. Tough for a proud girl her age to come up here."

"Not too hard for Tom."

"Tom's different. Tom's mature. Tom's responsible. When Ellen gets Tom's age I'm sure she'll be mature and responsible too."

Half hour goes back before Sis comes. Almost time to leave. She walks over and sits down.

"You give your Dad a hug now," Ma says.

Sis looks at Dad. She stands up then and goes over and puts her arms out. Dad stands up grinning and takes her to him and hugs her tighter than I've ever seen him hug anybody. It's funny because right then and there he starts crying. Just holding Sis so tight. Crying.

"I love you hon," Dad says to her. "I love you hon and I'm sorry for all the mistakes I've made and I'll never make them again I promise you."

Ma starts crying too.

Sis says nothing.

When Dad lets her go I look at her eyes. They're the same as they were before. She's staring right at him but she doesn't seem to see him somehow.

Mona picks up the microphone that blasts through the speakers hung from the ceiling. She doesn't need a speaker in a room this size but she obviously likes how loud it is and how it hurts your ears.

"Visiting hours are over. You've got fifteen seconds to say good-bye and then the inmates have to start filing over to the door."

"I miss you so much hon," Ma says and throws her arms around Dad.

He hugs Ma but over his shoulder he's looking at Sis. She is standing up. She has her head down again.

Dad looks so sad so sad.

"I'd like to know just who the hell you think you are treatin' your own father that way," Ma says on the way back to town.

The rain and the fog are real bad now so I have to concentrate on my driving. On the opposite side of the road cars appear quickly in the fog and then vanish. It's almost unreal.

The wipers are slapping loud and everything smells damp, the rubber of the car and the vinyl seat covers and the ashtray from Ma's menthol cigarettes. Damp.

"You hear me young lady?" Ma says.

Sis is in the backseat again alone. Staring out the window. At the fog I guess.

"Come on Ma, she hugged him," I say.

"Yeah when I practically had to twist her arm to do it." Ma shakes her head. "Her own flesh and blood."

Sometimes I want to get mad and really let it out but I know it would just hurt Ma to remind her what Dad was doing to Ellen those years after he came out of prison the first time. I know for a fact he was doing it because I walked in on them one day, little eleven-year-old Ellen there on the bed underneath my naked dad, staring off as he grunted and moved around inside her, staring off just the way she does now.

Staring off.

Ma knew about it all along of course but she wouldn't do anything about it. Wouldn't admit it probably not even to herself. In psychology, which I took last year at the junior college, that's called denial. I even brought it up a couple times but she just said I had a filthy mind and don't ever say nothing like that again.

Which is why I broke into that store that night and left Dad's billfold behind. Because I knew they'd arrest him and then he couldn't force Ellen into the bed anymore. Not that I blame Dad entirely. Prison makes you crazy no doubt about it and he was in there four years the first time. But even so I love Sis too much.

"Own flesh and blood," Ma says again lighting up one of her menthols and shaking her head.

I look into the rearview mirror at Sis's eyes. "Wish I could make you smile," I say to her. "Wish I could make you smile."

But she just stares out the window.

Sis hasn't smiled for a long time of course.

Not for a long time.

SUE GRAFTON

A POISON THAT LEAVES NO TRACE

To date, Sue Grafton has produced eight novels in her continuing series about California private eye Kinsey Millhone, running through the alphabet with ease to the current "H" Is for Homicide. *Kinsey's short cases have been less frequent but just as compelling, as in this MWA Edgar nominee.*

The woman was waiting outside my office when I arrived that morning. She was short and quite plump, wearing jeans in a size I've never seen on the rack. Her blouse was tunic-length, ostensibly to disguise her considerable rear end. Someone must have told her never to wear horizontal stripes, so the bold red-and-blue bands ran diagonally across her torso with a dizzying effect. Big red canvas tote, matching canvas wedgies. Her face was round, seamless, and smooth, her hair a uniformly dark shade that suggested a rinse. She might have been any age between forty and sixty. "You're not Kinsey Millhone," she said as I approached.

"Actually, I am. Would you like to come in?" I unlocked the door and stepped back so she could pass in front of me. She was giving me the once-over, as if my appearance was as remarkable to her as hers was to me.

She took a seat, keeping her tote squarely on her lap. I went around to my side of the desk, pausing to open the French doors before I sat down. "What can I help you with?"

She stared at me openly. "Well, I don't know. I thought you'd be a man. What kind of name is Kinsey? I never heard such a thing."

"My mother's maiden name. I take it you're in the market for a private investigator."

"I guess you could say that. I'm Shirese Dunaway, but everybody calls me Sis. Exactly how long have you been doing this?" Her tone was a perfect mating of skepticism and distrust.

"Six years in May. I was with the police department for two years before that. If my being a woman bothers you, I can recommend another agency. It won't offend me in the least."

"Well, I might as well talk to you as long as I'm here. I drove all the way up from Orange County. You don't charge for a consultation, I hope."

"Not at all. My regular fee is thirty dollars an hour plus expenses, but only if I believe I can be of help. What sort of problem are you dealing with?"

"Thirty dollars an hour! My stars. I had no idea it would cost so *much*."

"Lawyers charge a hundred and twenty," I said with a shrug.

"I know, but that's in case of a lawsuit. Contingency, or whatever they call that. Thirty dollars an *hour* . . ."

I closed my mouth and let her work it out for herself. I didn't want to get into an argument with the woman in the first five minutes of our relationship. I tuned her out, watching her lips move while she decided what to do.

"The problem is my sister," she said at long last. "Here, look at this." She handed me a little clipping from the Santa Teresa newspaper. The death notice read: "Crispin, Margery, beloved mother of Justine, passed away on December 10. Private arrangements. Wynington-Blake Mortuary."

"Nearly two months ago," I remarked.

"Nobody even told me she was sick! That's the point," Sis Dunaway snapped. "I wouldn't know to this day if a former neighbor hadn't spotted this and cut it out." She tended to speak in an indignant tone regardless of the subject.

"You just received this?"

"Well, no. It came back in January, but of course I couldn't drop everything and rush right up. This is the first chance I've had. You can probably appreciate that, upset as I was."

"Absolutely," I said. "When did you last talk to Margery?"

"I don't remember the exact date. It had to be eight or ten years back. You can imagine my shock! To get something like this out of a clear blue sky."

I shook my head. "Terrible," I murmured. "Have you talked to your niece?"

She gestured dismissively. "That Justine's a mess. Marge had her hands full with that one," she said. "I stopped over to her place and you should have seen the look I got. I said, 'Justine, whatever in the world did Margery die of?' And you know what she said? Said, 'Aunt Sis, her heart give out.' Well, I knew that was bull the minute she said it. We have never had heart trouble in our family. . . ."

She went on for a while about what everybody'd died of; Mom, Dad, Uncle Buster, Rita Sue. We're talking cancer, lung disorders, an aneurysm or two. Sure enough, no heart trouble. I was making sympathetic noises, just to keep the tale afloat until she got to the point. I jotted down a few notes, though I never did quite understand how Rita Sue was related. Finally, I said, "Is it your feeling there was something unusual in your sister's death?"

She pursed her lips and lowered her gaze. "Let's put it this way. I can smell a rat. I'd be willing to *bet* Justine had a hand in it."

"Why would she do that?"

"Well, Marge had that big insurance policy. The one Harley took out in 1966. If that's not a motive for murder, I don't know what is." She sat back in her chair, content that she'd made her case.

"Harley?"

"Her husband . . . until he passed on, of course. They took out policies on each other and after he went, she kept up the premiums on hers. Justine was made the beneficiary. Marge never remarried and with Justine on the policy, I guess she'll get all the money and do I don't know what. It just doesn't seem right. She's been a sneak all ner natural life. A regular con artist. She's been in jail four times! My sister talked till she was blue in the face, but she never could get Justine to straighten up her act."

"How much money are we talking about?"

"A hundred thousand dollars," she said. "Furthermore, them two never did get along. Fought like cats and dogs since the day Justine was born. Competitive? My God. Always trying to get the better of each other. Justine as good as told me they had a falling-out not two months before her mother died! The two had not exchanged a word since the day Marge got mad and stomped off."

"They lived together?"

"Well, yes, until this big fight. Next thing you know, Marge is dead. You tell me there's not something funny going on."

"Have you talked to the police?"

"How can I do that? I don't have any *proof.*"

"What about the insurance company? Surely, if there were something irregular about Marge's death, the claims investigator would have picked up on it."

"Oh, honey, you'd think so, but you know how it is. Once a claim's been paid, the insurance company doesn't want to hear. Admit they made a mistake? Uh-uh, no thanks. Too much trouble going back through all the paperwork. Besides, Justine would probably turn around and sue 'em within an inch of their life. They'd rather turn a deaf ear and write the money off."

"When was the claim paid?"

"A week ago, they said."

I stared at her for a moment, considering. "I don't know what to tell you, Ms. Dunaway. . . ."

"Call me Sis. I don't go for that Ms. bull."

"All right, Sis. If you're really convinced Justine's implicated in her mother's death, of course I'll try to help. I just don't want to waste your time."

"I can appreciae that," she said.

I stirred in my seat. "Look, I'll tell you what let's do. Why don't you pay me for two hours of my time. If I don't come up with anything concrete in that period, we can have another conversation and you can decide then if you want me to proceed."

"Sixty dollars," she said.

"That's right. Two hours."

"Well, all right. I guess I can do that." She opened her tote and peeled six tens off a roll of bills she'd secured with a rubber band. I wrote out an abbreviated version of a standard contract. She said she'd be staying in town overnight and gave me the telephone number at the motel where she'd checked in. She handed me the death notice. I made sure I had her sister's full name and the exact date of her death and told her I'd be in touch.

My first stop was the Hall of Records at the Santa Teresa County Courthouse two and a half blocks away. I filled out a copy order, supplying the necessary information, and paid seven bucks in cash. An hour later, I returned to pick up the certified copy of Margery Crispin's death certificate. Cause of death was listed as a "myocardial infarction." The certificate was signed by Dr. Yee, one of the contract pathologists out at the county morgue. If Marge Crispin had been the victim of foul play, it was hard to believe Dr. Yee wouldn't have spotted it.

I swung back by the office and picked up my car, driving over to Wynington-Blake, the mortuary listed in the newspaper clipping. I asked for Mr. Sharonson, whom I'd met when I was working on another case. He was wearing a somber charcoal gray suit, his tone of voice carefully modulated to reflect the solemnity of his work. When I mentioned Marge Crispin, a shadow crossed his face.

"You remember the woman?"

"Oh, yes," he said. He closed his mouth then, but the look he gave me was eloquent.

I wondered if funeral home employees took a loyalty oath, vowing never to divulge a single fact about the dead. I thought I'd prime the pump a bit. Men are worse gossips than women once you get 'em going. "Mrs. Crispin's sister was in my office a little while ago and she seems to think there was something . . . uh, irregular about the woman's death."

I could see Mr. Sharonson formulate his response. "I wouldn't say there was anything *irregular* about the woman's death, but there was certainly something sordid about the circumstances."

"Oh?" said I.

He lowered his voice, glancing around to make certain we couldn't be overheard. "The two were estranged. Hadn't spoken for months as I understand it. The woman died alone in a seedy hotel on lower State Street. She drank."

"Nooo," I said, conveying disapproval and disbelief.

"Oh, yes," he said. "The police picked up the body, but she

wasn't identified for weeks. If it hadn't been for the article in the paper, her daughter might not have ever known."

"What article?"

"Oh, you know the one. There's that columnist for the local paper who does all those articles about the homeless. He did a write-up about the poor woman. 'Alone in Death' I think it was called. He talked about how pathetic this woman was. Apparently, when Ms. Crispin read the article, she began to suspect it might be her mother. That's when she went out there to take a look."

"Must have been a shock," I said. "The woman did die of natural causes?"

"Oh, yes."

"No evidence of trauma, foul play, anything like that?"

"No, no, no. I tended her myself and I know they ran toxicology tests. I guess at first they thought it might be acute alcohol poisoning, but it turned out to be her heart."

I quizzed him on a number of possibilities, but I couldn't come up with anything out of the ordinary. I thanked him for his time, got back in my car, and drove over to the trailer park where Justine Crispin lived.

The trailer itself had seen better days. It was moored in a dirt patch with a wooden crate for an outside step. I knocked on the door, which opened about an inch to show a short strip of round face peering out at me. "Yes?"

"Are you Justine Crispin?"

"Yes."

"I hope I'm not bothering you. My name is Kinsey Millhone. I'm an old friend of your mother's and I just heard she passed away."

The silence was cautious. "Who'd you hear that from?"

I showed her the clipping. "Someone sent me this. I couldn't believe my eyes. I didn't even know she was sick."

Justine's eyes darkened with suspicion. "When did you see her last?"

I did my best to imitate Sis Dunaway's folksy tone. "Oh, gee. Must have been last summer. I moved away in June and it was probably some time around then because I remember giving her my address. It was awfully sudden, wasn't it?"

"Her heart give out."

"Well, the poor thing, and she was such a love." I wondered if I'd laid it on too thick. Justine was staring at me like I'd come to the wrong place. "Would you happen to know if she got my last note?" I asked.

"I wouldn't know anything about that."

"Because I wasn't sure what to do about the money."

"She owed you money?"

"No, no. I owed *her* . . . which is why I wrote."

Justine hesitated. "How much?"

"Well, it wasn't much," I said, with embarrassment. "Six hundred dollars, but she was such a doll to lend it to me and then I felt so bad when I couldn't pay her back right away. I asked her if I could wait and pay her this month, but then I never heard. Now I don't know what to do."

I could sense the shift in her attitude. Greed seems to do that in record time. "You could pay it to me and I could see it went into her estate," she said helpfully.

"Oh, I don't want to put you to any trouble."

"I don't mind," she said. "You want to come in?"

"I shouldn't. You're probably busy and you've already been so nice. . . ."

"I can take a few minutes."

"Well. If you're sure," I said.

Justine held the door open and I stepped into the trailer, where I got my first clear look at her. This girl was probably thirty pounds overweight with listless brown hair pulled into an oily ponytail. Like Sis, she was decked out in a pair of jeans, with an oversize T-shirt hanging almost to her knees. It was clear big butts ran in the family. She shoved some junk aside so I could sit down on the banquette, a fancy word for the ripped plastic seat that extended along one wall in the kitchenette.

"Did she suffer much?" I asked.

"Doctor said not. He said it was quick, as far as he could tell. Her heart probably seized up and she fell down dead before she could draw a breath."

"It must have been just terrible for you."

Her cheeks flushed with guilt. "You know, her and me had a falling out."

"Really? Well, I'm sorry to hear that. Of course, she always said you two had your differences. I hope it wasn't anything serious."

"She drank. I begged her and begged her to give it up, but she wouldn't pay me no mind," Justine said.

"Did she 'go' here at home?"

She shook her head. "In a welfare hotel. Down on her luck. Drink had done her in. If only I'd known . . . if only she'd reached out."

I thought she was going to weep, but shc couldn't quitc manage it. I clutched her hand. "She was too proud," I said.

"I guess that's what it was. I've been thinking to make some kind of contribution to AA, or something like that. You know, in her name."

"A Marge Crispin Memorial Fund," I suggested.

"Like that, yes. I was thinking this money you're talking about might be a start."

"That's a beautiful thought. I'm going right out to the car for my checkbook so I can write you a check."

It was a relief to get out into the fresh air again. I'd never heard so much horsepuckey in all my life. Still, it hardly constituted proof she was a murderess.

I hopped in my car and headed for a pay phone, spotting one in a gas station half a block away. I pulled change out of the bottom of my handbag and dialed Sis Dunaway's motel room. She was not very happy to her my report.

"You didn't find anything?" she said. "Are you positive?"

"Well, of course I'm not positive. All I'm saying is that so far, there's no evidence that anything's amiss. If Justine contributed to her mother's death, she was damned clever about it. I gather the autopsy didn't show a thing."

"Maybe it was some kind of poison that leaves no trace."

"Uh, Sis? I hate to tell you this, but there really isn't such a poison that I ever heard of. I know it's a common fantasy, but there's just no such thing."

Her tone turned stubborn. "But it's possible. You have to admit that. There could be such a thing. It might be from South America . . . darkest Africa, someplace like that."

Oh, boy. We were really tripping out on this one. I squinted at the receiver. "How would Justine acquire the stuff?"

"How do I know? I'm not going to set here and solve the whole case for you! You're the one gets paid thirty dollars an hour, not me."

"Do you want me to pursue it?"

"Not if you mean to charge me an arm and a leg!" she said. "Listen here, I'll pay sixty dollars more, but you better come up with something or I want my money back."

She hung up before I could protest. How could she get her money back when she hadn't paid this portion? I stood in the phone booth and thought about things. In spite of myself, I'll admit I was hooked. Sis Dunaway might harbor a lot of foolish ideas, but her conviction was unshakable. Add to that the fact that Justice was lying about *something* and you have the kind of situation I can't walk away from.

I drove back to the trailer park and eased my car into a shady spot just across the street. Within moments, Justine appeared in a banged-up white Pinto, trailing smoke out of the tail pipe. Following her wasn't hard. I just hung my nose out the window and kept an eye on the haze. Shd drove over to Milagro Street to the branch office of a savings and loan. I pulled into a parking spot a few doors down and followed her in, keeping well out of sight. She was dealing with the branch manager, who eventually walked her over to a teller and authorized the cashing of a quite large check, judging from the number of bills the teller counted out.

Justine departed moments later, clutching her handbag protectively. I would have been willing to bet she'd been cashing that insurance check. She drove back to the trailer where she made a brief stop, probably to drop the money off.

She got back in her car and drove out of the trailer park. I followed discreetly as she headed into town. She pulled into a public parking lot and I eased in after her, finding an empty slot far enough away to disguise my purposes. So far, she didn't seem to have any idea she was being tailed. I kept my distance as she cut through to State Street and walked up a block to Santa Teresa Travel. I pretended to peruse the posters in the window while I watched her chat with the travel agent sitting at a desk just inside the front door. The two transacted business, the agent handing over what apparently were prearranged tickets. Justine wrote out a check. I busied myself at a newspaper rack, extracting a paper as she came out again. She walked down State Street half a block to a hobby shop where she purchased one of life's ugliest plastic floral wreaths. Busy little lady, this one, I thought.

She emerged from the hobby shop and headed down a side street, moving into the front entrance of a beauty salon. A surreptitious glance through the window showed her, moments later, in a green plastic cape, having a long conversation with the stylist about a cut. I checked my watch. It was almost twelve-thirty. I scooted back to the travel agency and waited until I saw Justine's travel agent leave the premises for lunch. As soon as she was out of sight, I went in, glancing at the nameplate on the edge of her desk.

The blond agent across the aisle caught my eye and smiled.

"What happened to Kathleen?" I asked.

"She went out to lunch. You just missed her. Is there something I can help you with?"

"Gee, I hope so. I picked up some tickets a little while ago and now I can't find the itinerary she tucked in the envelope. Is there any way you could run me a copy real quick? I'm in a hurry and I really can't afford to wait until she gets back."

"Sure, no problem. What's the name?"

"Justine Crispin," I said.

I found the nearest public phone and dialed Sis's motel room again. "Catch this," I said. "At four o'clock, Justine takes off for Los Angeles. From there, she flies to Mexico City."

"Well, that little shit."

"It gets worse. It's one-way."

"I knew it! I just knew she was up to no good. Where is she now?"

"Getting her hair done. She went to the bank first and cashed a big check—"

"I bet it was the insurance."

"That'd be my guess."

"She's got all that money *on* her?"

"Well, no. She stopped by the trailer first and then went and picked up her plane ticket. I think she intends to stop by the cemetery and put a wreath on Marge's grave. . . ."

"I can't stand this. I just can't stand it. She's going to take all that money and make a mockery of Marge's death."

"Hey, Sis, come on. If Justine's listed as the beneficiary, there's nothing you can do."

"That's what you think. I'll make her pay for this, I swear to God I will!" Sis slammed the phone down.

I could feel my heart sink. Uh-oh. I tried to think whether I'd mentioned the name of the beauty salon. I had visions of Sis descending on Justine with a tommy gun. I loitered uneasily outside the shop, watching traffic in both directions. There was no sign of Sis. Maybe she was going to wait until Justine went out to the gravesite before she mowed her down.

At two-fifteen, Justine came out of the beauty shop and passed me on the street. She was nearly unrecognizable. Her hair had been cut and permed and it fell in soft curls around her freshly made-up face. The beautician had found ways to bring out her eyes, subtly heightening her coloring with a touch of blusher on her cheeks. She looked like a million bucks—or a hundred thousand, at any rate. She was in a jaunty mood, paying more attention to her own reflection in the passing store windows than she was to me, hovering half a block behind.

She returned to the parking lot and retrieved her Pinto, easing into the flow of traffic as it moved up State. I tucked in a few cars back, all the while scanning for some sign of Sis. I couldn't imagine what she'd try to do, but as mad as she was, I had to guess she had some scheme in the works.

Fifteen minutes later, we were turning into the trailer park, Justine leading while I lollygagged along behind. I had already used up the money Sis had authorized, but by this time I had my own stake in the outcome. For all I knew, I was going to end up protecting Justine from an assassination attempt. She stopped by the trailer just long enough to load her bags in the car and then she drove out to the Santa Teresa Memorial Park, which was out by the airport.

The cemetery was deserted, a sunny field of gravestones among flowering shrubs. When the road forked, I watched Justine wind up the lane to the right while I headed left, keeping an eye on her car, which I could see across a wide patch of grass. She parked and got out, carrying the wreath to an oblong depression in the ground where a temporary marker had been set, awaiting the permanent monument. She rested the wreath against the marker and stood there looking down. She seemed awfully exposed and I couldn't help but wish she'd duck down some to grieve. Sis was probably crouched somewhere with a knife between her teeth, ready to leap out and stab Justine in the neck.

Respects paid, Justine got back into her car and drove to the airport, where she checked in for her flight. By now, I was feeling baffled. She had less than an hour before her plane was scheduled to depart and there was still no sign of Sis. If there was going to be a showdown, it was bound to happen soon. I ambled into the gift shop and inserted myself between the wall and a book rack, watching Justine through windows nearly obscured by a display of Santa Teresa T-shirts. She sat on a bench and calmly read a paperback.

What was going on here?

Sis Dunaway had seemed hell-bent on avenging Marge's death, but where was she? Had she gone to the cops? I kept one eye on the clock and one eye on Justine. Whatever Sis was up to, she had better do it quick. Finally, mere minutes before the flight was due to be called, I left the newsstand, crossed the gate area, and took a seat beside Justine. "Hi," I said, "Nice permanent. Looks good."

She glanced at me and then did a classic double take. "What are you doing here?"

"Keeping an eye on you."

"What for?"

"I thought someone should see you off. I suspect your Aunt Sis is en route, so I decided to keep you company until she gets here."

"Aunt *Sis*?" she said, incredulously.

"I gotta warn you, she's not convinced your mother had a heart attack."

"What are you talking about? Aunt Sis is dead"

I could feel myself smirk. "Yeah, sure. Since when?"

"Five years ago."

"Bullshit."

"It's not bullshit. An aneurysm burst and she dropped in her tracks."

"Come on," I scoffed.

"It's the truth," she said emphatically. By that time, she'd recovered her composure and she went on the offensive. "Where's my money? You said you'd write a check for six hundred bucks."

"Completely dead?" I asked.

The loudspeaker came on. "May I have your attention, please. United Flight 3440 for Los Angeles is now ready for boarding at Gate Five. Please have your boarding pass available and prepare for security check."

Justine began to gather up her belongings. I'd been wondering how she was going to get all that cash through the security checkpoint, but one look at her lumpy waistline and it was obvious she'd strapped on a money belt. She picked up her carryon, her shoulder bag, her jacket, and her paperback and clopped, in spike heels, over to the line of waiting passengers.

I followed, befuddled, reviewing the entire sequence of events. It had all happened today. Within hours. It wasn't like I was suffering brain damage or memory loss. And I hadn't seen a ghost. Sis had come to my office and laid out the whole tale about Marge and Justine. She'd told me all about their relationship, Justine's history as a con, the way the two women tried to outdo each other, the insurance, Marge's death. How could a murder have gotten past Dr. Yee? Unless the woman wasn't murdered, I thought suddenly.

Oh.

Once I saw it in *that* light, it was obvious.

Justine got in line between a young man with a duffel bag and a woman toting a cranky baby. There was some delay up ahead while the ticket agent got set. The line started to move and Justine advanced a step with me right beside her.

"I understand you and your mother had quite a competitive relationship."

"What's it to you," she said. She kept her eyes averted, facing dead ahead, willing the line to move so she could get away from me.

"I understand you were always trying to get the better of each other."

"What's your point?" she said, annoyed.

I shrugged. "I figure you read the article about the unidentified dead woman in the welfare hotel. You went out to the morgue and claimed the body as your mom's. The two of you agreed to split the insurance money, but your mother got worried about a double cross, which is exactly what this is."

"You don't know what you're talking about."

The line moved up again and I stayed right next to her. "She hired me to keep an eye on you, so when I realized you were leaving town, I called her and told her what was going on. She really hit the roof and I thought she'd charge right out, but so far there's been no sign of her. . . ."

Justine showed her ticket to the agent and he motioned her on. She moved through the metal detector without setting it off.

I gave the agent a smile. "Saying good-bye to a friend," I said, and passed through the wooden arch right after she did. She was picking up the pace, anxious to reach the plane.

I was still talking, nearly jogging to keep up with her. "I couldn't figure out why she wasn't trying to stop you and then I realized what she must have done—"

"Get away from me. I don't want to talk to you."

"She took the money, Justine. There's probably nothing in the belt but old papers. She had plenty of time to make the switch while you were getting your hair done."

"Ha, ha," she said sarcastically. "Tell me another one."

I stopped in my tracks. "All right. That's all I'm gonna say. I just didn't want you to reach Mexico City and find yourself flat broke."

"Blow it out your buns," she hissed. She showed her boarding pass to the woman at the gate and passed on through. I could hear her spike heels tip-tapping out of ear range.

I reversed myself, walked back through the gate area and out to the walled exterior courtyard, where I could see the planes through a windbreak of protective glass. Justine crossed the tarmac to the waiting plane, her shoulders set. I didn't think she'd heard me, but then I saw her hand stray to her waist. She walked a few more steps and then halted, dumping her belongings in a pile at her feet. She pulled her shirt up and checked the money belt. At that distance, I saw her mouth open, but it took a second for the shrieks of outrage to reach me.

Ah, well, I thought. Sometimes a mother's love is like a poison that leaves no trace. You bop along through life, thinking you've got it made, and next thing you know, you're dead.

JOYCE HARRINGTON

ANDREW, MY SON

The stories of Edgar-winning author Joyce Harrington are not always pleasant. She examines the workings of the criminal mind with a chilling intensity that is often uncompromising. It's a pleasure to welcome her back to these pages.

"Do you hear the cats?" Andrew asks me. He is standing by the window, peering out into the deep winter darkness.

I have heard no cats, but I listen carefully. If I could make my ears twitch, I would. It's always best, with Andrew, to put on a good show.

I make a noncommittal sound, "Um-hum," which could mean yes. Or no. A mistake. Andrew can't abide inattention or ambivalence.

"Listen, will you!" he shouts. "They're out there yowling. I'll put poison out. I swear I will." He paces in front of the fireplace. The flickering logs light his narrow face from below. His eyes are fierce, feral. This is my son.

"Alley cats," I murmur. "A female in heat. They're fighting over her. It's what they do." I still haven't heard them.

"Disgusting." He bends over me to spit the words into my face. "You're disgusting. To even think such a thing." He flings himself away and into the tall armchair opposite mine. Then he simply sprawls and stares at me. I wonder what he's thinking.

Andrew was a pretty child—fine golden curls, an angelic smile, huge eyes of a deep indigo verging on purple. Now he is a handsome young man. The golden curls have thickened and burnished; the eyes have narrowed with intelligence and temperament.

The smile is still angelic, but wasn't Lucifer once an angel? I do not like my son.

I rise from my chair. My neglected book falls to the floor,

facedown, its pages crumpled. "Good night, Andrew," I say. "Sleep well."

"Pleasant dreams, Mother," he says. His tone conveys unmistakably that he wishes me nothing of the kind. It was a mistake telling him of the nightmares that have begun to plague me. I am always making mistakes with Andrew. Do all mothers make mistakes with their sons?

I stoop to pick up my book. His foot extends to kick it out of my reach. I straighten to gaze sorrowfully down at him, lolling and smirking in his chair.

"You shouldn't read such trash," he says.

"It's harmless. It helps me sleep." Once again, I bend and reach for it.

He swoops to pick it up and tosses it into the fire.

It's only a paperback, a romance of other times and of people engaged in passion and adventure. It can be replaced. I stand and watch the flames flirt with its pages. When it is fully ablaze, I turn and stride from the room. My shoulders are straight and my head erect.

Andrew's merry laughter follows me.

In the morning, the house is cold and Andrew is gone. He hasn't slept in his bed. He's turned the thermostat down. Another of his tricks. I turn it up and get back into bed to wait for the heat to rise. It would be nice to have a cup of hot tea, but I lack the energy to go down to the kitchen to make it. Or am I afraid?

Alone in the darkened bedroom, waiting for heat and daylight, I argue the point with myself. What is there to be afraid of? That he has left surprises for me? Constructed booby traps? In many ways, Andrew is still a child, dependent on me for what little love there is in his life. And like a child, reaching for independence, he resents me. I try to make allowances for that.

Often, I wish that he would marry. I dream of a lovely young woman for him and sons of his own. The little family would live nearby, but not too near. They would visit occasionally, but not too often. Christmas, Thanksgiving, the Fourth of July. We would have laughter and feasting. I would make the peach cobbler that Andrew's father loved so well.

There are tears on my cheeks and I wipe them away with the

back of my hand. The radiator clanks and pale gray daylight shows outside my window. Bare branches gleam with a frosting of ice.

It's silly to be afraid of the kitchen. I get up and wrap my fleecy robe over my flannel nightgown. My slippers are lined with lambswool. I will drink my cup of tea and go about my business until Andrew returns. Today will be a good day to work on the sweater I am secretly knitting for his birthday.

And then there is my appointment this afternoon.

The doctor sits as usual in his wheelchair, his fat legs and little feet hanging motionless down. I wonder, as I always do, why his legs are so fat if they are paralyzed. But I don't know what disease confines him to the chair, and I would never dream of asking. He probably wouldn't tell me. We are here to talk about me, not about him.

He waits, with infinite patience, for me to begin.

I tell him about Andrew burning my book.

"Was it a good book?" he asks.

"It was just a book." I know I am being evasive.

"Were you enjoying it?"

"Ummm. Yes."

"Is that why Andrew burned it?"

"I suppose so. We hadn't talked about it. He couldn't know whether I was enjoying it or not."

There is a long pause.

Then I tell him about Andrew turning the thermostat down. "I think he's trying to freeze me to death." I laugh a little to show I don't mean it literally.

But the doctor doesn't laugh. "Do you think Andrew would kill you?" he asks.

"No!" I exclaim. "What would he do without me?"

"Exactly," says the doctor.

There is another long pause. Long enough for the doctor to start the next round.

"Tell me about the accident," he says.

"I've told you about that. Many times."

"Yes. But each time, we learn something new. Isn't it so?"

I nod. And then I begin. "It was winter. This time of year. The anniversary is in a few weeks. Twenty years ago. Andrew was eight years old. Carl had sprained his ankle, so I was driving him to the station. He was taking a later train that morning. Andrew was in the backseat. I was going to drop him off at school. The roads were icy." My voice tapers off. This part is always so difficult.

"Go on," the doctor prompts.

"The roads were icy. I was supposed to have had the snow tires put on, but I hadn't got around to it yet. I was in the early months of pregnancy and not very energetic. Lazy, I suppose. Andrew was leaning over the backseat with his arms around my neck. I had told him to sit down, but he wouldn't. Carl started scolding him. I couldn't bear for anyone to scold Andrew, not even his father. We began to argue. Carl said I was pampering the boy, making a sissy out of him. Andrew was crying. His arms tightened around my neck. I couldn't breathe. I took my hands off the steering wheel to loosen his grip. We were cresting a hill. The car swerved into the other lane just as another car came up from the other side. We crashed. That's all."

I had been speaking rapidly, repeating the facts as I had repeated them so many times in this heavy room. I am out of breath and sitting bolt upright in my chair, reliving the moment. The doctor does not use a couch. I think he likes to watch the faces of his patients. Sometimes, I think he lives their lives in these tormented moments. In that wheelchair, he can't have much of a life of his own.

"Relax now," he says softly. "There is more."

"More," I murmur. "Yes. Of course there's more. The aftermath. Carl died. I lost the baby."

"And Andrew?"

"Andrew was . . . seriously injured. He flew over my shoulder and went through the windshield. His head . . ."

"Yes?"

"He has scars to this day. Fortunately his hair is thick and they can't be seen."

The doctor sighs. I don't blame him. It's a sad story.

"Do you blame yourself?" he asks.

"I guess I do. I was driving."

"Do you blame Andrew?"

"No. How could I? He was only a child."

"His arms around your neck, choking you?"

"He was frightened. His father was angry with him."

"Do you blame Carl?"

"How can you blame a dead man?"

The doctor sighs again. "It's hard work," he says. "It goes slowly. But you must try to be honest. For your own sake. So Andrew . . . he was seriously hurt?"

"I thought he would die."

"And . . . ?"

"He didn't."

"He didn't," the doctor repeats. "He got well and went back to school?"

I have to think about that. "He got well and . . . and I had a teacher come to the house."

"What was her name?"

"It wasn't a woman. It was a man."

"What was his name?"

"I can't remember. It was so long ago."

The doctor rolls his wheelchair behind his desk, a sign that our time is up. "Will you try to remember for next time? Perhaps there are some records you could look up."

"Yes," I promise earnestly. "I'll try. I'll look."

His attention is on his desk calendar and I know I am dismissed. Somehow, I feel that he is disappointed with me. I leave the dark cave of his office, wondering if I will return next week. What began as something to cure my nightmares has suddenly turned threatening.

Andrew doesn't like his dinner. He sits at the table, moodily pushing his food around on his plate. "Why don't we ever have fish?" he whines. "Don't you know that red meat is bad for you?"

"You don't like fish," I tell him. "You've always liked rare roast beef, just like your father."

"You killed my father. If you hadn't killed him in the car, you would have killed him with roast beef." He picks up his plate and dumps his dinner into my lap.

I sit there with gravy soaking through the skirt of my green wool jersey dress. It brings a heat and wetness to my thighs, a mockery of the ancient act of love. Carefully, I gather the mess into my napkin and carry it into the kitchen. The dress may not be ruined. I sponge it off as best I can, and then go upstairs to change. There is no point in being angry with Andrew. He will not listen. I think it's better not to provoke him. Tomorrow, I'll get some nice fillet of sole.

Instead of going downstairs to sit with Andrew in the living room, I climb on a chair to reach into the top of the closet. There, in an old suitcase, I know are papers, old photographs. I had promised the doctor to look. The suitcase is dusty. I wipe it off before putting it on the bed. I have not looked into this suitcase for many years. My hands fumble reluctantly with the latches. Before I can open them, Andrew appears in the doorway.

"Having a nostalgia trip?" he sneers.

"I thought I'd look," I mumble.

"Want to twine my innocent baby curls around your finger? I'll bet you saved each tooth I put under my pillow. Go ahead and open it. I'd like to see too."

"You've seen already." I know I am accusing him, but suddenly, I don't care. "You've been snooping into this. How dare you?"

"Snooping, Mother?" He is sly, self-righteous. "But it's my life too. Isn't it? Isn't that what you've got stored away in there? My brief life?"

"What are you talking about?" I realize I am shrieking like a madwoman. I say it again, softly and reasonably. "What are you talking about, Andrew?"

"You don't really want me to say it. Come downstairs and have some coffee. I've made it. It's all ready and waiting for you."

I am overcome by his sudden kindness. Perhaps we can have a pleasant evening together. We'll talk about the future. He'll tell me of his fiancée, his *secret* fiancée, whom I've never met. He'll ask me if she may come to dinner, and we'll plan together for a wedding in the summer.

He has gotten out the silver coffee service and my best china cups and saucers. "Andrew! How nice!" I exclaim. I can smell the fragrant fresh-brewed coffee.

Andrew, solicitous, takes my arm and ushers me to my chair. He pours a cup of coffee and brings it to me. He smiles benignly as I lift the cup to my lips. I sip. And the cup flies out of my hand, my lips sting, my tongue is seared. "Water!" I gasp.

Andrew laughs. His bitter laughter rings in my ears as I run to the kitchen and rinse my mouth directly under the faucet. When the awful burning in my mouth recedes to a prickling, stinging pain, I raise my head and turn the water off. There on the counter is an open can of Drāno.

"What's wrong, Mother? Don't you like my coffee?" He is hovering nearby, his face a mask of solicitude.

I cannot speak. My lips will crack. I walk past him and go back upstairs to my room. I lock the door. In the mirror, I see that my mouth and tongue are blistered. I also see the reflection of the old suitcase, just where I left it on the bed. I turn and stare at it. Is it time to open it? Now? After all these years?

I sit on the bed and remember a trip when the suitcase was new. Yes, it was our honeymoon. Carl's and mine. We had no knowledge then of Andrew. We were only and selfishly together, the two of us. We went to San Francisco, a city neither of us had seen and we both had dreamed of. We thought of living there, if Carl could arrange a transfer. But he couldn't and so that part of our dream faded. San Francisco does not have icy roads. I have often thought that Andrew was conceived in a room at the Palace Hotel. The timing was right. We should never have left that room. Or, perhaps, never have found it.

I open the suitcase. It's not so difficult after all to release the latches and raise the lid. Inside, I find old rags, shreds of yellowed newspapers, broken toys. No documents. No photographs. Ah, Andrew.

For a week, I have been left in peace. Andrew does this from time to time. Usually after one of his more outrageous pranks. I don't know where he goes, nor do I ever ask. Some things, it's better not to know. He will return filthy and repentant. He will say, "Mother, I'm sorry."

And I will forgive him. What else can I do?

The blisters on my mouth are almost healed, but the doctor notices immediately. I tell him about Andrew's coffee. I tell him I could find no papers.

"Would you like to take a rest?" he says. "I can get you a room."

"A rest? You mean in a hospital?" I am shocked that he would suggest such a thing. And yet, I am tempted. Yes, very tempted.

"It's not a hospital. It's a private facility. For people who just need a little time out from their worries. I would like you to consider it." His voice is so soothing. It seems like such a good idea.

"Oh, no," I hear myself saying. "I couldn't do that. Andrew needs me. He'll be coming home soon. I've bought him new clothes. I've almost finished his sweater. His birthday will be soon. He'll be home for that."

The doctor is silent. Waiting.

I try to wait him out, in silence. But I can't do it. I've become too accustomed to the luxury of talking. I haven't told Andrew of my visits to the doctor. In the beginning, the doctor wanted to speak to Andrew, but I told him that would be dangerous. He believed me.

At last, I am forced to ask the question that has troubled me for years. "Why does he do these things? I've been so good to him. I've tried so hard to make up to him for all that he's lost."

"What has he lost?" the doctor asks in that quiet, insistent voice of his.

"Why, you know. I've told you."

"Tell me again."

It's not possible that he doesn't remember. He just wants to torture me by going over and over it. I shake my head. I simply cannot do it again.

"What has Andrew lost?" He is implacable. Cruel.

"His father," I mutter.

"What else?"

"I don't know." I seldom perspire, but now my hands, my face, my entire body, even my feet are slick and damp. My whispered words reverberate in the hazy room.

"You know," the doctor insists.

I try to get out of the chair. I don't have to stay and submit to this. I can get into my car and drive home. I have a feeling that Andrew will come home tonight. I can't get up. Something keeps me nailed to the chair.

"Try to say it. I know it's difficult for you. But you'll feel so much better. What has Andrew lost?"

I remain mute. The words will not come. And yet, the thought is there. Oh, yes. The thought. It's always been there. Hasn't it? Yes.

The doctor is giving up. I can see it in his eyes. He's losing interest. A patient who will not speak is useless. I hate to feel useless. I begin to chatter. I intend to use up my hour. After all, I'm paying for it.

He listens, not interrupting, until I've exhausted my store of trifles. Then he says, "Will you come in tomorrow? I think it's important. We've reached a crucial point."

"Tomorrow? I don't know. It depends." But I am flattered by this attention. I make a show of consulting my date book. There is nothing written on tomorrow's page, yet I frown over it as if I had appointments of great moment. "Yes, all right," I allow. "I can make it. Same time?"

As I am driving away from the medical center where the doctor has his office, I see Andrew walking toward me along the street. This is an unpleasant part of town, old and seedy, inhabited by riffraff. He is walking with a woman. She is not young. She wears too much makeup to compensate for her loss of youth. She teeters along on extravagantly high heels, and she is wrapped in an imitation fur coat. I drive on past them, hoping that Andrew has not seen me or recognized the car. He has given no sign, but Andrew wouldn't. Why is he here? What has Andrew lost?

"Hello, Mother,"

He has caught me by surprise, my knitting in my lap. I try to hide it under a magazine. Even from across the room, I can smell the liquor on him and the cheap perfume. "Would you like some shrimp salad?" I ask. I'll never risk roast beef again.

Andrew makes a rude, gagging noise like a child rejecting a dish he does not like. Then he asks, "What were you doing in town today, Mother? Spying on me?"

"No, of course not. I had an appointment."

"Oh, an appointment. Not with a doctor, by any chance?"

"No. I . . . I went to see a decorator. Don't you think it's time I redid this room?"

He strolls around the living room, examining the wallpaper, kicking at the chairs. "Don't change it," he says. "I like it this way. Just the way it was twenty years ago." Then he swings on me, his face contorted with fury. "And don't lie to me! Don't ever lie to me. You went to see a psychiatrist. A nut doctor. Are you crazy, Mother?"

I remain outwardly calm, but my hands clutching my knitting are clammy. "I am not crazy, Andrew. And *you* have been spying on *me*."

He laughs at that. "Don't you know by now that you have no secrets from me? That thing in your lap, for instance. It's a sweater, isn't it? To keep your little boy warm and cozy. Too bad he'll never wear it. I wouldn't be caught dead in that ugly piece of trash."

It's so hard to keep from crying, but I've learned that that's the biggest mistake of all. To let Andrew see my weakness. "Go take a bath," I tell him. "You smell."

"Ah, but I smell of life, Mother. Something you know nothing about." Nevertheless, he disappears up the stairs and I am left alone.

I pick up my knitting and try to concentrate, but it's useless. I might as well rip it all out and make pot holders out of the yarn.

The next day, Andrew is repentant. He brings me breakfast in bed. Two soft-boiled eggs, buttered toast, fresh orange juice, a pot of tea. The white wicker bed tray is one I used during Andrew's long recuperation after the accident.

"How lovely!" I exclaim. "Andrew, you can be so thoughtful."

He sits at the foot of the bed and smiles at me. "You're the only mother I have." Angelic. "I don't know why I do the things I do."

"Let's forget all that," I tell him. "We'll go on from here, this moment. You have your whole life ahead of you."

"Yes," he broods. "And yours is almost over. I haven't given you much joy."

"Oh, yes, you have. Why, I remember . . ."

"Please, Mother. Don't remember. It makes me sad." But then he grins impishly and says, "Let's do something special today. Let's start redoing the living room. You were right about that. It's old and gloomy. I'd like to tear that old wallpaper right off the walls. It's peeling off anyway. Come on, Mom. Put on your working clothes and let's get busy." He leaps off the bed and dashes out the door.

"Wait!" I call after him. "We can't do it all ourselves."

"Yes, we can!" he shouts back as he goes thundering down the stairs.

By the time I am dressed, he has already torn long strips of wallpaper off the wall. He has taken the draperies off the windows, and the room, in the cold winter daylight, looks shabbier than I realized it was.

"You'd better make a list," he tells me. "New draperies, new furniture; the piano can stay but only if you play it for me."

"I haven't played for years," I tell him. "I don't know if I remember how. You always said it made you nervous."

"Sit down and play," he commands, "while I get on with the wallpaper. It's all got to go. Every scrap of it."

I sit on the bench and open the lid covering the keys. "It's probably out of tune," I murmur. But I tentatively finger the keys and begin with something simple. Carl always like me to play "Smoke Gets in Your Eyes."

"That's right, Mom." Andrew is on top of the ladder, scraping away at the wallpaper near the ceiling. "Sing for me. I want to hear you sing."

"Oh, no," I protest. "I never could sing. Even your father had to admit that."

Andrew turns and stares down at me. "Sing," he says softly.

And I do. I can't remember all the words and my voice creaks and cracks, but it seems to please Andrew. He hums along and works steadily. Soon one entire wall of the living room is bare, down to the plaster, except for some places where the paper refuses to peel away.

"I'll have to get a blowtorch," he says. "That's the only way.

And I can use it to strip the old paint off the woodwork. Oh, we're going to have fun. This room is going to look wonderful! And then we can start in on the rest of the house."

"I don't know, " I whisper weakly. "Isn't a blowtorch dangerous?"

"Not if you know how to use it."

And then he is gone.

Maybe he won't come back. I have spent the past two hours waiting for him. I have missed my appointment with the doctor, but I can't leave with the house in such a mess and Andrew not back yet. I know I should be doing something, but I don't know what to do. I haven't even washed my breakfast dishes. I want to be happy that Andrew is finally taking an interest in the house and I am, really, but all this sudden change is making me uneasy. I prowl the disheveled living room, fingering the dusty old draperies, crackling the torn wallpaper under foot, remembering when it was all new and gleaming and I was young and proud.

The phone rings, but I can't bring myself to answer it. It might be the doctor, wanting to know why I didn't show up. How can I tell him that I don't need him anymore? That Andrew has changed and we are going to be all right now, a family. I won't have any more nightmares. The phone stops ringing.

He's back, carrying a blowtorch and a big greasy can of some kind of fuel.

"Don't put it on the rug," I warn him.

"It doesn't matter," he says. "The rug has got to go. We'll have a new one. Pale green, I think. Like the grass in springtime." And he smiles.

"What took you so long?" I ask.

"You weren't supposed to ask," he says, "but since you did, I might as well tell you. I was getting a surprise for you." He reaches into his pocket and pulls out a small white box. "This is for you," he says. "Because I've been such a bad boy." He hands me the box.

I am thunderstruck. It is the first time Andrew has ever given me a gift.

"Open it," he urges.

I open it and there on a bed of soft blue velvet lies a gold heart-shaped locket on a thin gold chain. "Andrew!" I exclaim. "How pretty!"

"Open the locket," he says.

My hands can hardly manage the delicate latch, but at last the locket springs open. On one side, there is a picture of me as I was twenty years ago. On the other, Andrew's baby face beams up at me, golden curls, huge eyes, sweet innocent smile. "Oh, Andrew!" is all I can say before the tears gush forth.

"Now, Mom," he says. "It's nothing to cry about. Here, let me put it on for you."

While he fastens the golden chain around my neck, I wipe my eyes and try to compose myself. When he finishes, he is all business once again. "Back to work for me," he says, "and back to the piano for you. Music makes the time fly."

I am in an ecstasy of delight and I try to play the old songs as best I can. I am dimly aware of Andrew doing something with the blowtorch and the can of fuel. I play on, one song after another. Andrew goes quietly about his work. For the first time in years, we are happy with each other. What more could a mother ask?

The doorbell rings, but I can't stop to answer it. I don't want anyone to interrupt this precious time. There is a pounding at the door and I hear voices calling my name. "Go away!" I shout, before starting another song.

The flames are licking at the torn wallpaper now. And Andrew is smiling. Somehow he seems younger, as if the years are rolling back and he is becoming a boy again. The rug is smoldering. Andrew was never a gawky adolescent. He was a handsome teenager, never a spot of acne, never an awkward moment. The smoke brings tears to my eyes, but after so many years of not crying, I don't mind. Andrew looks about twelve years old, but that could be an illusion caused by the smoke. It's very warm in the room. The old sofa is burning now. The piano is near the picture window and hasn't caught fire yet.

Andrew stands in the flames and smiles at me. He beckons to me, this ten-year-old boy. "Mommy, Mommy," he calls. "Isn't this fun?"

On the other side of the picture window, I can see agitated

faces. The doctor is there, in his wheelchair. And the woman from his office. I am astonished and secretly pleased that he's come all this way just for me. Sirens wail in the distance, coming closer.

Andrew's eyes are closing. Blood gushes from his head and cascades down his pale face. He crumples and falls to the floor. I have seen him this way before. It is the way he was after the accident. I rise from the piano bench. This time I am determined I will save him.

But before I can reach him, there is a trememdous crash of glass behind me. Two tall men leap through the broken window and pick me up. "My son! My son! Andrew, my son! Save him first."

But they pay no attention. It is all so undignified. They bundle me into an ambulance, but not before I notice the great hoses they are aiming into my house. I can hear my doctor talking to the ambulance attendants. "Suicidal," he says. "But I never thought she'd do something like this."

How little he understands. Andrew will be back. Andrew *always* comes back. The fire is a good thing. It has burned away the past. Now we'll really fix up the house, make it better than new, with no memories. Andrew and I will be happy together. Forever.

EDWARD D. HOCH

THE DETECTIVE'S WIFE

This story of mine appeared in a special mystery and suspense issue of the California literary quarterly Cross-currents. *I have included it here because it's quite different from my usual work.*

When they were first married, before she realized what it would be like having a police detective for a husband, Jenny used to kid with him about his cases. Sometimes when he got home early enough for dinner he'd entertain her with accounts of the latest felonies around town. Most cases were solved by the testimony of eyewitnesses or the tips of informers, but once in a while there was the storybook crime that demanded a certain skill in the science of deduction.

It was these cases, especially, that Roger liked to explore with Jenny. He would go over the facts in careful detail; presenting what clues they'd been able to uncover, giving a brief account of suspects' testimony and alibis, if there were any. Then, invariably, he would look at her and say, "You know my methods, Watson. Who is the guilty party?"

She almost never came up with the correct solution, but that didn't seem to matter. It was a game both of them enjoyed. She was Watson to his Holmes, and, "You know my methods, Watson," became their own private joke. Once when he spoke the line in bed during their lovemaking, she broke into a fit of giggles.

That was in the early years, when life was simpler for them both. As they passed into their thirties, still childless, something changed. "There's just more crime these days," Roger told her when she questioned him about his late hours.

"You never tell me about your cases any more."

He sighed and turned away. "What's there to tell about a drug dealer who gets cut up by an Uzi? It's the same thing every day, and I get tired of talking about it."

His words made sense, she knew. Other cops, friends of theirs, had gotten burnt out. It could happen to Roger too.

But there was more. The sex between them wasn't as good or as spontaneous as it had been during those first years. Sometimes she wondered if he had found someone else. She made a special effort to interest herself in his cases, and to act as his Watson once more.

"They can't all be drug killings, Roger," she argued one night. "Tell me something interesting."

"A bartender shot to death on the west side? Is that interesting?"

"Any motive?"

"Robbery, I suppose. It was after closing time when he was alone. The cash register wasn't touched but something might have scared the killer away. Or maybe there was another motive. Some seventeen-year-old kid he refused to serve goes home and gets his father's gun. The victim must have let the killer in, so he probably knew him."

That was in February, during the eighth year of their marriage.

Jenny worked in the production department of a small advertising agency downtown. Sometimes she had lunch with the other women in the office, but more often she ate a sandwich at her desk. Occasionally, if the weather was nice, she'd venture out on a summer's day to eat her sandwich in a little park across the street where the local utility company sponsored jazz concerts on Fridays. It was here that one of the agency's artists, a bearded young man named Carl, found her on a hot August afternoon. She'd heard he was leaving soon for a better job.

"How you doing, Jenny girl? Enjoying the music?"

"It's a break from the office," she told him with a smile. "I can just take so much of ordering typesetting and engravings and printing."

He sat down beside her on the smooth stone seat. "How's hubby?"

"Roger is fine," she answered defensively. The people at work, especially the men, seemed to treat him with thinly veiled disdain because of his position with the police.

"He catch any bad guys lately?"

"A drug dealer who—"

"What about the serial killer?" Carl asked, unwrapping a candy bar and starting to munch on it. "The one who's been shooting the bartenders."

It was true that three bartenders had been slain since February, at roughly two-month intervals. One paper had spoken of a serial killer, and there was a fear that August might bring a fourth killing. She'd spoken of it to Roger once or twice, but he preferred talking about the small everyday triumphs of his job. "I don't think he's working on that," she answered, though she knew he was in charge of it.

"That's the trouble with cops." He took a bite of his Mr. Smiley Nut Cluster. "They waste their time on unimportant crimes while the big stuff gets by them."

She suddenly felt the need to defend her husband. "Roger says most crimes are solved by informers. Someone like a serial killer acts alone. No one else knows about it, so no one can inform on him."

Carl finished his candy bar and leaned back, letting the music wash over him. Jenny recognized it as an old Duke Ellington tune, one that her father had liked to play when she was growing up. "I'll have to meet Roger sometime," Carl commented. "Why don't you ever bring him around to the office parties?"

"He works a lot of nights," she answered lamely. The truth of the matter was that she tried to keep her two lives separate. Roger wouldn't like the people she worked with, and they would have little respect for him. Many of them were artistic types, who wore torn jeans to work and thought of the police as right-wing oppressors.

"Yeah," Carl said, getting to his feet. "Well, I'll see you back at the office, Jenny girl. Hope you're coming to my party."

She watched him cross the little park and enter the side door of their building. He'd left the crumpled candy wrapper on the ground by their bench, twisted into a knot.

Roger was moody all through dinner that night. He picked at his food and didn't say much. She tried to ask him about the day's routine, about any new crimes, but he had nothing to contribute. Finally, over coffee, he said, "I was driving around downtown this noon. I passed your building."

"Oh? You should have stopped to see me. We could have had lunch together."

"I did see you, in that little park where they have the jazz concerts. You were with another man."

She had to laugh at this evidence of his jealousy. "That was just Carl, one of our artists. I don't take him too seriously—you shouldn't either."

"When I saw you from the car you looked like you were enjoying each other."

She could see he wasn't joking and this annoyed her. "If he bothers you, take heart. He's leaving in two weeks. He's found a better job in the art department at a printer."

"I was just *asking,* for God's sake!"

"What's happening to you? What's happening to *us?* You used to talk about your job, about the cases you worked on. You made it sound like fun, like a game!"

"It isn't a game any more. After so many bodies it stops being a game."

Jenny tried to soothe him. "I just remember how you used to describe a case and give me the clues and let me try to solve it. You called me Watson."

"Yeah, I guess I did." He smiled at the memory.

A few nights later Roger surprised her with his suddenly buoyant spirits. He suggested they go out to dinner and took her to a neighborhood restaurant they'd frequented when they were first married. "I cracked a case today," he told her over drinks. "An interesting one I've been working on all week."

She knew he was going to tell her about it, and she felt a glow of anticipation. It was almost like the old days. "Do you have pictures?" she asked, remembering the large manila envelope he'd brought home earlier.

"Not before dinner. I'll show you back at the house."

"Tell me about it, at least."

"A man reported that his wife had committed suicide, hanged herself from a rafter in the garage."

"Did she leave a note?"

"No, which is one of the reasons we started investigating."

"What was the other reason?"

"Well, her car was outside in the driveway. Death by carbon monoxide is a lot tidier than hanging."

Their food arrived and the conversation shifted to pleasanter topics. She talked about the office, and some of the ad campaigns they were working on. It was the most pleasant dinner they'd enjoyed in months. Home was within walking distance, and the few blocks' stroll on a late summer evening was invigorating. The cool air against Jenny's face reminded her of the coming of autumn.

Back at the house he showed her the eight-by-ten glossies he'd brought from the office file. Crime scene photographs were usually in color now, and she was thankful at least that there'd been no blood. The woman's stockinged feet dangled about two feet from the floor, next to an overturned crate of rough wood. "She climbed up on that and put the rope around her neck?"

"Apparently," Roger said with a slight smile. "Come on—you know my methods, Watson."

"First of all, the crate is too flimsy. I can see she's a good-sized woman. More important, in this shot of her from the rear, showing the bottoms of her feet, there are no snags in her stockings. She couldn't have climbed up on that flimsy crate in her stocking feet, adjusted the rope, and then kicked it away, all without getting a run or at least a snag from those wood splinters."

"Go to the head of the class! That's basically what I told her husband, and we had a confession within an hour."

"I'm glad," she whispered into his ear. She was glad he'd caught a murderer and glad he was back to the same old Roger she loved so much.

That night the serial killer struck again.

The following evening he was worse than ever. "I told you the games were over and I meant it! My job's on the line now. Four killings of bartenders since February is too much for the city fathers to sit still for. If we don't make quick progress they're taking me off the case, and that means I can say good-bye to any chance of promotion. I'll be lucky if I'm not back giving traffic tickets."

"I didn't see the papers. Tell me about it. Was it like the others, in a restaurant?"

"This one was different. He was shot on his way home from work, around three in the morning. The killer apparently was waiting in an alley next to his apartment house."

"But he was a bartender?"

Roger nodded. "He was helping out at the Platt Street Bowling Lanes. Before that he worked at Max's Party House, the same place as victim number two."

"That might be a lead. Maybe they owed gambling debts to one of the customers. Or maybe someone owed them money. Maybe they were dealing drugs on the side."

"We checked all that out on the others. We'll try again but it doesn't look promising. The latest victim was a fill-in bartender. Even when he worked at Max's it was only when they needed extra people for a big party. Victims two and four probably met, but they hardly knew each other, as near as we can tell."

"How about the other victims?"

"No connection."

"And it wasn't robbery?"

"His wallet wasn't touched."

"Could it be just a coincidence?"

Roger shook his head. "Ballistics says it was the same gun all four times—a nine millimeter automatic pistol."

He was glum for the rest of the night, and she could do nothing to shake him out of it. Finally she asked, "Did they give you any sort of deadline?"

"A week or two. They want some action."

"Maybe I can help."

He only sighed and walked away. As he'd told her earlier, the games were over.

Roger didn't attend the office farewell party for Carl. She hadn't really expected that he would, and when she mentioned it he didn't even bother to reply. Most nights she ate alone, knowing it would be nine or ten or later before she saw him. She'd never thought it would be like this, being married to a detective.

The party, at one of downtown's fancier hotels, was a welcome relief. Carl himself hadn't had a drink in two years, since his wife was killed in an auto accident, but that didn't stop the rest of the staff from having a good time. Jenny's boss, the production manager, was a beefy man named Herb who imagined every young woman in the office to be fair game, married or not. At one point he had her pressed into a corner, but he was already too far gone to be a real threat. It was the president of the agency who suggested a bit later that perhaps Jenny could drive Herb home.

"He can't drive himself and I don't want another accident, Jenny. If I help you get him into the car could you take him home? It's less than a mile away."

"Certainly, Mr. Miller." She dreaded the idea, but she could hardly suggest that he call a cab for Herb. Miller didn't like anyone to know about drunken employees.

It wasn't till they were on the way that she remembered she hadn't even said good-bye to Carl.

Herb mumbled and snored all the way home, but he came awake as she brought the car to a stop in front of his apartment building and tried to make a pass without fully realizing who she was. She brushed his hand from her breast and he reached into his pocket for a handkerchief, pulling matches, gum and keys with it.

Jenny ran around to the passenger door and helped him out, retrieving his keys and whatever else she could find. The doorman at the building took charge then, betraying no surprise. Perhaps he'd seen Herb in this condition before.

When she got back to her own house, Roger was in the kitchen preparing a sandwich for himself. "I forgot you were going to be out tonight. How was the party?"

She shrugged, dropped her keys on the table. "The usual. My boss got drunk and I had to drive him home. How's the case coming?"

"It's not. Four murders now and we're no closer to an arrest than we were after the first one. My time is running out. The commissioner wants action before the November election."

"Won't you let me work on it with you?" she asked. "Bring

home some of the pictures for me to look at. Remember, I spotted the clue in that hanging case right away."

"There's nothing in the pictures," he insisted. "I've been over them a dozen times."

The following morning she found an excuse to leave the office and do some library research. While there she checked the microfilmed copies of the daily papers and read about each of the earlier killings. There was nothing new, nothing to connect the four men except for their occupation. The second victim had worked exclusively at Max's Party House but the others had moved around, mostly filling in part-time at neighborhood places. The first victim had been the youngest, at twenty-six. The other three were all in their thirties or forties. They lived in different parts of the city and seemed to have been nothing more than passing acquaintances, if that much. Only one had been married at the time of his death. Two of the others were divorced. The youngest victim had never been married.

Was it a random thing, she wondered, just killing bartenders? Or had these four been chosen for a reason?

That night Roger seemed more depressed than ever. He'd brought home some of the crime scene photographs but he never took them out of the envelope. He'd spent the entire day interviewing the girlfriends and ex-wives of the victims, and had nothing to show for it. "No girls in common, no jealous lovers."

Finally, just before bedtime, she asked, "Can I look at these pictures."

"Go ahead. I have to take them back in the morning."

Jenny opened the clasp on the envelope and pulled out a dozen pictures of the various crime scenes. Bodies, four bodies. All shot at fairly close range. The first three were in the barrooms where the men had worked, as they prepared to close up for the night. The fourth was at the mouth of an alley where the killer had waited. One photo showed the cartridge case ejected from the killer's automatic pistol, lying amidst the dirt and trash of the alley.

An empty pack of cigarettes, a torn stub from a nearby movie, the spilled remains of a half-finished container of popcorn, the knotted wrapper off a candy bar, a broken piece of brick—

She went on to the next photo, then quickly turned back to the picture of the alley pavement. Where had she seen a candy wrapper tied in a knot like that? Was it something that people often did, or was it unique?

Then she remembered. Carl had dropped his candy wrapper on the ground that day they'd been listening to the jazz concert on the lunch hour. It was the same brand, Mr. Smiley Nut Cluster, and the wrapper had been twisted and knotted in the same manner.

Of course it proved nothing.

When she slid into bed next to Roger she said, "Those pictures gave me an idea. I want to check on something tomorrow."

"I need all the help I can get. I also need your car in the morning."

"How come?"

"The brakes aren't working on mine. I'll take it in over the weekend."

"You'll have to drop me off at work."

"Can you get home on your own?"

"Sue will give me a ride."

"Fine." He rolled over and was snoring within minutes.

Jenny searched through the newspaper files for an account of the accident that had killed Carl's wife two years earlier. She'd never heard the details of it, and it had happened before she came to the agency, but something Mr. Miller said—"I don't want another accident"—made her wonder if it might have happened after an office party. It took her a long time to find it, but there it was. Carl's wife had been hit by a truck as she pulled out of the parking lot at Max's Party House shortly after midnight. They'd come to the party in separate cars and he was still inside when it happened. Her blood alcohol level was extremely high at the time, and no charges were placed against the truck driver.

A later article talked about the liability of a place like Max's that continued serving someone who was obviously drunk.

There was talk of a lawsuit and the owner stated he was unable to determine which of the four bartenders on duty had been responsible.

Four bartenders.

Why hadn't they seen it? Why hadn't anyone seen it?

The answer to that was simple enough. They had approached the problem from the opposite direction, through the four victims. Jenny was approaching through Carl, and his dead wife, and the accident, and Max's Party House.

That had to be her next stop. Max's.

What a day for Roger to borrow her car!

Back at the office she arranged to take Sue's little Volvo. "I won't be more than an hour," she promised.

She struck it lucky at Max's Party House. Max himself was there, preparing for a big retirement dinner that evening. "Is this more about that lawsuit?" he asked when she told him what she wanted. "That whole thing was settled last January."

"The newspaper quoted you as saying there were four bartenders working the night of the accident. I want their names."

"Look, the case was settled out of court for a few thousand dollars. The husband's attorney convinced him he couldn't get any more than that. The only reason I paid anything was that she was hit driving out of our parking lot. As for the bartenders, I couldn't tell you if I wanted to. A couple of them were working off the books that night, to avoid paying taxes. It's not unusual in this business."

Jenny opened her purse and took out the list of names. "Just tell me one thing. Are these the four men?"

He glanced at it and then at her. "All right, those are the ones. A couple of them are dead now."

"You don't keep up with the papers. All four of them are dead now."

Jenny felt a rising excitement all the way home in the car with Sue. She barely heard her friend's chatter as she ran over the facts in her mind. Carl had settled the lawsuit in January, against his wishes, for a figure far less than he thought was justified. A month later, in February, the killings had begun, spaced two months apart in hopes no one would notice the connection right away. They had, of course, by the time of the third one, but then he only had to risk one more.

Four dead—one or more of them the ones who'd been directly responsible for his wife's tragic death. And he'd have gotten away with it if it hadn't been for that knotted candy wrapper dropped to the ground while he waited for the final victim to appear. How had he found out the identity of the four? Probably by getting friendly with the first victim and asking him in some innocent way. That helped explain how he came to be in the bar long after closing. He'd made friends with the first victim, and then killed him when he'd learned the names of the other three.

"Here we are," Sue said, pulling into her driveway. "Home at last. I don't see your car. Roger must be still working."

"He's been working every night lately. Thanks, Sue."

"See you in the morning."

Jenny hurried into the house and got out of her sweaty clothes, silently rehearsing how she'd tell Roger. She slipped into her robe and switched on the television, settling down opposite it without really seeing it.

Roger was very late that night and when he came in she could see that his mood was bad. He unbuckled his holster and tossed the gun onto a chair before he even spoke to her. "What does this mean, Jenny?" he said at last.

"What?" She tried to see what he was holding in his outstretched hand. "What is it?"

"A sealed packet containing an unused condom. I found it under the passenger seat of your car."

"I—"

"Do you have an explanation?"

Her mind was whirling. She could barely recognize this man standing before her. "Roger, let me think—!"

"Make it good—for whatever it's worth."

"My God, Roger! You can't think I was making love to someone in my car!" Then suddenly it came to her. "Herb, my boss! I told you I drove him home from the party because he was drunk. When we got to his apartment he pulled out his handkerchief and a lot of things came with it. I picked them up but I must have missed this."

"Herb, your boss. Am I supposed to believe that?"

All at once the unfairness of his constant jealously and suspicion moved her to a fury. "I don't give a damn what you believe!" She ripped open the top of her robe. "Here! Do you want to dust my breasts for fingerprints?"

That was when he slapped her. Hard.

Jenny slept that night curled up on the sofa, somehow protecting herself from further blows. When she awoke, just after dawn, it was raining. Roger came downstairs a little while later, and walked over to her. "I'm sorry about last night. This case has just got me down. I have to see the commissioner this morning and I've got nothing for him."

She got up, wrapping the robe around her, and started making breakfast. Later, while she was drinking her coffee, he remembered to ask, "Did you think of anything yesterday, about the killings?"

"No," she answered softly, staring straight ahead at the rain-streaked window. "Nothing at all."

CLARK HOWARD

CHALLENGE THE WIDOW-MAKER

For the fourth time, EQMM's annual Reader's Award went to Clark Howard, two of whose stories ended in a virtual tie for first place. One of them, "Deeds of Valor," is far too long to include here, but we're happy to offer the other readers' favorite, which also brought Howard another Edgar nomination. It's a shimmering tale of pearls and surfing in modern Hawaii.

They buried old Terangi in a small country cemetery several miles below the crater of Kaneakala volcano. It was a simple funeral. Most of Terangi's neighbors made the drive up-mountain from Lahaina Town to attend, and a few of his fellow merchants who had small stores near Terangi's surfboard shop on the waterfront also attended. Because there were no other family members, Terangi's widow, Marama, was escorted to the services by George Hill, her late husband's sole employee, who was like a son to them. George had been with Terangi when the massive heart attack struck. They had been sanding separate ends of a new competition board Terangi was making for one of the Maui surfers to use in the next big North Shore finals on Oahu.

When the services were over and the other mourners had left, Marama leaned her head against George's arm. "Life will seem very strange without him, Keoki," she said, using the Polynesian form of George.

"Yes, it will," George replied, just as quietly. "I hate to think what my life would have been like if it hadn't been for him. And you."

"You have been a great comfort to us, Keoki," she assured him. "You'll stay on and run the shop, won't you?"

"Yes." George shrugged. "I wouldn't know how to do anything else. All I've ever been was a soldier, a convict, and a surfboard maker."

"And a son," Marama reminded him, squeezing his arm. "You've been a son to two lonely people."

As they walked away from Terangi's grave, George noticed that not all the mourners had gone. A solitary figure stood well back at the edge of the cemetery, watching. Wearing a flowered Hawaiian shirt, his hands shoved into his pants pockets, he was a once-husky islander who had gone to fat. In one corner of his mouth was an ever-present toothpick. His name was Charley Kula. He was George Hill's parole officer from Oahu.

George drove Marama back down-mountain in Terangi's old Plymouth, which he supposed would now become his because Marama had never learned to drive. George had a lot on his mind at the moment. He was wondering how life was going to be without Terangi's wise counseling. He was wondering whether he could run the surfboard shop by himself. And he was wondering what was on Charley Kula's mind. In the rear-view mirror he could see Kula following them down-mountain in the white state-owned pool car he used when he was on Maui. Kula was, in George's opinion, exactly what old Terangi had called him in private for years: a *haahaa na mea kino me ka hanu ola*. Literally translated, it meant a low creature, unworthy of a name.

George had been under Charley Kula's thumb for five years, living with the constant threat of being returned to Oahu Prison on the whim of an unfavorable monthly report. For five years George had loaned Kula money—twenty dollars here, twenty dollars there—money that was never paid back; or given him free surfboards for his supervisor's kids; or fixed him up with one of the *wahines* from the Cloud Nine Massage Parlor, at George's expense; or bought his dinner, his lunch, his breakfast, his haircuts, his shoeshines. When Kula came over from Oahu once a month, George always paid for one thing or another.

"Never mind," Terangi had always counseled him, "keep your *hu'ihu'i* [your cool]. Don't let a robber like him upset you. Be happy. Take one of the boards and go surf for an hour."

For five years George had worked off his anger out on the

waves. For five years he had kept his *hu'ihu'i.* But he had not been happy about it.

When George and Marama got back to Lahaina Town, to the little frame house on Lani Street where Terangi and Marama had lived for forty years, the ladies of the neighborhood were there with dishes of food and doses of comfort, so George only stayed a little while before telling Marama he was going to the shop for a couple of hours.

Then he left to go see what Charley Kula wanted.

Kula was in the bar of the old Missionary Inn, sipping a gin and tonic around his toothpick, shooting the breeze with the bartender. When George came in, he moved to a back table, taking his drink with him.

"Aloha, Georgie," he said with a smile. George sat down and a bored cocktail waitress in a sarong came over to take his order.

"Just a Coke," George said.

"I'll have another gin and tonic," Kula added. Then to George, he said, "Listen, have something stronger if you want it. I know how much you liked the old man."

George shook his head. "Just a Coke," he repeated. He remembered Terangi's words from the very first day of his parole: *Never let him get anything on you. Never break the rules, even if he tells you it's okay.* Paroless weren't allowed to drink alcoholic beverages.

"I guess the old lady wants you to stay on and run the shop, huh?" Kula asked when the waitress left.

"Yes."

"There's no other family, is there? They all died in that car wreck, didn't they?"

"Yes. I mean no, there's no other family."

"Well, that leaves you pretty well fixed, I guess. I mean, the shop will be all yours someday, won't it?"

"I suppose."

"Lucky day for you when old Terangi helped you make parole and gave you a job in his shop."

"Yes. Lucky day."

The waitress brought their drinks and George paid for them.

Kula sat back and patted his ample belly with both hands. "You know, what happened to old Terangi makes a man realize just how short life is. A man's a fool if he don't make the most of the time he's got left. Take me, for instance. Next month's my birthday. I'll be fifty-five. That makes me eligible for early retirement. Know what I'd like to do? Buy a little corn farm in Kansas."

George looked at him incredulously and Kula chuckled. "Yeah, I know that's funny. Probably half the people in Kansas would like to come here to retire, and I want to go back there." He leaned forward on his elbows. "But I'm sick of the islands. I'd like to get up in the mornings and know I can hop in my car and drive more than thirty miles without running into the ocean. I want to live someplace where they have seasons, not the same boring perfect weather all the time.

"But why a corn farm?" George asked.

"I like to grow things," Kula said, taking the toothpick out of his mouth for the first time. "I've got a little garden at home right now. Tomatoes, radishes, carrots. But you need a field for corn—all I've got is the patio of my bachelor apartment. I get this realty catalogue every month. It's got a section on rural properties, with photographs, in color. I'll tell you something: a field of growing corn is a real pretty sight." Kula sat back again, taking a sip of his drink. "Only thing is, it takes a hefty down payment to buy a decent-sized farm in Kansas."

George sat back, too, and drank some of his Coke. "What's on your mind, Mr. Kula?"

The parole officer smiled. "Know what I like about you, Georgie? You cooperate. You always cooperate." The smile faded and the voice lowered. "I've got a parolee over on Oahu named Nicky Dade. Did five for burglary. Young guy, midtwenties, real hip—he's a surfer, like you. The kid's old man was a locksmith. Nicky can pick damn near any lock there is."

George nodded. "So?"

"So there's a wholesale costume jewelry merchant on Oahu that gets a shipment of pearls from Hong Kong the first of every month. They're supposed to be fake, but they're not, they're *real*—the kind divers bring up from the ocean. Nobody knows they're real, of course—everybody assumes they're fake because the business is set up as a costume jewelry company. It's a perfect cover. The guy doesn't have to pay a big insurance premium, doesn't have to have fancy security at his offices. I mean, who's going to steal a few hundred bucks' worth of fake pearls, right?" Kula sat forward again and his voice became even lower. "This guy brings in between a half and three-quarters of a million dollars' worth every month and nobody's the wiser. I only found out about it by accident, from this guy I know who works for the air courier service that brings the stuff from Hong Kong."

"What's the point?" George asked.

"The point is that my boy Nicky can pick the locks to this guy's offices *and* his safe."

"Sounds like your boy Nicky's heading for trouble."

"Not at all," Kula said emphatically. "It's a walk-in, walk-out job, sixty minutes from start to finish. It's all set to go on the first of the month. All I have to do is find my boy Nicky a partner. A helper. Nothing heavy—a bag holder, lookout man, that sort of thing. Very easy work."

"Why don't you do it yourself if it's so easy?" George asked flatly.

"Me?" Kula said. There seemed to be genuine surprise in his expression. "Hell, Georgie, I couldn't do a thing like that. I'm no thief."

"Neither am I," George reminded him. "I did time for manslaughter, remember?"

Kula's eyes narrowed a fraction. "Like I said, Georgie, I like you because I figure you always cooperate. But maybe I'm wrong. Maybe I've been wrong writing good parole reports on you all these years."

Sighing quietly, George looked away for a moment. There was hurt in his eyes, and helplessness. Presently he looked back and said, "No, Mr. Kula, you aren't wrong. What do you want me to do?"

Charley Kula smiled.

Two days later, the girl came into his shop. She had what islanders called "mixed-up blood," and it was obvious from her appearance: the brown hair of the Portuguese, the blue eyes of the *keokeos* (whites), the flat lips of the Tahitians, the wide nostrils of the Filipinos, and the long body of the Spaniards. She was almost pretty.

"Hi. You Georgie?" she asked.

"I'm George," he replied.

"I'm Mileka. Nicky's friend. He wants to see you."

"I'm right here," George said. He went on waxing the competition board he was working on.

"Not here," Mileka said. "Nicky doesn't talk business in rooms, only on beaches. He got sent to prison because of a microphone in a motel room." She jerked her head toward the ocean. "He's out surfing."

George thought about it for a moment, then put the board aside and reached under the counter for a printed sign that read: BACK IN TEN MINUTES. Terangi had used a felt-tip marker to cross out IN TEN MINUTES and in its place had hand lettered SOON.

"Let's go," George said, putting the sign in the door.

He and the girl walked down Front Street a couple of blocks, then cut over to where the beach began. Neither of them tried to make conversation. George was pushing thirty-six and the girl couldn't have been more than twenty, so each assumed they had nothing to say to the other. When they reached the sand, both took off their sandals and left them on the curb with a dozen other pairs. Then they walked along the beach, up away from the water, until they came to a couple of towels with a beach bag on them.

"Nicky's out there." The girl pointed to a figure lying flat on a surfboard on the water fifty yards out, waiting for a swell. As George looked seaward, Mileka dropped her shorts onto one of the towels and pulled her polo shirt over her head. When George looked back, she was stretched out on the towel in a yellow French-cut bikini that made her tanned body look like a warm caramel. Sun bunny, George thought derisively.

He waited for five minutes until the figure on the board caught a soft wave and stood up to surf back onto the beach. As the surfer walked toward him, George saw that he was a typical young white islander: blond, golden-tanned, supple, muscular, handsome, confident. Like I used to be, George thought before he could help himself.

"Hi, I'm Nicky Dade," the young man said, not offering to shake hands.

"George Hill," said George.

"I thought we ought to meet once before the job," Nicky said easily. "I guess Kula told you it's a real piece of cake. All you'll really have to do is what I tell you to. I thought we ought to have a look at each other, but Kula says you're okay so that's good enough for me."

"He told me you were okay, too," George countered. He didn't like being talked to as if he were a flunky.

"Of course I'm okay," Nicky retorted, annoyed. "It's my job, man. I'm the one that's doing it. Of course I'm okay."

"Of course."

Nicky stuck his surfboard upright in the sand. It was, George observed, one of the most expensive factory-made boards.

"Kula tells me you surf," Nicky said, seeming to get over his pique as quickly as it came.

"Yes."

"A little old for it, aren't you?"

"I do it anyway," George told him. He noticed that Mileka was leaning up on her elbows, looking curiously at him.

"Maybe we can go out together sometime," Nicky suggested, bobbing his head at the water. "Early in the morning, before you open your shop."

"I don't surf in the harbor," George said. He didn't even try to keep the disdain out of his voice.

"That right?" Nicky said, with a trace of amusement. "Where do you surf?"

"Kaanapali," said George.

Nicky frowned slightly. "*You* surf Kaanapali?"

"I surf Kaanapali."

"At your age?"

"At my age." George could feel himself blush. He wished the girl wasn't there. Or at least that she wasn't looking at him. He forced himself to smile. "The waves aren't big at Kaanapali, but they're tricky. Harbor surfing's too tame for me. Look, I've got to get back to my shop. You can find me there whenever you want me."

He knew their eyes followed him all the way off the beach.

At noon the next day, Marama, as usual, brought George his lunch, as she had always done for Terangi and him. "Couple of nice *opakapaka* sandwiches today," she said. George went into the bathroom at the back of the shop and washed his hands. When he came back out, Marama had his lunch set out on the desk behind the counter. As he started to eat, Mileka came in. Marama got up to leave. "I've got marketing to do, Keoki. Don't be late for supper."

After Marama left, Mileka raised her eyebrows inquiringly. "Keoki?"

"Polynesian for George," he said. "You've got Poly blood—don't you know the dialect?"

"If I spoke the language of every kind of blood *I've* got in me, man, I'd be—what do you call it?—multilingual. I'm not real big on being a native girl. What's that you're eating?"

"*Opakapaka.* Pink snapper. Want some?"

"No, thanks. I'm strictly a hamburger-and-fries person. Listen, the reason I'm here is that Nicky wants to surf Kaanapali with you. He wants to know if tomorrow morning's okay."

"I'm too busy," George said. "I'm all alone in the shop now and I'm getting behind in the work." He saw that she had pursed her lips and was nodding knowingly.

"Nicky said you were probably all talk. I'll tell him you can't make it."

As she started to leave, George said, "Wait a minute. Tell him I'll be at Black Rock at daybreak."

"I'll tell him," she said, a little smugly. Walking out, she looked back over her shoulder. " 'Bye, *Keoki.*"

At sunrise, George was sitting on the beach at the foot of Black Rock, a dark outcropping of lava rock that stood eighty feet high and jutted into the sea like a driven fist, dividing the long, beautiful beach into two lengths. Legend had it that Pele, the ancient fire goddess, had built the rock as a throne for herself. Terangi and Marama believed the story, so George believed it, too. As he sat on the sand, a thick beach towel around his shoulders for warmth, his surfboard resting familiarly between his legs, he wasn't afraid of the shadows of the rock that seemed to shift and adjust as if they had life, or of the eerie noises the wind made as it dervished its way through the throne's crags and crevices.

The sun rose at the edge of Lanai, ten miles away on the horizon, and in an instant sent warm yellow light across the dark water, changing its surface from black to an azure blue that perfectly matched the lightening sky above it. George heard a whistle and turned to see Nicky Dade and Mileka walking down the beach toward him. He rose and was pulling his sweatshirt off over his head as they came up.

"Hello, Keoki," Mileka said pertly. George ignored her.

"These waves look kind of soft to me," Nicky said.

"Like I told you, they're not big but they're tricky." George looked at him. "You a wave counter?"

"What do you mean?"

"On this side of the island, every ninth wave is a good one. So we wait here on the beach for a good one to break, then we start out, counting the incoming waves as we go. When the ninth one is about to come in, we get up and go with it. Clear?"

"Yeah, sure," Nicky said. "Where'd you learn all that?"

"Here and there."

As they waited, Nicky studied George's board. It was a handmade, tapered, hollow board ten feet long and eighteen inches wide, with a skeg, or stabilizing fin, near its back. Etched in a curve across the upper front were the words CHALLENGE THE WIDOW-MAKER.

"What's that mean?" Mileka asked, seeing the inscription.

"The widow-maker is what the old merchant seamen used to call the ocean. The man who helped me make this board said every time a person goes out to ride the water on a piece of wood, that person is challenging the widow-maker. He wanted me to remember that, so he put it on the board." At that moment a good wave broke in the surf and George turned to Nicky. Ready?"

"Ready, man."

"Let's go."

They walked into the water until they were chest-deep, then belly-flopped onto their boards and began paddling seaward. A low wave rolled in and they pushed easily through it. "That's number one!" George shouted. They kept paddling. Twenty yards, thirty. Another wave rolled in. "Number two!" Fifty yards, sixty. A third wave, perceptibly higher. "Three!"

They paddled in as straight a line as the sea would allow, their bodies flat on the narrow boards, their hands moving rapidly, their faces raised to the mass of water confronting them. In that juxtaposition, their relationship to the ocean was perilous and unpredictable, but at the same time almost carnal. Behind them, the safety of land grew farther and farther away. Ahead of them, the waves grew higher and began rolling and twisting as, far beneath the surface the water encountered deep reefs and sandbars.

"Number six."

One hundred eighty yards, one ninety.

Arm, shoulder, and neck muscles began to burn as if raw rope had been pulled across them.

"Seven!"

Two hundred ten yards. Two twenty.

The throat and groin began to react now, tightening, tensing, tickling oddly.

"Eight—!"

Two hundred and fifty yards away from the land, a six-foot wall of water rolled toward them.

"Number nine coming up!" George shouted. He leaped upright and with his feet turned the board so that it was diagonally facing the beach in the path of the wave. In his peripheral vision, he saw Nicky do the same thing. Then both of them were being lifted and carried like feathers on the wind as the swell of ocean rolled, shifted to the right, and rolled some more, taking them back where they belonged. Knees bent, bodies arched, arms akimbo, hearts pounding, faces glowing with the thrill of it, they rode the ocean. It was exhilarating.

When their boards hit sand, they leaped off and grabbed them up, then stood panting and smiling. They had come as close as any mortal ever comes to walking on water.

"Man, I see what you mean about tricky!" Nicky exclaimed as they walked back to where Mileka waited. "But I did all right, didn't I!" It was a boast more than a question.

"You did okay," George allowed. "Good thing the wave wasn't any higher."

"What do you mean?"

"I'm not sure you could have handled a higher swell."

"Oh, yeah? Could you have?"

"Sure, I handle them all the time," George replied confidently. He noticed that Mileka was taking in every word.

"Oh, yeah? Where at?" Nicky demanded.

"Kahana," George said. "The other side of Black Rock."

"Okay, let's surf there tomorrow," Nicky said.

"Look, I've got a business to run."

"You chicken?" Nicky taunted. "Afraid I'll show you up?"

George didn't have to look at Mileka to know she was again appraising him. What the hell do you care? he asked himself. She's just another sun bunny—Lahaina Town was crawling with them. Nevertheless, he said, "Okay, Kahana tomorrow at sunrise."

As George walked away, he heard Nicky ask, "Did I look better than him out there?"

And he heard Mileka reply, "You both looked about the same to me."

George couldn't help smiling.

That night George met Nicky and Charley Kula at a small café in Wailea. Mileka was with Nicky, but he sent her to play the pinball machines while the men talked.

"You two getting acquainted?" Kula asked, shifting a toothpick from one side of his mouth to the other.

"Yeah, we're surfing buddies now," Nicky said. Something in his tone told George that Nicky didn't like the fat parole officer any more than he did.

"What do you think of my boy Nicky?" Kula asked George.

"Great guy," George replied blandly.

"I knew you two'd get on." Kula leaned forward. "Speaking of business, I checked on the pearl shipment. It'll be in right on schedule Friday afternoon." He looked at Nicky. "You ready to go to work Friday night?"

"I'm ready," Nicky assured him.

"Good. Now, remember, you have to be in and out of the

building before eleven o'clock—that's when the night watchman comes on duty. I'll be at my house all evening, so I'll be able to provide an alibi for either of you on the outside chance you need one—I'll say you were with me all evening, helping me in my garden. After the job, you bring the pearls directly to me, Nicky. I'll hang on to them until it's safe to approach a fence to buy the stuff."

"How long before we get any bread out of this?" Nicky wanted to know.

"You'll get your cut as soon as I make the sale. A month, probably. Georgie, I'll take care of you out of my share."

I can hardly wait, George thought. Just then a waiter brought their dinner and Nicky waved to Mileka to come join them. "I ordered you a steak and fries," he told her when she came over.

"Okay." She glanced at the plate that was set in front of George. Everyone had steak and fries except him. "What's that?" she asked.

"*Ahi*," he said. When she frowned, he translated, "Yellowfin. It's a tuna."

"You ought to try steak sometime, Keoki," she said.

"Keoki?" Nicky asked, raising his eyebrows.

"That's his Polynesian name."

"Cute," Nicky said drily.

George felt himself turn red again. Silently he called Mileka a little bitch.

The next morning, George was waiting on Kahana beach when Nicky and Mileka got there.

"Hello, Keoki," Mileka teased at once.

"Hello, Mildred," he replied.

Nicky's mouth dropped open. "Mildred?"

"That's what Mileka means in English," George told him. He looked innocently at Mileka, who was glaring at him. "I asked my foster mother last night."

Nicky looked at her incredulously. "I don't believe it. Mildred?" After a moment, he laughed. "That's funny. Mildred!"

"Oh, shut up!" she snapped. "I thought you came here to surf."

Nicky was still laughing as he and George walked down to

the water's edge. George looked over his shoulder at Mileka and smiled. She made an obscene gesture at him.

After a good wave broke, George and Nicky put their boards in the water and began paddling out, counting waves as they went. "Remember," George reminded him, "these aren't as tricky as the ones at Kaanapali, they don't twist as much, but they're higher. You'll need a tighter crouch to keep your balance."

"I know how to surf, man," Nicky said.

Okay, big shot, let's see, George thought. He began to paddle a little faster, to get farther out before the ninth wave swelled. Nicky increased his own paddling to keep up. By the time eight waves had rolled under them, they were nearly three hundred yards from shore. When number nine began to rise up in front of them, George yelled, "Looks like a ten-footer!"

Both of them stood and planted their feet firmly against the boards. Their arms extended like gulls spreading their wings. With the lift of the water, they turned, and as they felt themselves being lifted lightly with the swell they had a brief glimpse of Mileka, far away on the beach, standing with her hands on her hips, looking out at them.

Then they made the oblique shift to ride diagonally and she passed from their line of sight as they faced Kahana far to the right of where she stood. It *was* a ten-footer and it lifted them high and sped them along on its sheet of water as if it were frozen and they were city kids sliding on an icy sidewalk.

They rode in until the big wave broke, then maneuvered their boards into calmer water and coasted until it was shallow enough to jump off.

"Great! That was great!" Nicky exclaimed as they waded in. "Man, it can't get any better than that!"

"Sure it can," George said.

"Huh? What do you mean?"

"At Kapalua," George told him. "Farther up the coast. There the waves are high *and* tricky."

"Let's go there, then," Nicky said at once. "Tomorrow."

George shrugged. "Why not?"

Mileka didn't say good-bye to George when she and Nicky

left, but as they were walking away George heard Nicky ask, "How did I look out there?"

"You looked good," Mileka said. Then, after a moment she added, "But he looked better . . ."

Early that afternoon, Mileka came into the surfboard shop. Marama had already been there and George was eating his lunch.

"Fish again?" she asked. "What is it this time?"

"*Ono*," he said. "The fishermen call it wahoo. It's a gray game fish."

"Do you eat fish all the time?"

"Yes. My foster father said if a man ate fish every day he'd become a better swimmer and surfer because he'd feel more at home in the ocean."

"Come on, you don't really believe that, do you?"

"Yes, I do." Her tone irritated him. "What are you doing here, anyway? Another message from Nicky?"

"No. Nicky's taking a nap." Now it was she who blushed slightly. "Look, I came to say I'm sorry. About the name business, teasing you like I was doing. I didn't realize how you felt until you did the same thing to me. Then I realized how dumb it was. Sometimes I can be really stupid."

George grunted softly. "Can't we all."

"Anyway, I'm sorry."

"Forget it," he said. He pushed his plate toward her. "Want half a wahoo sandwich?" She hesitated. "Go on, try it, you might like it."

"Okay." Mileka sat and joined him for lunch. Presently she asked, "So how'd you get Poly foster parents? Did they adopt you?"

"Kind of." George turned to gaze out the window, across Front Street at the harbor.

"Maybe I shouldn't have asked," she said when he didn't elaborate.

George shrugged. "It's no secret, really. Thirteen years ago I was in the army, stationed at Fort Shafter over on Oahu. I loved the army—I was going to be a thirty-year man. To me it was the perfect life: soldier all week, drink beer, surf, and get laid every weekend. Except that one weekend it didn't quite work out that way. Four of us were coming back from surfing the north shore and we'd had a little too much to drink. We were cruising along the Nimitz Highway in a convertible one of the guys owned, when he lost control of the car, crossed the center line, and crashed head-on into an oncoming car.

"A Hawaiian couple and their two children were killed. My three buddies were killed, too. Seven dead—and I survived. I guess they wanted to make an example out of me as a warning to other servicemen stationed on the island, so they indicted me for manslaughter. I hadn't been driving—but I couldn't prove it. The prosecution couldn't prove that I *had*, but there was enough doubt for the jury to convict me. I got fifteen years. I did eight and then Terangi and Marama helped me get out. They offered to provide me with a job and a place to live, and talked to the parole board. The parole board was very impressed by their interest—because the woman killed in the other car had been their daughter. I guess the board figured that if Terangi and Marama could forgive me, so could they. So five years ago I got out and came here to Maui. Terangi and Marama treated me like a son from the first day."

"They sound like wonderful people," Mileka said quietly.

"The best," George said.

Mileka studied him for a moment, then asked, "You don't like being in on this job Nicky's doing, do you?"

He shook his head. "I'm in it because of Kula. I don't want to go back to prison."

"Neither does Nicky." She took one of his hands and held it for a moment. "It'll be okay, Keoki," she said, and this time she spoke his Polynesian name naturally, without teasing. "Things will work out all right."

Yes, they would, George thought, nodding slightly.

Because he would *make* them work out all right.

Off Kapalua beach the next morning, George and Nicky paddled out a hundred yards, let a six-foot wave roll under them, and *then* began to count waves as they pushed farther out to sea. By the time they had counted eight waves, they were four hundred yards from the beach and facing a twelve-foot swell that was twisting forty degrees to their right. Getting upright on their boards, they turned almost fully around instead of diagonally, braced, crouched, sucked in air, and stopped breathing as the water lifted them like so much driftwood and seemed to hold them aloft for a split instant before rolling under them and rushing them back toward the beach. As their journey began, they breathed again, moving as if in flight, seemingly weightless, soaring along smoothly in defiance of magnetic gravity, marine physics, and mortal fear. For as long as they rode the crest of the wave, they were greater than other men.

When it was over, they waded back onto the beach and dropped to the sand, their chests heaving as the tension of the ride slowly gave way to the calm and safety of land.

"Man," said Nicky, "I never got a charge out of surfing like I get when I surf with you. There's something about the way you know the ocean—it's almost spooky." He propped up on one elbow and glanced at Mileka, who lay sunning farther up the beach. "Look, tonight's the job. When it's over, I figured we'd go our separate ways. But I been thinking. After the payoff, why don't we take a trip together? A surfing trip. We could head down to Peru for the season there, then move on to eastern Australia—hell, we could just follow the waves wherever they were breaking."

George sat up and hugged his knees. "What about her?" he asked, bobbing his chin at Mileka.

"I'll dump her," Nicky said without hesitation. "She's just a sun bunny—there'll be plenty like her wherever we go. Look, my share of tonight's job, and whatever Kula gives you for helping me, ought to last us a year, maybe a year and a half. And when it's gone, we'll find a way to get more. It's the chance of a lifetime, Georgie. What do you say, man?"

George seemed to ponder the proposition for a long moment, but presently he nodded and smiled at Nicky Dade. "Count me in."

"Far out!" Nicky all but cheered. Glancing toward Mileka again, he quickly lowered his voice. "Our little secret, right?"

George winked at him. "Right."

* * *

That evening, George flew to Oahu on the six o'clock Aloha flight. Nicky, who had gone over at noon, met him outside the airport in a rental car. When Nicky saw the look on George's face, he asked at once, "What's wrong, man?"

"We've got a problem," George said tensely. He handed Nicky the pink carbon of an airline ticket confirmation from a Maui travel agency. It was a one-way ticket on the next morning's Continental flight to San Francisco in the name of Charles Kula. Looking at it, Nicky frowned.

"I don't understand."

"A friend of mine works in the travel agency," George said. "He knows Kula's my parole officer. This afternoon he mentioned to me that Kula was flying to the mainland tomorrow. I had my friend get me a copy of the ticket confirmation, just to be sure." Nicky was now staring incredulously at George. "He's crossing us, man," George concluded simply. "It's a one-way ticket. He's taking the pearls and skipping."

Nicky's eyes scanned the confirmation again. "The dirty bastard," he whispered.

"We'll have to call off the job," George said.

"No!" Nicky snapped. "We're not calling off nothing! I'm not giving up my surfing trip because of this bastard. Besides, this job is too cushy to call off. We'll just do to him what he was going to do to us: take the pearls and skip."

"No good," George vetoed. "He'd find a way to finger us without involving himself. He's the law, remember, and we're ex-cons. We'd better call it off."

"No! We're going to pull this job, man, just like we planned!" Nicky was staring out the windshield as if transfixed. "After we pull it, I'll figure out how to handle Mr. Charles Kula."

Nicky pulled away from the airport and drove into Honolulu. He parked on a side street off busy Kalakaua Avenue, where the costume jewelry firm's office building was located. He and George walked around the area for an hour as Nicky briefed him. "Kalakaua's a big tourist street now: lots of shops, places to eat, lots of bars. There's usually people on the street until midnight or later. That's our building over there—"

George looked at a rather ordinary five-story structure that rose above a large drugstore. On one side of the drugstore was the entrance to an underground garage. Stretching beyond it was a string of souvenir shops: T-shirts, seashells, monkey-pod carvings, muumuus. Shoppers were everywhere.

Just before nine o'clock, Nicky said, "Okay, let's go."

They returned to the car and Nicky drove directly to the building and into the underground garage. It was only about one-third full, most of the building's employees having left for the day. Nicky parked as close as he could to a door marked: ELECTRICAL ROOM—AUTHORIZED PERSONNEL ONLY. Opening the trunk of the car, he said, "Stay here. Bend over the trunk like you're looking for something. If anybody comes, drop the tire iron on the floor."

He walked away, pulling on a pair of gloves. George saw him take something from his pocket and briefly do something with the lock of the electrical room door. The door opened almost at once and Nicky disappeared inside. Waiting at the trunk, George began to sweat.

In less than five minutes, Nicky was back. "Okay, the alarm's crossed," he said. He took a briefcase from the trunk. "Come on."

They rode the elevator from the garage up to three. No one got on with them and they encountered no one in the hall. "I can't believe there's a fortune in pearls just lying around this place," George said in a tense whisper.

"I told you, it's a cushy job," Nicky whispered back. "Now you see why I wouldn't call it off?" They reached a door with lettering on a frosted-glass pane that read PACIFIC-ORIENT COSTUME JEWELRY CO., LTD. "Watch the elevator indicator," Nicky instructed. "If the light comes on, nudge me and we'll both walk away from the door. Same thing if anyone comes out of another office." He immediately went to work on the door's lock.

The elevator light did not come on, and within a minute Nicky had the door open and was pulling George inside. Nicky had him wait just inside the door to listen for any sound from the hallway. He himself disappeared into one of the inner offices. George began to sweat again. At one point while he was standing there, he heard the sound of footsteps going by in the hall, and for a fleeting moment he thought he was going to be sick. He could challenge the widow-maker atop a rolling wave twice his height, but standing in a dark office at night was something else entirely.

Nicky seemed to take forever in the other room. Several times George heard vague metallic sounds and soft, muted tapping, but aside from that there was only silence. In the light from a nearby outside window, George could see a water cooler. It was sorely tempting as he felt his mouth go drier and drier, but he didn't want to leave his place at the door—somehow being next to the door seemed safer.

After what seemed like half the night, Nicky was suddenly back at his side. "Check the hall."

George opened the door a crack, using a handkerchief around the doorknob. The hall was clear. They left quickly, walking briskly back down to the elevator. Waiting there, Nicky grinned and shook the briefcase once. It sounded as if it was full of dried peas.

Back in the car, Nicky handed the briefcase to George. "I'm gonna drop you at a taxi stand. Go back out to the airport and wait for me around the Aloha ticket counter."

"Where are you going?"

"To see Kula." Nicky smiled coldly. "I want to be the one to tell him that his trip to San Francisco tomorrow has been canceled."

"You sure you know what you're doing?" George asked.

"I know exactly what I'm doing, man."

At the Royal Hawaiian taxi queue, Nicky pulled over and left the engine running. For just an instant, he seemed to hesitate. George knew at once what he was thinking.

"Don't worry," he said easily. "I'll be at the airport when you get there." He patted the briefcase. "And so will this."

Nicky nodded and drove off.

George had to wait in the airport four hours. Then he and Nicky had to wait another two hours for the first early-morning commuter flight back to Maui. The sun was just breaking on the ocean horizon as the twin-engine Otter set down on the airstrip at Kahului.

Both men had been silent during the flight. The night's events lay heavily between them. When Nicky had arrived back at the Honolulu airport, George had immediately asked, "What happened?"

"It's all settled with Kula," Nicky had replied tightly.

"What happened?" George asked again. Nicky glanced around. They were sitting alone in a corner of the passenger terminal.

"I bashed his double-crossing head in with a tire iron," Nicky told him coldly. "Then I put him in the trunk and drove out to Kaneana. You know where that is?"

George nodded. "It's out the Farrington Highway. Out where the underwater caves are."

"Right. I dumped him off the cliff right above the caves."

George swallowed. "Sharks feed in those caves."

"All the time," Nicky had confirmed in a whisper.

Now they were walking out of the Kahului airport toward the parking lot where George had left the old Plymouth that used to belong to Terangi. Nicky, carrying the briefcase, put it on his lap when he got in the car. As George started the engine, he said almost to himself, "Man, I've got an edge on. I need to unwind. After I drop you, I'm hitting the waves."

"I'll go with you," Nicky said. "We'll just stop by and pick up my board."

George shook his head. "Not today. I need a real challenge. I'm going out to Mokolea Point."

"Where's that?"

"It's out past where the highway ends. Out past Lipoa, where the lighthouse is."

"What's out there?"

"Pipelines," George said. "You ever surf a pipeline?"

Nicky shook his head. Pipelines were the twelve-to-eighteen-foot waves that rolled all the way over to form a moving channel of water through which a person could surf—if they were good enough. Fearless enough. Crazy enough.

"I'm going with you," Nicky said.

"You're not good enough to do a pipeline." George kept his tone clinical.

"Up yours," Nicky said. "I'm as good as you are. I'm going."

"Suit yourself," George told him.

They stopped at a little motel in Kahaina Town where Nicky and Mileka had been living. Nicky slipped in and got his board without waking her. Then George headed out Honoapiilani Highway and followed it past all the beaches they had surfed together—Kaanapali, Kahana, Kapalua—then on past Lipoa, where the lighthouse stood, and on around to where the paved highway ended and a dirt road began.

The road curved and wound around the natural lay of the craggy rock on which it rested, twisting and turning as if teasing the great ocean with its presence. George drove slowly, guiding the car carefully in tracks left by other vehicles. As on the plane, the two men did not talk. But George noticed that Nicky drummed his fingertips soundlessly on the briefcase that he again held on his lap.

Finally they arrived at a high point above the beach with a precarious path leading down to it. Beyond the beach, the ocean seemed angry. Great churning waves roiled up and rushed the shore as if in attack, not merely to erode but to shatter, to break apart this speck of rock that usurped its vastness.

Nicky put the briefcase of pearls under a blanket in the backseat and George locked the car, hiding the keys under a rock. Then the two men changed into their swim trunks and stood with their boards, looking out from the point.

"This is a *uhane lele*," George said quietly. "It's a sacred place where the souls of the dead leap into their ancestral spirit land."

"You don't really believe that bullshit, do you?" Nicky asked derisively.

"Yes, I do," George replied, staring at the sea.

Shaking his head disdainfully, Nicky started down the steep path. Then he turned back, eyes suspicious, and said, "You first." Containing a knowing smile, George led the way down to the beach.

There they waited for the next pipline to break, then plunged in and started paddling. Even though the sea was turbulent, moving against the tide wasn't difficult—the slender boards pierced the oncoming water with almost no resistance, needling through the waves or dipping over them as if without purpose, yet steadily leaving the land behind. They stayed close together, counting the waves. When the ninth one broke before them, Nicky yelled, "It's not the pipeline!"

"The *ninth* ninth wave is the pipeline!" George yelled back. "We've got a long way to go!" Nicky was looking at him in astonishment. "Want to turn back?" George challenged.

"Not me, man! I'm in all the way!"

They kept paddling. And counting. The second ninth wave broke. The third ninth wave. Periodically they rested, letting several waves go past without paddling through or over them, moving their hands only enough to keep from losing distance, then they began thrusting again. They passed the fourth ninth wave, the fifth, the sixth, and rested some more. Their upper arms burned, hot with fatigue. Their breath came in bursts.

"How far—out are we?" Nicky asked.

"About—eight hundred yards."

"God!"

"It'll be—a great ride!" George bolstered. "Probably—half a mile!"

The seventh ninth wave broke.

The eighth.

Then it came. The pipeline, rolling up in front of them as if the ocean had been tilted on edge. A sixteen-foot wave that looped back to embrace itself and form a tunnel of spiraling water that skimmed toward landfall with unbridled power.

"Waaaa-hoooo!" George yelled as he rose upright on his board. He caught only a brief glimpse of Nicky, just long enough to see the terror in his face, then the pipeline was upon him and he was in the vortex of it. An embryo in the womb of mother ocean.

George rode the great whirlpool all the way back to the beach. And he was right: it *was* a half-mile ride.

He sat on the bluff with a blanket around his shoulders for an hour, but Nicky never came out of the water. Score one more for the widow-maker, he thought.

He got the briefcase out of the car and opened it. The pearls lay spread inside like white caviar from some giant fish. They came from the ocean, they might as well go back to the ocean, he thought. Scooping up a handful, he flung them from the high bluff out into the water. Then he flung a second handful, a third. At some point, he began to laugh at what he was doing. It was a loud, uncontrollable laugh, growing in volume with each new handful of pearls he threw back to the ocean. He kept throwing and laughing, throwing and laughing. Finally, the pearls were all gone and he put a couple of rocks in the briefcase and threw that off the edge, too, watching it sink into the water.

From the glove compartment, he took the airline ticket he had bought in Charley Kula's name, and tore it into tiny pieces, releasing the bits to the sea breeze. Then he got into Terangi's old Plymouth and drove back toward Lahaina Town to open his shop.

BILL PRONZINI

STAKEOUT

The life of a private investigator isn't always quite so glamorous or exciting as the books and films of the past six decades may have led us to believe. Often it's a matter of sitting alone behind the wheel of a car on a rainy night, watching for someone to come out of a house. Bill Pronzini's Nameless, one of the most realistic of today's private eyes, knows what a stakeout can be like. In this unusual tale, virtually the entire story comes to us while he sits behind the wheel of that car in the rain.

Four o'clock in the morning. And I was sitting huddled and ass-numb in my car in a freezing rainstorm, waiting for a guy I had never seen in person to get out of a nice warm bed and drive off in his Mercedes, thus enabling me to follow him so I could find out where he lived.

Thrilling work if you can get it. The kind that makes any self-respecting detective wonder why he didn't become a plumber instead.

Rain hammered against the car's metal surfaces, sluiced so thickly down the windshield that it transformed the glass into an opaque screen; all I could see were smeary blobs of light that marked the street lamps along this block of 47th Avenue. Wind buffeted the car in forty-mile-an-hour gusts off the ocean nearby. Condensation had formed again on the driver's door window, even though I had rolled it down half an inch; I rubbed some of the mist away and took another bleary-eyed look across the street.

This was one of San Francisco's older middle-class residential neighborhoods, desirable—as long as you didn't mind fog-belt living—because Sutro Heights Park was just a block away and you were also within walking distance of Ocean Beach, the Cliff House, and Land's End. Most of the houses had been built in the thirties and stood shoulder-to-shoulder with their neighbors, but they seemed to havc more individuality than the bland row houses dominating the avenues farther inland; out here, California Spanish was the dominant style. Asians had bought up much of the city's west side housing in recent years, but fewer of those close to the ocean than anywhere else. A lot of homes in pockets such as this were still owned by older-generation, blue-collar San Franciscans.

The house I had under surveillance, number 9279, was one of the Spanish stucco jobs, painted white with a red tile roof. Yucca palms, one large and three small, dominated its tiny front yard. The three-year-old Mercedes with the Washington state license plates was still parked, illegally, across the driveway. Above it, the house's front windows remained dark. If anybody was up yet I couldn't tell it from where I was sitting.

I shifted position for the hundredth time, wincing as my stiffened joints protested with creaks and twinges. I had been here four and a half hours now, with nothing to do except to sit and wait and try not to fall asleep; to listen to the rain and the rattle and stutter of my thoughts. I was weary and irritable and I wanted some hot coffee and my own warm bed. It would be well past dawn, I thought bleakly, before I got either one.

Stakeouts . . . God, how I hated them. The passive waiting, the boredom, the slow, slow passage of dead time. How many did this make over the past thirty-odd years? How many empty, wasted, lost hours? Too damn many, whatever the actual figure. The physical discomfort was also becoming less tolerable, especially on nights like this, when not even a heavy overcoat and gloves kept the chill from penetrating bone-deep. I had lived fifty-eight years; fifty-eight is too old to sit all-night stakeouts on the best of cases, much less on a lousy split-fee skip-trace.

I was starting to hate Randolph Hixley, too, sight unseen. He was the owner of the Mercedes across the street and my reason for being here. To his various and sundry employers, past and no doubt present, he was a highly paid free-lance computer consultant. To his ex-wife and two kids, he was a probable deadbeat who currently owed some $14,000 in back alimony and child support. To me and Puget Sound Investigations of

Seattle, he was what should have been a small but adequate fee for routine work. Instead, he had developed into a minor pain in the ass. Mine.

Hixley had quit Seattle for parts unknown some four months ago, shortly after his wife divorced him for what she referred to as "sexual misconduct," and had yet to make a single alimony or child support payment. For reasons of her own, the wife had let the first two barren months go by without doing anything about it. On the occasion of the third due date, she had received a brief letter from Hixley informing her in tear-jerk language that he was so despondent over the breakup of their marriage he hadn't worked since leaving Seattle and was on the verge of becoming one of the homeless. He had every intention of fulfilling his obligations, though, the letter said; he would send money as soon as he got back on his feet. So would she bear with him for a while and please not sic the law on him? The letter was postmarked San Francisco, but with no return address.

The ex-wife, who was no dummy, smelled a rat. But because she still harbored some feelings for him, she had gone to Puget Sound Investigations rather than to the authorities, the object being to locate Hixley and determine if he really was broke and despondent. If so, then she would show the poor dear compassion and understanding. If not, then she would obtain a judgment against the son-of-a-bitch and force him to pay up or get thrown in the slammer.

Puget Sound had taken the job, done some preliminary work, and then called a San Francisco detective—me—and farmed out the tough part for half the fee. That kind of cooperative thing is done all the time when the client isn't wealthy enough and the fee isn't large enough for the primary agency to send one of its own operatives to another state. No private detective likes to split fees, particularly when he's the one doing most of the work, but ours is sometimes a back-scratching business. Puget Sound had done a favor for me once; now it was my turn.

Skip-tracing can be easy or it can be difficult, depending on the individual you're trying to find. At first I figured Randolph Hixley, broke or not, might be one of the difficult ones. He had no known relatives or friends in the Bay Area. He had stopped using his credit cards after the divorce, and had not applied for new ones, which meant that if he was working and had money, he was paying his bills in cash. In Seattle, he'd provided consultancy services to a variety of different companies, large and small, doing most of the work at home by computer link. If he'd hired out to one or more outfits in the Bay Area, Puget Sound had not been able to turn up a lead as to which they might be, so I probably wouldn't be able to either. There is no easy way to track down that information, not without some kind of insider pull with the IRS.

And yet despite all of that, I got lucky right away—so lucky I revised my thinking and decided, prematurely and falsely, that Hixley was going to be one of the easy traces after all. The third call I made was to a contact in the San Francisco City Clerk's office, and it netted me the information that the 1987 Mercedes 280 XL registered in Hixley's name had received two parking tickets on successive Thursday mornings, the most recent of which was the previous week. The tickets were for identical violations: illegal parking across a private driveway and illegal parking during posted street-cleaning hours. Both citations had been issued between seven and seven-thirty A.M. And in both instances, the address was the same: 9279 47th Avenue.

I looked up the address in my copy of the reverse city directory. 9279 47th Avenue was a private house occupied by one Anne Carswell, a commercial artist, and two other Carswells, Bonnie and Margo, whose ages were given as eighteen and nineteen, respectively, and who I presumed were her daughters. The Carswells didn't own the house; they had been renting it for a little over two years.

Since there had been no change of registration on the Mercedes—I checked on that with the DMV—I assumed that the car still belonged to Randolph Hixley. And I figured things this way: Hixley, who was no more broke and despondent than I was, had met and established a relationship with Anne Carswell, and taken to spending Wednesday nights at her house. Why only Wednesdays? For all I knew, once a week was as much passion as Randy and Anne could muster up. Or it could be the two daughters slept elsewhere that night. In any case, Wednesday was Hixley's night to howl.

So the next Wednesday evening I drove out there, looking for his Mercedes. No Mercedes. I made my last check at midnight, went home to bed, got up at six A.M., and drove back to 47th Avenue for another look. Still no Mercedes.

Well, I thought, they skipped a week. Or for some reason they'd altered their routine. I went back on Thursday night. And Friday night and Saturday night. I made spot checks during the day. On one occasion I saw a tall, willowy redhead in her late thirties—Anne Carswell, no doubt—driving out of the garage. On another occasion I saw the two daughters, one blond, one brunette, both attractive, having a conversation with a couple of sly college types. But that was all I saw. Still no Mercedes, still no Randolph Hixley.

I considered bracing one of the Carswell women on a ruse, trying to find out that way where Hixley was living. But I didn't do it. He might have put them wise to his background and the money he owed, and asked them to keep mum if anyone ever approached them. Or I might slip somehow in my questioning and make her suspicious enough to call Hixley. I did not want to take the chance of warning him off.

Last Wednesday had been another bust. So had early Thursday—I drove out there at five A.M. that time. And so had the rest of the week. I was wasting time and gas and sleep, but it was the only lead I had. All the other skip-trace avenues I'd explored had led me nowhere near my elusive quarry.

Patience and perseverance are a detective's best assets; hang in there long enough and as often as not you find what you're looking for. Tonight I'd finally found Hixley and his Mercedes, back at the Carswell house after a two-week absence.

The car hadn't been there the first two times I drove by, but when I made what would have been my last pass, at twenty of twelve, there it was, once again illegally parked across the driveway. Maybe he didn't give a damn about parking tickets because he had no intention of paying them. Or maybe he disliked walking fifty feet or so, which was how far away the nearest legal curb space was. Or, hell, maybe he was just an arrogant bastard who thumbed his nose at the law any time it inconvenienced him. Whatever his reason for blocking Anne Carswell's driveway, it was a dumb mistake.

The only choice I had, spotting his car so late, was to stake it out and wait for him to show. I would have liked to go home and catch a couple of hours sleep, but for all I knew he wouldn't spend the entire night this time. If I left and came back and he was gone, I'd have to go through this whole rigmarole yet again.

So I parked and settled in. The lights in the Carswell house had gone off at twelve-fifteen and hadn't come back on since. It had rained off and on all evening, but the first hard rain started a little past one. The storm had steadily worsened until, now, it was a full-fledged howling, ripping blow. And still I sat and still I waited . . .

A blurred set of headlights came boring up 47th toward Geary, the first car to pass in close to an hour. When it went swishing by I held my watch up close to my eyes: 4:07. Suppose he stays in there until eight or nine? I thought. Four or five more hours of this and I'd be too stiff to move. It was meat-locker cold in the car. I couldn't start the engine and put the heater on because the exhaust, if not the idle, would call attention to my presence. I'd wrapped my legs and feet in the car blanket, which provided some relief; even so, I could no longer feel my toes when I tried to wiggle them.

The hard drumming beat of the rain seemed to be easing a little. Not the wind, though; a pair of back-to-back gusts shook the car, as if it were a toy in the hands of a destructive child. I shifted position again, pulled the blanket more tightly around my ankles.

A light went on in the Carswell house.

I scrubbed mist off the driver's door window, peered through the wet glass. The big front window was alight over there, behind drawn curtains. That was a good sign: People don't usually put their living room lights on at four A.M. unless somebody plans to be leaving soon.

Five minutes passed while I sat chafing my gloved hands together and moving my feet up and down to improve circulation. Then another light went on—the front porch light this time. And a few seconds after that, the door opened and somebody came out onto the stoop.

It wasn't Randolph Hixley; it was a young blond woman wearing a trenchcoat over what looked to be a lacy nightgown.

One of the Carswell daughters. She stood still for a moment, looking out over the empty street. Then she drew the trench-coat collar up around her throat and ran down the stairs and over to Hixley's Mercedes.

For a few seconds she stood hunched on the sidewalk on the passenger side, apparently unlocking the front door with a set of keys. She pulled the door open, as if making sure it was unlocked, then slammed it shut again. She turned and ran back up the stairs and vanished into the house.

I thought: Now what was that all about?

The porch light stayed on. So did the light in the front room. Another three minutes dribbled away. The rain slackened a little more, so that it was no longer sheeting; the wind continued to wail and moan. And then things got even stranger over there.

First the porch light went off. Then the door opened and somebody exited onto the stoop, followed a few seconds later by a cluster of shadow-shapes moving in an awkward, confused fashion. I couldn't identify them or tell what they were doing while they were all grouped on the porch; the tallest yucca palm cast too much shadow and I was too far away. But when they started down the stairs, there was just enough extension of light from the front window to individuate the shapes for me.

There were four of them, by God—three in an uneven line on the same step, the fourth backing down in front of them as though guiding the way. Three women, one man. The man—several inches taller, wearing an overcoat and hat, head lolling forward as if he were drunk or unconscious—was being supported by two of the women.

They all managed to make it down the slippery stairs without any of them suffering a misstep. When they reached the sidewalk, the one who had been guiding ran ahead to the Mercedes and dragged the front passenger door open. In the faint outspill from the dome light, I watched the other two women, with the third one's help, push and prod the man inside. Once they had the door shut again, they didn't waste any time catching their breaths. Two of them went running back to the house; the third hurried around to the driver's door, bent to unlock it. She was the only one of the three, I realized then, who was fully dressed: raincoat, rainhat, slacks, boots. When she slid in under the wheel I had a dome-lit glimpse of reddish hair and a white, late-thirties face under the rainhat. Anne Carswell.

She fired up the Mercedes, let the engine warm up for all of five seconds, switched on the headlights, and eased away from the curb at a crawl, the way you'd drive over a surface of broken glass. The two daughters were already back inside the house, with the door shut behind them. I had long since unwrapped the blanket from around my legs; I didn't hesitate in starting my car. Or in trying to start it: The engine was cold and it took three whirring tries before it caught and held. If Anne Carswell had been driving fast, I might have lost her. As it was, with her creeping along, she was only halfway along the next block behind me when I swung out into a tight U-turn.

I ran dark through the rain until she completed a slow turn west on Point Lobos and passed out of sight. Then I put on my lights and accelerated across Geary to the Point Lobos intersection. I got there in time to pick up the Mercedes' taillights as it went through the flashing yellow traffic signal at 48th Avenue. I let it travel another fifty yards downhill before I turned onto Point Lobos in pursuit.

Five seconds later, Anne Carswell had another surprise for me.

I expected her to continue down past the Cliff House and around onto the Great Highway; there is no other through direction once you pass 48th. But she seemed not to be leaving the general area after all. The Mercedes' brake lights came on and she slow-turned into the Merrie Way parking area above the ruins of the old Sutro Baths. The combination lot and overlook had only the one entrance/exit; it was surrounded on its other three sides by cliffs and clusters of wind-shaped cypress trees and a rocky nature trail that led out beyond the ruins of Land's End.

Without slowing, I drove on past. She was crawling straight down the center of the unpaved, potholed lot, toward the trees at the far end. Except for the Mercedes, the rain-drenched expanse appeared deserted.

Below Merrie Way, on the other side of Point Lobos, there is a newer, paved parking area carved out of Sutro Heights park, for sightseers and patrons of Louis' Restaurant opposite and the Cliff House bars and eateries farther down. It, too, was deserted at this hour. From the overlook above, you can't see this curving downhill section of Point Lobos; I swung across into the paved lot, cut my lights, looped around to where I had a clear view of the Merrie Way entrance. Then I parked, shut off the engine, and waited.

For a few seconds I could see a haze of slowly moving light up there, but not the Mercedes itself. Then the light winked out and there was nothing to see except wind-whipped rain and dark. Five minutes went by. Still nothing to see. She must have parked, I thought—but to do what?

Six minutes, seven. At seven and a half, a shape materialized out of the gloom above the entrance—somebody on foot, walking fast, bent against the lashing wind. Anne Carswell. She was moving at an uphill angle out of the overlook, climbing to 48th Avenue.

When she reached the sidewalk, a car came through the flashing yellow at the intersection and its headlight beams swept over her; she turned away from them, as if to make sure her face wasn't seen. The car swished down past where I was, disappeared beyond the Cliff House. I watched Anne Carswell cross Point Lobos and hurry into 48th at the upper edge of the park.

Going home, I thought. Abandoned Hixley and his Mercedes on the overlook and now she's hoofing it back to her daughters.

What the hell?

I started the car and drove up to 48th and turned there. Anne Carswell was now on the opposite side of the street, near where Geary dead-ends at the park; when my lights caught her she turned her head away as she had a couple of minutes ago. I drove two blocks, circled around onto 47th, came back a block and then parked and shut down again within fifty yards of the Carswell house. Its porch light was back on, which indicated that the daughters were anticipating her imminent return. Two minutes later she came fast-walking out of Geary onto 47th. One minute after that, she climbed the stairs to her house and let herself in. The porch light went out immediately, followed fifteen seconds later by the light in the front room.

I got the car moving again and made my way back down to the Merrie Way overlook.

The Mercedes was still the only vehicle on the lot, parked at an angle just beyond the long terraced staircase that leads down the cliffisde to the pitlike bottom of the ruins. I pulled in alongside, snuffed my lights. Before I got out, I armed myself with the flashlight I keep clipped under the dash.

Icy wind and rain slashed at me as I crossed to the Mercedes. Even above the racket made by the storm, I could hear the barking of sea lions on the offshore rocks beyond the Cliff House. Surf boiled frothing over those rocks, up along the cliffs and among the concrete foundations that are all that's left of the old bathhouse. Nasty night, and a nasty business here to go with it. I was sure of that now.

I put the flashlight up against the Mercedes' passenger window, flicked it on briefly. He was in there, all right; she'd shoved him over so that he lay half sprawled under the wheel, his head tipped back against the driver's door. The passenger door was unlocked. I opened it and got in and shut the door again to extinguish the dome light. I put the flash beam on his face, shielding it with my hand.

Randolph Hixley, no doubt of that; the photograph Puget Sound Investigations had sent me was a good one. No doubt, either, that he was dead. I checked his pulse, just to make sure. Then I moved the light over him, slowly, to see if I could find out what had killed him.

There weren't any discernible wounds or bruises or other marks on his body; no holes or tears or bloodstains on his damp clothing. Poison? Not that, either. Most any deadly poison produces convulsions, vomiting, rictus; his facial muscles were smooth and when I sniffed at his mouth I smelled nothing except Listerine.

Natural causes, then? Heart attack, stroke, aneurysm? Sure, maybe. But if he'd died of natural causes, why would Anne Carswell and her daughters have gone to all the trouble of moving his body and car down here? Why not just call Emergency Services?

On impulse I probed Hixley's clothing and found his wallet. It was empty—no cash, no credit cards, nothing except some old photos. Odd. He'd quit using credit cards after his divorce; he should have been carrying at least a few dollars. I took a close look at his hands and wrists. He was wearing a watch, a fairly new and fairly expensive one. No rings or other jewelry—but there was a white mark on his otherwise tanned left pinkie, as if a ring had been recently removed.

They rolled him, I thought. All the cash in his wallet and a ring off his finger. Not the watch because it isn't made of gold or platinum and you can't get much for a watch, anyway, these days.

But why? Why would they kill a man for a few hundred bucks? Or rob a dead man and then try to dump the body? In either case, the actions of those three women made no damn sense . . .

Or did they?

I was beginning to get a notion.

I backed out of the Mercedes and went to sit and think in my own car. I remembered some things, and added them together with some other things, and did a little speculating, and the notion wasn't a notion anymore—it was the answer.

Hell, I thought then, I'm getting old. Old and slow on the uptake. I should have seen this part of it as soon as they brought the body out. And I should have tumbled to the other part a week ago, if not sooner.

I sat there for another minute, feeling my age and a little sorry for myself because it was going to be quite a while yet before I got any sleep. Then, dutifully, I hauled up my mobile phone and called in the law.

They arrested the three women a few minutes past seven A.M. at the house on 47th Avenue. I was present for identification purposes. Anne Carswell put up a blustery protest of innocence until the inspector in charge, a veteran named Ginzberg, tossed the words "foul play" into the conversation; then the two girls broke down simultaneously and soon there were loud squawks of denial from all three: "We didn't hurt him! He had a heart attack, he died of a heart attack!" The girls, it turned out, were not named Carswell and were not Anne Carswell's daughters. The blonde was Bonnie Harper; the brunette was Margo LaFond. They were both former runaways from southern California.

The charges against the trio included failure to report a death, unlawful removal of a corpse, and felony theft. But the main charge was something else entirely.

The main charge was operating a house of prostitution.

Later that day, after I had gone home for a few hours' sleep, I laid the whole thing out for my partner, Eberhardt.

"I should have known they were hookers and Hixley was a customer," I said. "There were enough signs. His wife divorced him for 'sexual misconduct'; that was one. Another was how unalike those three women were—different hair colors, which isn't typical in a mother and her daughters. Then there were those sly young guys I saw with the two girls. They weren't boyfriends, they were customers too."

"Hixley really did die of a heart attack?" Eberhardt asked.

"Yeah. Carswell couldn't risk notifying Emergency Services; she didn't know much about Hixley and she was afraid somebody would come around asking questions. She had a nice discreet operation going there, with a small but high-paying clientele, and she didn't want a dead man to rock the boat. So she and the girls dressed the corpse and hustled it out of there. First, though, they emptied Hixley's wallet and she stripped a valuable garnet ring off his pinkie. She figured it was safe to do that; if anybody questioned the empty wallet and missing ring, it would look like the body had been rolled on the Merrie Way overlook, after he'd driven in there himself and had his fatal heart attack. As far as she knew, there was nothing to tie Hixley to her and her girls—no direct link, anyhow. He hadn't told her about the two parking tickets."

"Uh-huh. And he was in bed with all three of them when he croaked?"

"So they said. Right in the middle of a round of fun and games. That was what he paid them for each of the times he went there—seven hundred and fifty bucks for all three, all night."

"Jeez, three women at one time." Eberhardt paused, thinking about it. Then he shook his head. "*How?*" he said.

I shrugged. "Where there's a will, there's a way."

"Kinky sex—I never did understand it. I guess I'm old-fashioned."

"Me too. But Hixley's brand is pretty tame, really, compared to some of the things that go on nowadays."

"Seems like the whole damn world gets a little kinkier every day," Eberhardt said, "A little crazier every day, too. You know what I mean?"

"Yeah," I said, "I know what you mean."

RUTH RENDELL

AN UNWANTED WOMAN

Most of the critical praise (and awards) for Ruth Rendell's work has been directed toward the long list of novels and short stories of psychological suspense that she publishes under her own name and as by "Barbara Vine." However the past few years have seen an upsurge in popularity for her Inspector Wexford novels, due in part to a successful television series, which has been shown in England and on cable channels in America. There are fourteen Wexford novels to date, plus one collection of stories and novelettes, Means of Evil. *Here is the first new Wexford short story since 1979.*

"It's not a matter for the police."

Burden had said it before—to his wife, if not to this woman. The affair of Sophie Grant, bizarre, nearly incomprehensible, was outside the range of his experience. Deeply conservative, convinced of the superiority of past ways to those of the present, he was inclined to blame events on the decadence of the times he lived in. He repeated what he had said and added, "There's nothing we can do."

Jenny's friend, who was not crying yet, who seemed on the verge of crying or even screaming, a desperate woman, said in the voice she could only just control, "Then who am I to turn to? What can I do?"

"I've already suggested the Social Services," said Jenny, "but it's true what Hilary says, all they can do is take her into care, apply for a care order."

"She's not in need of care," Hilary said with bitterness, with venom. "She doesn't need protecting. It's me, I'm the one who's suffering. I ought to be taken into care and looked after." She had her voice and herself under control again. Her wineglass was empty. She took hold of it and, after a small hesitation, held it up. "I'm sorry, Jenny. I *need* it. It's not as if it was the hard stuff."

Jenny refilled the glass with Frascati. Hilary had got through half the bottle. They were sitting in the living room of the Burdens' house in Glenwood Road, Kingsmarkham. It was just after nine on a winter's evening—Christmas not far off, as evinced by the first few cards, greetings from the superpunctual, on the mantelpiece. A wooden engine, gaily painted, a worn rabbit, and a Russian doll, its interlocking pieces separated, lay on the carpet, and these several objects Jenny now began picking up and dropping into a toy chest. Hilary watched her with increasing misery.

"I know I'm a nuisance. I know I'm disturbing you when you'd like a quiet evening on your own. I'm sorry, but you—well, Jenny—you're all I've got. I don't know who else to talk to. Except to Martin and he—sometimes I think he's *glad*. Well, he's not, I shouldn't say that, but when she was there she was so hateful to him, it must be a relief. You see"— she looked away from them —"I'm so *ashamed*. That's why I can't tell other people, because of being ashamed."

Burden thought he would have a drink, if only to make Hilary feel better. He fetched himself a beer from the fridge. When he came back, Jenny had her arm round Hilary and Hilary had tears on her face.

"What is there to be ashamed of?"

"A woman whose child doesn't want to live with her? What sort of a mother can she be? What sort of a home has she got? Of course I'm ashamed. People look at me and they think, what was going on in that house? They must have been abusing her, they must have ill-treated her."

"People don't *know*, Hilary. Hardly anyone actually knows. You're imagining all this."

"I can see it in their eyes."

Buoyed up by his drink, resigned to the ruin of his evening, Burden thought he might as well go the whole hog. Get it firsthand, though he could do nothing. Nothing could come of it but the slight relief to Hilary Stacey of relating it once again.

Jenny said suddenly, "Does her father know?"

"Her father wouldn't care. It's once in a blue moon he writes to her—she hasn't heard from him in months."

"Tell me exactly what happened, would you, Hilary? Jenny's told me, but I'd like you to." Burden was painfully aware of sounding like a policeman. On the other hand, she had *wanted* a policeman. "Tell me from the beginning."

"I thought you were going to say 'in your own words,' Mike."

He inclined his head a little, not smiling.

"Sorry. Being so miserable makes me bitchy. What is this, therapy?"

"It might be that as well," said Burden. He was foraging in his knowledge of the law, thinking of such vague and insubstantial offenses as enticement and corruption of a minor. "Let me have the facts. I'm not saying we can do anything—I'm sure we can't—but just tell me what happened, will you?"

She looked him in the eye. Her own eyes were a startling turquoise blue, large and prominent. It was easy to see why she never wore makeup, she was colorful enough without it—that white and rosy skin, those eyes, flaxen hair straight and shining. A woman with those attributes should have been good-looking, but Hilary missed beauty by the length of her face that gave her a horsey look. She was very thin, thinner since this trouble started.

"It really began long before I married Martin," she said, "perhaps even when Peter and I were divorced five years ago. I didn't *want* a divorce, you know, I wanted to stay married for life. I know it sounds self-pitying, but it wasn't my fault, it really wasn't, I was hard done-by. Peter's girlfriend was pregnant. I still didn't want a divorce, but how long can you keep on fighting? I knew he'd never come back.

"Sophie was nine. She made a big thing about saying she hated Peter. She told people he'd left 'us'—not that he'd left me. She knew about the girlfriend, Monica, and she used to say her father preferred Monica to us. Well, she wouldn't see Peter for months, but gradually she came round. It was the baby, I think. He was her half brother and she liked the idea of a brother. She started to enjoy spending weekends with Peter and Monica and the baby. I will say for Monica that she was very nice to her, and of course it wasn't the usual situation where a child is jealous of a new sibling.

"I honestly think none of this would have happened if Peter and Monica were still here. I'm sure it's much more due to their going to America than to me marrying Martin. Peter had this job and no doubt it was the only course for him to take. He was always more or less indifferent to Sophie, anyway. Monica was much nicer to her than her father was and I don't think it bothered him that he wouldn't see his daughter for years. He could have afforded to pay her airfare to Washington but he wouldn't.

"It was a blow to her. It was a second blow. Okay, I suppose you'll say my remarrying was the third. But what's a woman to do, Mike? I was on my own with Sophie, I had a full-time job, and the school holidays were a nightmare. So I got a part-time job and even that was too much for me. And then when things were about as grim as they'd ever been, I fell in love with Martin and he fell in love with me. I mean, it was like a dream, it was like something that you daren't dream about because it just won't happen, things as good as that don't happen. But it did. A nice, kind, clever, successful, good-looking man was in love with me and wanted to marry me and liked my daughter and thought she could be his daughter, and everything was wonderful.

"And she thought so, too—Sophie thought so. She was happy, she was excited. I think she saw Martin as a wonderful new friend, hers as much as mine. Of course, we were very careful in front of her, she was thirteen and that's a very difficult age. For ages I never let Martin even kiss me in her presence and then when he did he'd always kiss her, too.

"We got married and she was at the wedding and she loved every minute of it. Next day she started to hate him. She loathed him. She did everything to try and split us up—she told lies to us about the other one, she'd seen Martin out with a woman, she'd heard me call a man 'darling' on the phone, she'd heard me telling Jenny I married him for his money. Yes, *truly*. You wouldn't credit it, would you?

"When she saw she couldn't separate us, she did what she's

done, walked out and went to live with Ann Waterton. That's where she is and where she intends to stay, she says.

"I've pleaded with her, I've begged her, I've even tried to bribe her to come back. I've pleaded with Ann Waterton. I've been there, I've even set it all down in writing, in letters to her. To do Ann justice, she hasn't enticed her or anything like that—she's lonely and she likes Sophie's company, but she's told her she ought to come home. Anyway, she says she has. Sophie won't. She's got a key to Ann's house, she comes and goes as she pleases, and she's very good to Ann, she looks after her. She likes cooking, which Ann doesn't, and she cooks special meals for them. She takes Ann her breakfast in bed before she goes to school.

"I've asked Ann to change the locks on the door but she won't, she says Sophie would stay out in the street all night, and I think she's right—Sophie would do that. She'd wrap herself in blankets and sit on the garden wall or sleep in Ann's garage."

Burden said, "Have you asked her what it is she wants?"

"Oh, yes." Hilary gave a short, bitter laugh. "I've asked her. 'Get rid of Martin,' she says, 'and then I'll come home.' "

"What's the bugger done to her?" said Chief Inspector Wexford.

It was the following day and he and Burden were on their way to London. Donaldson was driving and Wexford and Burden sat in the back of the car. Their mission was to interview two men suspected of being concerned in a raid on Barclay's Bank in Kingsmarkham High Street a week before. One lived in Hackney, the other was usually to be found around midday at a pub in Hanwell. Burden had been relating the story of Sophie Grant.

"Nothing," he siad. "I'm sure of it. Oh, I know you can't tell. It's no good saying, I know the guy, I've had a meal in his house, I know he's not like that. The most unexpected men are like that. But I'd say he just didn't have time. He didn't have the time or the opportunity. He and Hilary Grant, as she was, were newly married, sharing a bedroom—that was partly the trouble. Sophie stayed around for three weeks and then she left."

"But you say she seemed to like the chap before he married her mum?"

"I suppose she just didn't know, she didn't realize. She was nearly fourteen, but she didn't realize her mother would be sharing a bed with Martin Stacey. And I expect there was some kissing and cuddling and touching in her presence—well, there was bound to be."

"She thought it was a marriage for companionship, is that what you're saying? Yes, I can imagine. The mother was very careful, no doubt, *before* she was married—no physical contact when the girl was there, definitely no bed sharing, no good night kisses. And then, after the wedding, a kind of explosion of sensuality, mother and stepfather having no need to curb their ardor. Because it would be okay, wouldn't it, they were *married*, it was respectable, nothing to object to. A shock to the girl, wouldn't you say?"

"According to Hilary, it was pretty much like that." Burden began assembling in his mind the facts and details as Hilary Stacey had told them. "Sophie seems to have given him hell. Insulted him, told her mother lies about him, then refused to speak to him at all. That went on for a week, and one evening she just didn't come home from school. Her mother didn't have time to get worried before Sophie phoned her and said she was with Mrs. Waterton and there she intended to stay."

"Why Mrs. Waterton?" Wexford asked.

"That's rather interesting in itself. Sophie is a very bright child, good at her schoolwork, always in the top three. And she does a lot of community service, visiting the elderly and the bereaved, that sort of thing. She does their shopping and sits with them. There's a blind woman she calls on and reads the newspaper to her. As well as this, she does babysitting—she babysits for us—and she used to do a paper round, only her mother stopped that, quite rightly in my view. It's dangerous even in a place like this.

"Ann Waterton's in her sixties. She lost her husband in the spring and apparently it hit her very hard. There were no children. Sophie used to go to her house after school—just to talk, really. They seem to have got on very well."

"A girl of that age," Wexford said, "will often get on a great deal better with an older woman than with her own mother. I take it this Ann Waterton's no slouch—I mean, she's got something to give a lively, intelligent fourteen-year-old?"

"According to Hilary, she's a retired teacher. In his last years, she and her husband were both studying for Open University degrees but she gave that up when he died. At one time she used to write the nature column for the Kingsmarkham *Courier.*"

Wexford looked dubious. The car had joined the queue of vehicles lining up for the toll at the Dartford Tunnel. They were in for a long wait. Burden looked at his watch, a fairly useless exercise.

"One evening about a month after George Waterton died, Sophie called round there. It was about nine, but light still. She was on her bicycle. Hilary Stacey and Ann Waterton live about a mile apart, Hilary in Glendale Road—you know, the next street to me—and Mrs. Waterton in Coulson Gardens. Sophie couldn't make Mrs. Waterton hear, but the back door was unlocked and she went in, thinking she would find her fallen asleep over a book or the television.

"She did find her, in an armchair in the living room, and she appeared to be asleep. There was an empty pill bottle on the table beside her and a tumbler which seemed to have contained brandy. Sophie acted with great presence of mind. She phoned for an ambulance and then she phoned her mother. Of course, Hilary hadn't yet married Martin Stacey, though she was planning to marry him, the wedding being fixed for August.

"Hilary got there first. She and Sophie managed to get Ann Waterton onto her feet and were walking or dragging her up and down when the ambulance came. As we know, they were in time and Ann Waterton recovered."

Wexford said unexpectedly, "Was there a suicide note?"

"I don't know. Hilary didn't say. Apparently not. She and Sophie had been very anxious it shouldn't appear as a suicide attempt but as an accidental taking of an overdose."

"Bit indiscreet telling you then, wasn't it?" said Wexford derisively. "Why did she tell you?"

"I don't know, Reg. It was all part of the background, I suppose. She knew I wouldn't broadcast it around."

"You've told *me*. And Donaldson's not deaf."

"That's all right, sir," said Donaldson, no doubt indicating his willingness to be the soul of discretion.

"I imagine everybody knew about it," said Wexford. "Or guessed. And after that she and this Mrs. Waterton became fast friends, is that it? The house in Coulson Gardens was the natural place for the girl to decamp to." He pondered for a moment or two as the car moved sluggishly toward one of the toll booths. "The mother might be able to get a care order made or a supervision order," he said. "She could try to get her made a Ward of Court."

"She doesn't want to do that, and who can blame her? She wants the girl back living with her. Sophie's out of control, it's true—that is, her mother can't control her to the extent of making her come home—but she hasn't done anything wrong, she's broken no law."

"The danger," said Wexford, "with getting a care order for someone who's out of control might be that it contained a requirement for the subject—that is, Sophie Grant—to reside with a named individual. And suppose that named individual was Ann Waterton?"

The car began to head for London up the motorway.

From the tall, rather forbidding curtain wall of stone blocks rose thirteen towers. The arc lamps flooded them with white light and showed up the cloudly, smoky texture of the sky behind, purplish, very dark, starless. In the great wall, which had lost its roof some six centuries before, which was open to this heavy, rain-threatening sky, a performance of Elizabethan music was under way, drawing to its close just in time, thought Burden, before the heavens opened. He was there, sitting in the second row, because Jenny was singing in the choir.

This was the first time he had been to Myland Castle, a type of fortification (according to the program) innovative in Europe in the twelfth century. It was a huge fortress containing the remains of gateways and garderobes and kitchens and tunnel-vaulted rooms and features called rere-arches. Burden was more interested in the castle than the concert. It was too late in the year, in his opinion, for outdoor performances of anything. The evening was damp and raw rather than really cold but it was cold enough. The audience huddled inside sheepskin and anoraks.

It was a mystery why the organizers had picked on this place. Size alone must account for it, for the acoustics were so bad that the harpsichord was nearly inaudible and the sweet melodious voices were carried up into the sky where no doubt they could be clearly heard some two hundred feet in the air. As a soloist began on the final song, "Though Amaryllis Dance in Green," Burden let his eyes rove along the top of the walls and the catwalk between the towers. From the other side of the curtain wall, where the great buttresses fell steeply away to green slopes and a dry moat, the view across country must be very fine. Perhaps he'd come back in the spring and bring Mark.

The applause was enthusiastic. Relief, they're glad it's all over, thought Burden, the Philistine. That sort of thing was better at home, by the fire, on a compact disc.

Jenny, coming up to him, laying an icy hand on his, said, "You couldn't hear, could you?"

Burden grinned. "We couldn't hear as much as we were meant to." He was astonished and pleased to see it wasn't yet nine. Time had passed slowly. He took his wife's arm and they ran to the car park as the rain began.

The extreme youth of their babysitter, Sophie Grant, had worried him the first time she came. That she would phone her mother in the next street if there was any cause for alarm did a lot to calm his fears. By the time she had sat for them three times, he trusted her as entirely as he would have trusted someone three times her age. She might be fourteen but she looked seventeen. It was absurd, he reflected as he walked into his living room, to think of her in the context of care orders, of being in need of supervision or protection.

She was sitting on the sofa with her books beside her, writing an essay on unlined paper attached to a clipboard. Her handwriting was strong, clearly legible, slightly forward sloping. She looked up and said, "I haven't heard a sound from him. I went up three times and he was fast asleep." She smiled. "With his rabbit. He's inseparable from that rabbit."

"D'you want a drink, Sophie?" Jenny remembered she was a

child. It was easy to forget. "I mean hot chocolate or a cup of tea or something?"

"No, thanks—I'd better get off."

"What do we owe you?"

"Nine pounds, please, Jenny. Three hours at three pounds an hour. I started at six-thirty, I think." Sophie spoke in a crisp and businesslike way, without a hint of diffidence. She took the note and gave Jenny a pound coin.

Burden fetched her coat. It was a navy-blue duffel and in it she immediately shed a few years. She was a schoolgirl again, tall, rather gawky, pale-skinned and dark-haired, the hair long and straight, pushed behind her ears. The shape of her face and the blue eyes were her mother's, but she was prettier. She packed books and clipboard into a rather battered briefcase.

"I'll walk you home," said Burden. It was only round the corner, but these days you never knew. He had forgotten for the moment where home was for her now.

She said, "Coulson Gardens. It's a long walk."

Should he dispute it? Argue? "I'll drive you," he said.

They were uncomfortable together in the car. Or Burden was uncomfortable. The girl seemed tranquil enough. It was cowardice, he thought, that kept him from speaking. Was he afraid of a fourteen-year-old?

"How long are you going to keep this up, Sophie?" he said.

"Keep what up?" She wasn't going to help him.

"This business of living with Mrs. Waterton, of refusing to go home to your mother."

For a moment he thought she was going to tell him to mind his own business. She didn't. "I haven't refused to go home," she said. "I've said I'll go home when he's not there. When she gets rid of him, I'll go home."

"Come on, he's her husband."

"And I'm her daughter. You're going past it, Mike—it's the house with the white gate. She loves him, she doesn't love me. Why should I live with someone who doesn't care for me?"

She jumped out of the car before he could open the door for her. A small slim woman with short gray hair was looking out of a front window, the curtain caught on her shoulder. She smiled, gave a little wave, a flutter of fingers. Burden thought, I can't just leave it, I can't miss this opportunity. "What's Martin Stacey done, Sophie? Why don't you like him? He's a nice enough chap, he's all right."

"He made her deceive me. They pretended things. They both pretended he was going to look after us and earn money for us and like us both—not just her, not just want to be with her. And she pretended I was the most important person in the world to her. It was all false, all lies. I was nothing. He *made* me nothing and she *liked* it." She spoke in a low intense voice that was almost a growl.

There was a pause in which she drew a long breath, then: "Thanks for the lift, Mike. Good night." She ran up the path and the door opened for her. The figure of Mrs. Waterton was fleetingly visible.

On the way home, Burden thought, It's as much that woman's doing as the girl's. Why does she give her a room? Why does she feed her? She ought to go away for a bit, shut up the house. She would if she had any sense of responsibility.

He said something of this to his wife.

"Oh, think, Mike, how Ann Waterton must love it. She was all alone, a widow, no children, probably not many friends. People don't want to know widows, or so they say. And then suddenly along comes a ready-made granddaughter, someone who actually *prefers* her over her own mother and her own home. I'm not saying she deliberately encouraged Sophie, but I bet you she doesn't make any positive moves to send her home. It must have brought her a new lease on life. Did she look happy?"

"I suppose she did," said Burden.

"Well, then. And less than six months ago, she was suicidal."

It was a fortnight before he saw Sophie's mother again. Once more she was spending the evening with Jenny, Martin Stacey being away on a protracted business trip abroad.

"He's glad to get away from me, I expect. It's been nothing but trouble ever since we got married. Of course, he's been angelic but how long can that go on? I'm always miserable, I cry every day, I'm always in a state, he can't put up with that forever. So I've decided what to do. You tell him, Jenny. Tell him what I'm doing."

Jenny said drily, "It's a case of if you can't beat 'em, join 'em. Hilary's idea is that the best thing for her to do is make friends with Ann Waterton."

"I've stopped arguing about it. I've stopped telling her she has to send Sophie home and I've stopped threatening her."

"Threatening her?" said Burden, on the alert.

"I only mean telling her I'd get an injunction to stop her seeing Sophie. I don't suppose I ever would have. But now I've decided to *like* her. The way I see it, I don't have a choice. And if it works—well, oh, it's all in the air as yet, but I thought maybe we could all live together. If Sophie's that crazy about old Ann, the answer might be for us all to be together. Sell our houses and buy a big house for the lot of us."

Burden thought, But surely it's not that Sophie is especially "crazy" about Mrs. Waterton as that she's especially uncrazy about her stepfather. He didn't care to say this aloud. It occurred to him that Hilary Stacey, if not exactly unhinged by all this, was becoming rather strange.

"So what's happening?" said Jenny. "You're inviting her to tea, are you? Taking her out for drives?"

"She can drive herself," Hilary said shortly. "This is deadly serious, Jenny. This is my life, my whole future existence we're talking about. You could say I've lost my only child."

Jenny poured her another glass of wine.

"I reason," said Hilary, "that if my daughter likes someone that much, I could like her, too. After all, we used to be very close, Sophie and I—we used to like the same things, the same people, we had the same taste in clothes, we liked the same food. There's got to be something about old Ann that I can like. And there is, there is. I can see there's a lot more to her than I thought at first. I thought Sophie was flattered—you know, a sort of granny-substitute buttering her up and telling her how pretty and clever and mature she was, all that, but Ann's a very bright woman, she's very well read. It's just a matter of my meeting her more than halfway."

"I wonder what that poor devil of a husband's going to say," was Wexford's comment when Burden retailed all this to him, "having a supererogatory mother-in-law shacking up with him."

"Hardly shacking up," Burden protested. "And it hasn't come to that yet. Personally, I don't think it ever will."

"Does her mother make her an allowance? Give her pocket money?"

"I don't know. I never asked."

"I was thinking of a scene from *The Last Chronicle of Barset,*" said Wexford, who was rereading his Trollope. "The Archdeacon wants to know how to deal with a recalcitrant son. His daughter, who is a rich marchioness, asks him if he allows her brother an income and when he replies yes, she says, 'I should tell him that must depend upon his conduct.' "

"Does it work?" said Burden, interested in spite of himself.

"No," said Wexford rather sadly. "No, it doesn't. I shouldn't expect it to, not with anyone of spirit, would you?"

An inquiry about an attack on a cyclist took Wexford and Sergeant Martin to Myland Castle. It was the fourth in a series of such assaults, each apparently motiveless, for the amount of money the cyclists carried was negligible. Three were men, one a woman. Two of the attacks happened by day, two after dark. The only pattern discernible seemed to be that the attacks increased in severity. The first, on the woman, consisted in not much more than pushing her off her bicycle and damaging the machine to make it temporarily unusable, but the fourth had put the victim into intensive care with broken bones and a ruptured spleen.

All these seemingly pointless acts of violence had taken place in the Myfleet-Myland neighborhood, this last on the cycle path, which led from the Myfleet Road to Myland village and passed on the outer side of the castle moat.

Wexford had already questioned the staff at the castle. The purpose of this return visit was to reexamine one of the guides. Two members of staff, those manning the south gate and the turnstile, claimed to have seen the victim, a frequent cyclist on the path, but only the guide admitted to the possibility of having seen the perpetrator. Just before the castle closed to the public at four, he had been standing in the gathering dusk on the curtain wall between the two south towers.

It was a fine day, a sunny island of a day in a week of fog and rain, and the number of visitors to Myland Castle was nearer a midsummer than a December average. While Martin talked to the woman at the turnstile, Wexford went across the great hall in search of the guide. The two o'clock tour had five more minutes to run. Wexford could see the group of about ten people standing on the battlements, the guide pointing across the meadows toward Myland church where the tombs of the castle builders were.

While he waited, Wexford made his way to the remains of a chapel and hall embedded in the inner court. This had been a town rather than a dwelling house, with gatehouses and barracks, almshouses and courts. From the passage along which he was walking, a flight of stone stairs led up onto the curtain wall and these he took, emerging into the fresh air but also to deep shadow. It was possible to walk round the battlements on this walkway, occasionally passing up and down steps inside the turrets. The wall on the inner side was high enough—it came up to his waist—but rather lower on the outer and crenelated. However, the path was wide, the wall was more than small-child height, and even a venturesome older person would have had to lean over and lose balance in order to fall.

Falling would be an atrocious thing, Wexford thought. The battlements here were like cliffs, but with no merciful sea at their base. Their height was increased by the moat, a fifteen-feet-deep ditch whose northern side at this point continued downward the sheer slope of the castle wall. He walked along slowly, keeping in sight the guide, Peter Ratcliffe, and his group, now standing under the great bulwark of the gatehouse flanking tower.

He wasn't alone on the walkway. He could hear a party with children mounting the staircase behind him and in front, some twenty or thirty feet ahead, saw two women appear from the steps inside the first of the south turrets. It was probably his fancy that when she saw him—and saw also those behind him—the younger of the women whispered something to her companion and they turned back the way they had come. Most likely they had meant to turn back anyway and retrace their steps along the sunny side. An area of deep cold shade lay between them and Wexford.

He walked along and through it more quickly. Beyond the turret, the sun began, and it was warm and benign on his face. The two women were still ahead of him and as he observed them talking together, sometimes pointing across the fields or studying the guidebook the older one carried, he knew who they were. That was putting it rather too strongly, perhaps. He guessed who they might be, he *thought* he knew. The bright fair hair of one of them told him and her rather protuberant eyes, extraordinarily blue and clear just as Burden had described them. As if she sensed his watchfulness, she turned round and those eyes cast their blue beam on him.

The other woman was small and slight, very upright, perhaps sixty-five, with short gray hair. Hilary Stacey and Ann Waterton. He was so sure that he wouldn't have hesitated to address them by their names.

Inside the gatehouse tower, the main exit staircase went down. He saw them enter the arch to the tower and by the time he had reached it they had begun the descent. Ratcliffe's party immediately appeared, heading in their turn for the exit staircase. Wexford pressed himself against the wall to allow their passage, and when the last of them was through Ratcliffe came sauntering up, all smiles and helpfulness.

"Brain-picking time?" he said. "They tell me I'm needed to help you with your inquiries."

It was uttered in a facetious way, quotation marks very evident round the last words.

Wexford said quietly, "Perhaps we can go a few yards along the walkway, Mr. Ratcliffe, to the place from which you saw the attacker."

A neighbor called the police. It was nine o'clock on a Friday. He went out into his front garden and heard a car engine running. The only car nearby was shut up in Ann Waterton's garage. He opened the garage doors and the first thing he saw was the length of hose attached to the exhaust, passing in through the driver's window.

He switched off the engine and pulled Ann Waterton out. Giving the kiss of life, what he, an elderly man, called artificial respiration, had no effect. She was dead. When the police came, they found the house unlocked but empty. On the table in the dining room, in a sealed envelope marked *To the Coroner*, was what they concluded was a suicide note.

"Where was the girl?" Wexford asked when Martin told him about it the next day.

"Gone on a school trip to London," said Burden. "A theater visit, apparently. Shakespeare—something they were studying. They went in a coach, which didn't get back to Kingsmarkham until eleven-thirty."

"And Sophie, finding what had happened, at last went home to her mother?"

"It would seem so . . ."

At the inquest, a verdict was returned on Ann Waterton of suicide while the balance of her mind was disturbed. The suicide note, written in the firm, round, characterless hand of the primary-school teacher, was read aloud. *I cannot go on. Life has become a meaningless farce. I am totally alone now with no prospect of things ever changing. I am unwanted, an unnecessary woman, a useless drag on society. It is better for everyone this way, and much better for myself.*

Ann Waterton.

"Totally alone?" Burden said to Jenny. "She had Sophie, didn't she?"

"Sophie was going home."

"What, you mean Sophie meant to leave her? To go home? She'd given in at last?"

"Hilary said so in evidence at the inquest. The coroner asked her about her daughter living with Ann and she told him how Sophie was returning home. She told me privately, between ourselves, that she and Sophie had been talking it over. They had a talk with Ann there and some talks on their own and the upshot was that Sophie said, all right, she'd come home by Christmas and she made a few conditions, but the crux of it was she'd come home."

"Conditions?" Burden took his little boy on his knee. He was wondering, not for the first time, how he would feel in ten years' time if this child, this apple of his eye, upped and packed his bags and went to live in someone else's house. "What conditions?"

"Oh, they were to turn the attics into a sort of flat for her. It's quite a big house. She was to have her own kitchen and bathroom, live separately. Hilary must have agreed. She'd have agreed to almost anything to get Sophie back."

"And Ann Waterton knew this?" Mark was thrusting a book under his father's nose, demanding to be read to. "Yes, just a minute, I will, I promise I will." He said to his wife, "She knew it and that's what she meant by being 'totally alone,' and being 'an unnecessary woman'?"

"I suppose so. It's rather awful, but it's nobody's fault. You have to think of it that if the girl hadn't gone there in the first place Ann Waterton would be dead, anyway. She'd just have died six months sooner. She was determined to kill herself."

Burden nodded. Mark had opened the book and was pointing rather sternly at the first word of the first line. His father began reading the latest adventure of Postman Pat . . .

"Anthony Trollope," said Wexford, "wrote about fifty books. It's a lot, isn't it? One of them, a not very well known one, is called *Cousin Henry*. I've just finished reading it." He took note of the expression on Burden's face. "I know this bores you. I wouldn't be telling you about it if I didn't think it was important."

"Important?"

"Well, perhaps not important. Interesting. Significant. It gave me something to think about. Trollope wasn't what one would normally think of as a psychologist."

"Too long ago for that, wasn't it?" Burden said vaguely. "I mean, surely psychology wasn't invented till this century."

"I wouldn't say that. Psychology is one of those things that was always with us—before anyone gave it a name, that is. Like, well, linguistics, for instance. And 'invented' isn't quite the word. Discovered."

It was the end of the day. They were at a table in the saloon bar of the Olive and Dove. Earlier, Wexford had made an arrest, that of Peter Ratcliffe, the Myland Castle guide. His attacks on the cyclists he was unable adequately to account for, though he had fully confessed to all of them. The explanation he gave Wexford was a strange one—it almost pointed to a disturbance of the man's mind. His daily presence in the castle, year after year, day after day, had brought him to a curious identification with its former defenders. It impelled him to attack those he saw as intruders. Perhaps it would only have been a matter of time before the paying visitors appeared to him in the same light and he injured one of them.

Wexford didn't know whether he believed this or not. No court would. Burden had stared in incredulous disgust when Wexford repeated Ratcliffe's words. That was why—partly why—he had changed the subject onto *Cousin Henry*.

"Bear with me," he said, "while I give you a brief outline of the plot." Burden didn't exactly demur, not quite. His face was a sigh incarnate.

Wexford said, "I promise you it's relevant." He added, "It even gets exciting."

Burden nodded. He looked reflectively into his beer.

"The old squire dies," Wexford began, "and leaves all his property to his nephew Henry. Or that's how it appears, that's what everyone thinks, and Henry comes into his inheritance. Then he finds a later will which leaves everything to his cousin Isabel. Henry's best bet is to destroy this will, but he doesn't. He daren't. He hides it in a place where he thinks it will never be found—in a book in the library, a book that is so boring no one would ever want to take it down and open it.

"Why doesn't he destroy it? He's afraid. It's an official document, an almost sacred thing—it exercises an awesome power over him, it's almost as if he's afraid of some unnamed retribution. Yet if he destroys it—a simple thing to do, though Henry, in his mind, discovers terrible difficulties in the way of doing this—if he does, all will be secure forever and he the undisputed man in possession. But he can't destroy it, he dare not. Good psychology, don't you think? People behave like that, inexplicably, absurdly, but that's how they behave."

"I suppose so. Thousands would. Have destroyed it, I mean. Most would."

"Not the law-abiding. Not the conventional. Someone like you wouldn't."

"I wouldn't have nicked it in the first place," said Burden. "What's the point of all this? You said there was a point."

"Oh, yes. The Stacey-Grant-Waterton affair, that's the point."

Burden looked up at him, surprised. "No wills involved in that, so far as I know."

"No wills," said Wexford, "but another sort of document—a sacred sort of document. A suicide note."

Wexford was silent for a moment, enjoying the look on Burden's face, a mixture of incredulity and sheer alarm. "Let me give you a scenario," he said. "Let me give you an alternative to what actually happened—a lonely, unhappy woman at last succeeding at taking her own life."

"Why have an alternative to the facts?"

"Just listen to a theory, then. Ann Waterton didn't commit suicide. She had no reason to commit suicide. She was happy, she was happier than she'd been since her husband died. She had found an affectionate, charming granddaughter who wanted more than anything in the world to live with her."

"Wait a minute," said Burden. "Sophie may have been living with her, but she wasn't going to go on doing that. She was going home. She was going back to her mother and her stepfather."

"Was she? Do we have anyone's word for that but Hilary Stacey's?"

"She told the coroner under oath."

"Hmm," said Wexford. "D'you want another drink?"

"I don't think I do. I want to hear the rest of what you've got to say."

"All right. The fact is that we have no evidence that Sophie intended to go home but Hilary Stacey's word."

"Sophie herself. Sophie could presumably confirm it?"

Wexford smiled rather enigmatically. "Hilary Stacey's her mother. She may have been at odds with her but I don't think she'd shop her own mother."

"Shop her?"

"Hilary Stacey murdered Ann Waterton, Mike"

"You mean that's your theory, that's your alternative."

"I saw them at Myland Castle about ten days ago. I recognized them from your description. If I hadn't been there, if so many visitors hadn't been there, an exceptional number for December but it was an exceptionally nice day, I think Hilary—oh, yes, it's hindsight—was going to push Ann off that wall. It would have been, would have looked, like an accident. It was made impossible by the circumstances.

"Three days afterward, Sophie went on a school trip to a London theater. Hilary was often at the house in Coulson Gardens—it would have been nothing out of the way for her to drop in during the evening. The next step was to give Ann a sleeping pill. She would have made them both a drink and given her the pill in that. Ann was a small, slight woman—it looked to me as if she weighed about seven stone. Hilary Stacey, on the other hand, is tall and strong and no more than—what? Thirty-seven? Thirty-eight? She carried Ann out to the garage, by way of the communicating door from the house, sat her in the driver's seat, and fixed up that business with the hose pipe and the exhaust.

"No doubt she supposed Sophie would find the body. An unpleasant thought. Would a mother do that to her child? Perhaps not. Perhaps Hilary intended to come back later and find the body herself. In the event, the next-door neighbor found Ann Waterton."

Burden said, "It doesn't work, Reg. You're forgetting the suicide note. Ann left a note for the coroner."

"I'm not forgetting it. The suicide note is at the heart of all this. We have to go back to last May or June, whenever it was. Ann Waterton attempted to kill herself, but the attempt was frustrated by Sophie Grant and her mother. There was no suicide note—or was there? Has anyone heard of the existence of a suicide note? On the other hand, has the existence of such a note been denied? Let us postulate that there was such a note. On the mantelpiece or in a pocket of Ann's dress or by her bed. Remember that suicides, especially 'home' suicides, almost always leave a note."

"Yes, but we've discussed this. That first time, Hilary and

Sophie wanted to keep it dark that there had been a suicide attempt. For Mrs. Waterton's sake."

"What are you saying, Inspector Burden? And you a policeman! Are you saying they *destroyed a suicide note* for no more reason than to protect the reputation of a woman who was then a mere acquaintance? No, of course you aren't and of course they didn't. Isn't it quite reprehensible enough to remove and conceal such a note? It's quite possible indeed that Sophie knew nothing about it but that Hilary, spotting what it was, picked it up and took it away with her."

"But didn't destroy it?"

"No, no. Remember Cousin Henry. She took it. She had no prevision of any future need for it. Ann at that time had done her no harm and there was no hint that she would. She took it, as I say, and read it, as Cousin Henry read his uncle's will, and decided to tell no one about it. Ann had been found in time, Ann would survive. And, by the way, I'd suggest at that time the note was in its envelope but *unsealed*. Hilary later did the sealing.

"She preserved it. Not for any nefarious purpose then, but simply because it had become an official document, a document of great weight and significance, fraught almost with magic. Perhaps she thought she'd give it back to Ann one day. Ann would be happy again and they would—dare she expect it?—laugh about it together. But I think the real reason for preserving it was Cousin Henry's. She was *afraid* to destroy it. And why do so, anyway? Easier than destroying it was to slip it inside a book in the way Cousin Henry concealed the will, a book no one in the household was ever likely to want to read or even take down and look at.

"In Cousin Henry's case, it was Jeremy Taylor's sermons. What book Hilary Stacey used we'll never know and it doesn't matter. Perhaps, anyway, she kept it in a drawer with her underclothes.

"But possession of the suicide note gave her the idea for Ann Waterton's murder. After she had put Ann into the car, she had only to place the note on the table and, making sure she had left no fingerprints, return home and leave the body to be discovered."

Burden, who had listened to the last part of this in silence and with his head bowed, now looked up. He shook his head a little, but rather as if in wonder at human depravity than from any particular doubt at what Wexford had told him. It might be true. Hilary Stacey had been angry enough, desperate enough. He realized he had never really liked her.

"You'll never prove it," he said, and as he spoke he was confident Wexford would agree with him. Wexford would give him a rueful smile, accept the inevitable.

His chief often, still, surprised him.

"I shall have a damn good try," said Wexford.

Staying out drinking wasn't Burden's way. It never had been. He was an uxorious man, a home-loving man. Anyway, he liked to be with his little boy before Mark went to bed, liked if possible to put him to bed himself. If the licensing hours hadn't changed from a cast-iron regularity to depend upon the whim of the landlord, he wouldn't have been able to have a beer with Wexford at ten to five. As it was, he was still early, though the evening was as dark as midnight. He walked home, thinking about Hilary Stacey. It seemed to him unfortunate she had been Jenny's friend. How much, he wondered, did Jenny care for her? And should he tell Jenny something of all this?

It might be best to wait a while, see what unfolded, see how Wexford progressed. There would be a point at which he would know the time had come to divulge horrors, undreamt-of intrigue.

He found Jenny in an armchair by the fire, the child on her knee. Mark was in pajamas and a blue dressing gown of classic cut, piped in navy and tied with a silk cord. Jenny was reading to him, Beatrix Potter this time, the one about the kitten who traps a mouse in her pocket handkerchief, but the mouse escapes through a hole. Mark was mad about literature, he would soon be able to read himself. Rather gloomily, Burden saw a future with a son always talking about books.

Mark got down from Jenny's lap and came over to his father. Another adventure of some thwarted predator or enterprising rodent was demanded. While Burden was looking through the collection on the bookshelf, the doorbell rang.

After dark, he answered the door himself to unexpected visitors. You never could tell. He went out into the hall, Jenny behind him with the boy, holding his hand because he was nearly too heavy to carry.

Burden opened the door and the girl came in. She stepped in quickly and stood for a moment in the hall, a suitcase in each hand.

"I've come," Sophie said, smiling. "I'll cook for you, I'll look after Mark, I won't be any trouble. Don't bother to come with me, Mike, I'll just take these straight up to the spare room."

JULIAN SYMONS

THE CONJURING TRICK

Julian Symons, last year's winner of the Crime Writers Association's Diamond Dagger award for lifetime achievement, returns to these pages with a clever tale that more than lives up to its title.

A love affair may be like a conjuring trick. It is not always what it seems to be.

From the beginning, Robert Banister opposed the move to Marlborough Court from the house in Quinton Close. There was much more space in the house, he said, a garden at the back in which to sit out on sunny evenings, friendly neighbors. It was a community. To this Barbara responded that there was no comparison between the house and the apartment. If you lived in Quinton Close you stamped yourself as suburban and second-rate. Marlborough Court was in the city center, an address that would impress people, a place where Robert could invite one of the Multiplex directors to dinner without the humiliation of having to explain where they lived and how to get there.

She added a clincher: "We might get on better." It was true that they snapped at each other, were annoyed by trivialities, seemed to have little in common. They had been married four years, and after the first had occupied separate beds.

So they moved to Marlborough Court, an E-shaped block of luxury flats, with a restaurant, an indoor swimming pool, and, of course, a porter and caretaker. Three apartments were vacant, but Barbara particularly liked one on the sixth floor that faced inwards. It had a balcony with a delicate, though rather flimsy wrought-iron railing. It was protected from the wind, and so would be just as good as Quinton Close for sitting out on sunny evenings. There was a living room with a sliding door opening onto the balcony, their bedroom, a kitchen with a breakfast bar, and a bathroom in which all the fitments were gold-plated. And that was all. The space was less than half of that in Quinton Close and it cost twice as much. When Robert pointed this out, Barbara replied that he was unable to recognize anything first-class when he saw it. Within a week they were bickering as much as ever.

"It's like living in a rabbit hutch."

"With less than half the work for me, do you ever think of that?"

"I was stuck for twenty minutes in traffic this morning, getting to the office. From the house there were never any traffic jams."

"But if we wanted to go to the cinema, what then? I remember driving round and round to find a parking space. Now we can walk."

Such squabbling can be affectionate, but theirs had an unpleasant edge to it, as if each was trying to put the other down. In fact, they rarely went to the cinema, and didn't watch much television. In the evening, Robert listened to classical music—Brahms, Beethoven, and Mahler, in particular. Barbara was a member of a bridge club and spent two or three evenings a week there. Sometimes Robert brought work home with him. He was an accountant at Multiplex, a firm with subsidiaries that sold everything from biscuits to bicycles. He had hoped at one time to become *the* accountant, but he was in his midthirities and further promotion seemed unlikely. Barbara was a few years younger and worked as a dental hygienist. Without her income, they could not have afforded to buy the lease of the Marlborough Court apartment. There were no children, because Barbara had said decisively that they could not afford them.

Robert didn't argue about it. Sometimes now he wondered why they had got married, although there had seemed nothing strange about it at the time. He had recently moved from a smaller firm to Multiplex at a considerable increase in salary, and he was tired of living alone and doing his own cooking. He had had a half-hearted affair with a secretary at the smaller firm and was relieved rather than upset when she told him she was going to marry one of the salesmen. Shortly afterward, he had met Barbara on a visit to the dentist, where she had cleaned his teeth and said he looked after them beautifully.

As she bent over him, masked face within inches of his own, body slightly pressed against his as her powerful hands scraped at tartar, vaguely erotic feelings stirred in him. Her features, the hygienic mask removed, were strong and regular, thick brows almost met across her forehead, her chin was strong where his was indeterminate. She wasn't beautiful, but might have been called handsome. Everything about her was powerful in a way that impressed him, especially those strong managing hands. He pretended to an interest in bridge, she feigned a liking for concerts, and within a few weeks they were married.

Robert's parents had died when he was young and he was an only child—Barbara had been abandoned by hers and brought up by foster parents appointed by the local council. They had a brief honeymoon in the south of France, bought the house in Quinton Close, and settled to a kind of domesticity. But Barbara didn't much like cooking and Robert was not good at talking to the neighbors who came occasionally to dinner, and such occasions almost ceased after the first year. Barbara kept the house scrupulously clean and painfully tidy, Robert bought and planted annuals in the tiny garden. But that, too, was over now they were in Marlborough Court.

Robert couldn't have said what he expected from marriage, and so was not disappointed. When he looked in the glass he saw a tall, gangling man with regular features slightly flawed by the indeterminate chin, a trim figure in no need of dieting, small well-kept hands. He had never taken too much to drink, never looked at another woman after his marriage. If he had been asked whether he was happy, he would hardly have known how to answer, for he never asked himself such questions, any more than he took any interest in which political party governed the country, although he felt it a duty to vote at elections. Nor did it occur to him to wonder whether Barbara was happy, or to concern himself that at night they stayed in their separate beds. He was aware that they didn't get on as well as they had in the first year, but then perhaps that was the way with all married couples. He realized she had some desire for a different, more luxurious or wealthier life and so didn't seriously resist the move from house to apartment, although he didn't like it.

Two weeks after they moved to Marlborough Court, he saw Lucille.

It was early evening. He was alone in the apartment because this was one of Barbara's bridge-club days, and he had taken a chair onto the balcony and was sipping the first of the two whiskey and sodas he allowed himself after work while reading the evening paper. He glanced up from it, and saw a girl standing in the opposite window, naked from the waist up.

She had long, fair, almost golden hair, small beautiful breasts, and a look of childish innocence as she stared intently at something down in the street far below. As he watched, she stretched her arms upwards slowly, stroked one shoulder reflectively with the other hand, momentarily caressed a breast, smiled. Then she saw him and, still with the smile lingering on her lips, stepped back and out of sight.

His first reaction was to retreat from the balcony and close the sliding window. He felt ashamed of intruding on the girl's privacy, was aware of having relished the sight of that stretched arm moving lovingly over the shoulder and the hand lingering on the breast. He was also aware of feeling emotions Barbara had never aroused. She had impressed him by the self-confidence that he knew he lacked, but this girl looked frail, vulnerable, yet in movement and manner sensual.

He couldn't have said just when he began to try to work out what apartment she occupied and who she might be. His apartment, Number 65, was on a prong of an inner side of the E, he had looked sideways to the right when seeing her, so the girl's apartment, or that of her parents, must be next door. He opened the door, looked across the thick dark-blue Wilton landing carpet, and saw 64 in gold numbers. She must be behind that door.

When Barbara returned, he asked if she knew the name of their neighbors and she said she had no idea, adding surprise that he was interested.

He was disturbed to find that the vision of the girl remained with him, distracting him from some dull but complicated calculations about the financial position of a small company Multiplex thought of acquiring. He found himself looking out for her in the lift, and asked the porter the name of the occupants of Number 64, saying he thought he had recognized one of them as an acquaintance.

"That'd be Mr. Delaporte. Can't be him, though—he's away on business."

Robert mumbled that he must have been mistaken, the name was not Delaporte. The porter, young and curly-haired, looked at him a little oddly, and he realized he could have seen the name on the entry phone outside the entrance.

He saw her again a little less than a week later. He was coming back from the office and saw her at the entrance, carrying a bag containing several parcels. She put it down to open the entrance door and two small parcels spilled onto the pavement. He picked them up. She thanked him, speaking in slightly accented English. They got into the lift together, and at the sixth floor he realized he still had hold of the parcels. At her door she hesitated, then said, "Please come in."

They were in a large hall and passage, with several doors leading off it, then in a sitting room much larger than the Banisters', with several pictures on the walls. He had the parcels in his arms.

"Put them—oh, we will put them in Pierre's study, he is away."

She led the way to a room as big as their bedroom, with a desk, easy chairs, more pictures. Robert had known theirs was one of the smaller apartments, but as he looked at the striped sofa in the sitting room, the elaborate flower arrangement, the pieces of china displayed in alcoves—Dresden or Meissen, perhaps, but obviously valuable—he realized fully that life in Marlborough Court was something to which he and Barbara should not have aspired. He should have said so, have said it firmly.

But now the girl was telling him to sit down, offering a cigarette, asking if he would like a drink. He said something about being her neighbor.

"I know. You saw me the other day." He was overwhelmed with confusion, said he was sorry. "Why should you be? I am stupid, I think here I am high up, nobody can see, but of course it isn't so. Anyway, what does it matter? My name is Lucille Delaporte. Chin chin." She had poured him a whiskey and soda, now raised her glass, and they drank together. He asked, half question and half statement, if her father was away. She laughed.

"Pierre is away, yes, but he is not my father, he is my husband."

That made him more confused. He didn't know what to say, although looking at her now more closely, hair piled on top of her head instead of hanging loose, he realized she was not a girl but a young woman, although an impression of childishness and physical frailty remained. He remembered the sight of those girlish breasts, felt embarrassed, looked away, and saw in a corner of the room a brass-legged table with chessmen laid out on top. She followed his gaze.

"You like to play chess? I play with Pierre, but he beats me, he is so good." They went over to look at it. He picked up two of the chessmen, and saw that they were real ivory and ebony.

"You will like to have a game sometime? But I tell you, I am not good. Perhaps you play Pierre when he comes back. He travels a lot. He is in France now or perhaps in Germany—he deals in art and also in jewelry. He has a gallery here—the Deux Arts, do you know it?" He had seen the gallery, which was in the city's most fashionable street. "He travels to buy and sell things. He has a gallery also in Cologne, he says that is the great European center for art. We have an apartment there in Cologne, but I like it here, except when he is away it is a little boring. I sometimes travel with him, but"—she shrugged—"he is always so busy, and I have nothing to do."

He finished his drink and said he must go. She came to the door and said now he knew who she was and where she lived, they were neighbors, perhaps one day they could have a game of chess.

He didn't mention the meeting to Barbara. To do so, he told himself, would have meant talking about the evident wealth of the Delaportes and saying how foolish they were to have come to Marlborough Court. That was no good, they were stuck with it now and could afford it—just. But he found himself looking at Barbara's scowling handsomeness, comparing it with Lucille's delicacy and fragility, and remembering that glimpse of her half naked. He longed to see her again but was too shy to telephone, or knock on the door of Number 64. One day he went into the Deux Arts Gallery, and was astonished by the prices asked for pictures, which seemed to him mostly splodges of paint laid on very thick in vivid colors. The supercilious young man who gave him the price list said they were a new school of Latin American painters coming into fashion. The gallery also had a collection of modern jewelry, French and Italian, and again the prices seemed to him immense.

Ten days elapsed. He had been working late at the office. When he got home Barbara said, "The people next door telephoned and asked us for dinner tomorrow. She said she'd met you. You never told me." She barely listened to his explanation and seemed more interested in the fact that both the Delaportes had undergone teeth scraping at her hands.

Pierre Delaporte was a surprise to Robert. He was very small, a little smiling man who wore gold-rimmed spectacles hanging on a chain. He lifted these spectacles to look at things and people, perched them on his nose, then dropped them again so that they hung on his chest. The surprise was his age. Although lively in his movements, he was obviously between fifty and sixty years old, while Lucille could be no more than twenty-five.

They drank champagne and Pierre talked about his latest trip, which had taken him to five European countries. "I bought only three paintings. That was in Copenhagen, a young Danish artist, he is going to be important. Lucille tells me you play chess. She says also you are very kind, you carry her parcels. We have a game one day, what do you say?" Robert said he'd like that, and agreed to come in for a game at the weekend. "My Lucille, she is beautiful but she does not have a chess brain." He pulled Lucille to him and held her close while kissing her lips, cheek, neck.

Barbara watched, cold-eyed. When they were back home she said, "What a disgusting little man, slobbering over his wife." Robert said he was exuberant. "Is that what you call it?"

He asked what she thought of the apartment, and she replied

that it was very fancy. "They have lots of money," he said. "He has another flat in Cologne."

"She told you that, did she?" Her dark intense gaze was bent on him. "I could see the way she looked at you."

Had she looked at him in a particular way? The idea had not occurred to him, and he found it attractive.

When he went round to play chess, Lucille watched them for a little, then sat on a sofa with her legs curled under her, reading a book, went onto the balcony, poured drinks for them, returned to the sofa. He was disturbed by her presence when for a moment she stood near to him, and distracted by it even when she was on the sofa.

Delaporte made his moves quickly, not always with much thought. After an hour, he threw up his hands in surrender, let the little gold glasses drop to his chest. "You are too good, my friend—tonight, at least. You give me my revenge another time. But it will have to wait—we fly to New York next Wednesday."

He said inanely to Lucille that she was going, too, and she screwed up her face. "Pierre says I must, he wants me. I do not like the city, it is so noisy, so busy."

"I give a little party there, my wife must be my hostess, that is her place, her job," Pierre said, laughing. Still laughing, he put out finger and thumb and pulled at the lobe of her ear—as, Robert remembered, Napoleon had tweaked the ears of his favorite soldiers. Her reaction was not that of Napoleon's young men. She cried out that he was hurting her and ran out of the room. Pierre shook his head. "Women, they like to live well, wear nice clothes, spend money. Sometimes they must be reminded they have duties."

They had drinks, ate bits of things in pastry cases. Lucille was lively, even flirtatious. Pierre laughed and joked, yet there seemed to Robert something odd in their relationship, a passion that remained unexpressed.

He tried to explain what he felt to Barbara, who said he was imagining things. He also mentioned the prices of the pictures and jewelry at the Deux Arts, and that was perhaps what prompted her to remember the star cuff links. They were gold links with tiny rubies and diamonds inlaid in the shape of a star, the only heirloom that had come to him from his father. He thought them rather showy and wore them only on occasions like the twice-yearly office dinner dance. She suggested he should ask Pierre how much they were worth, and was irritated when he said he would never sell them.

"Suppose they're worth a lot of money, two or three times as much as you expect?" she said. "Anyway, I'm not saying we should sell them, only find out how much they're worth." He shook his head. "You're so feeble. Don't you see it might be a way of getting to know them better, they're the kind of people who might be helpful."

"How?"

"How do I know? It was to meet people like them that we came here, wasn't it?"

"I thought we came here because we might get on better. That doesn't seem to be happening."

She stared at him, then said she was sorry.

That night, for the first time in weeks, she came to his bed.

When he learned from the curly-haired porter that the Delaportes had returned from their trip, he telephoned. Lucille answered and said Pierre had gone away again for a couple of days, but, yes, she would love to come in for a drink.

She came, exclaimed at the prettiness of this and the cleverness of that in their living room, went out to the balcony and said the view was nicer than that from their apartment that looked the other way (a quick glance at Robert when she said that, a reminder of what he had seen). New York was always exciting and Pierre had done some business, but really she did not like it. She spoke mostly to Robert, as if she knew he would be a sympathetic listener, and Barbara said little, sitting with her heavy brows drawn together in a frown. He was surprised when she produced a little red morocco box containing the cuff links and opened it.

Lucille exclaimed with pleasure and said she had seen nothing like them. He found himself tongue-tied, and it was Barbara who asked if Pierre would say what he thought they might be worth.

"Of course, he will be pleased. You would like him to make an offer for them?"

Robert broke in before Barbara could speak, to say no, all they wanted was that he should value them, so that they would know their worth for insurance purposes.

When Lucille had gone, he asked why Barbara hadn't spoken to him before showing the links. She glared at him and said she knew if it had been left to him he would have done nothing about it. They nagged at each other for half an hour.

In bed that night he compared Barbara with Lucille and wondered why he had married her. At breakfast next morning they hardly spoke. It was a relief to get to the office and bury himself in work.

The call came in the afternoon. When he lifted the telephone and heard Lucille's voice, he could hardly believe it. Nor had he heard her like this, obviously distressed, the words jumbled together, foreign accent pronounced, as she said she must see him. What about? She could not say on the telephone, but she must see him.

He rang the bell and she opened the door, her face anguished, took him into the big room with its china, ornaments, and pictures, and held out to him with a dramatic gesture the morocco box. He opened it and saw one cuff link. He stared at her.

"What happened?"

"I do not know." Her hands were clasped tightly together. "I take them out, look at them, they are so pretty—not pretty, beautiful. I put them on the dressing table. Then I am trying on clothes, I put on a shirt with holes so you can use buttons or links, I put your links in them to try. They are charming. I come in here, do this, do that, then I see one is not there anymore. I am so sorry, so very sorry." She began to cry.

It is not easy to cry without looking ugly, but she seemed to him just as beautiful crying as smiling. She also looked, as when he had first seen her, no more than sixteen years old. He put an arm round her, no more than that, and told her not to worry, it must be somewhere, they would look together and find it.

They searched the apartment, searched it thoroughly. They didn't find the cuff link.

When they were in the bedroom, both kneeling, looking under the bed, she began to giggle. It *was* funny, he saw that, two adults crawling over a bedroom floor looking for a cuff link. He began to laugh, too. Naturally—as it seemed, inevitably—she came into his arms, her face smudged with tears.

It was the first time he had been unfaithful to Barbara—which was the word he used to himself when he was back in their own little apartment and waiting for her to return. He felt ashamed. The most shameful thing was that he wanted to do it again, that when Lucille said she could see him tomorrow he had said yes. And that seemed possible, for next day was Wednesday, one of Barbara's bridge days.

The telephone call to him at the office on the following morning was hardly more than a whisper down the line, a whisper in which she said again she must see him.

"You've found it?"

She seemed not to hear the question, but asked him to meet her at lunchtime at the entrance to the Royal Arcade, which contained several of the city's most expensive shops. When he got there, she stood waiting. He asked again if she had found the cuff link. She shook her head, her expression that of a mischievous child.

"Then what are we doing here?"

She answered with another question. "You have what they call a boiled shirt?"

"A dress shirt, yes, but why do you ask?"

She took his hand, led him into the Arcade, entered a shop that had in the window only a rope of pearls, a diamond pendant, and an emerald necklace, all unpriced. Inside, a man in frock coat and wing collar bowed, smiled, laid reverentially on a bed of black velvet three dress studs. In each of them a diamond glittered.

"What do you think? You like?"

He said they were beautiful, and before he could go on to the reasons why he could not accept them she had nodded to the frock coat, he was putting them into a little red box that looked identical to the one that held his cuff links, she was saying they could be charged to Mrs. Delaporte, and they were out of the shop.

"I have been careless, I lose something, I could not find cuff links so I give a little present. There is no more to be said." That was her reply to his stumbling objections, and when he tried to pursue them she said, "Please, you must take them. If you don't, I shall not forgive myself."

What happened after that again seemed inevitable. The curly-haired porter saw them as they walked through the entrance hall together and got into the lift. When it stopped at the sixth floor, Robert went without question into that grand apartment and there made love. He got back to the office very late, and it seemed to him that his secretary looked at him strangely. He found it impossible to concentrate on work, told her he had a bad headache, and left early.

He put the diamond studs into a drawer that he kept locked, and when Barbara came home she found him lying on the bed, staring at the ceiling. He told her he felt ill, and in a way that was true. The images of their lovemaking rose up before him and were played over and over in his mind, a tape endlessly repeated. He was repelled by what he had done, yet longed to see Lucille again.

For three days, he heard nothing from her. Returning home on another evening before Barbara, he stood out on the balcony for several minutes, as if by doing so he could rewind the tape back to the beginning, the vision of the golden-haired girl looking down into the street. But the French windows of the Delaporte apartment remained closed. Each morning and evening, going to and from the office, he looked at the blue door with its gold number, unsuccessfully willing it to open.

After those three days, he could bear it no longer and rang her from the office. There was a moment of silence when she heard him, then she said brightly, "Hallo, how are you? Did you want to speak to Pierre? He is here." Then Delaporte was on the line saying something about his revenge at chess, and also that Lucille had complained of boredom, they were having a small party in a week's time and hoped he and Barbara would come. Robert said they would be delighted and put down the telephone with a feeling of overwhelming relief. Why had it not occurred to him that Pierre might have come home?

Who would be at the party? Should they after all go to it? Robert had a sudden feeling of revulsion, mixed with an unidentifiable fear. He had no particular wish to see Pierre again or to meet Pierre's friends. His only interest was in Lucille. And the fear, what did that come from? Perhaps from worry that the Delaportes' friends would be immensely sophisticated and talk about things in a way that left him looking and sounding foolish. Barbara became angry when he said something of this. Her eyes sparkled with a blend of indignation and contempt. She repeated those remarks about meeting people who might be helpful and said she didn't want to work for a dentist all her life.

So they went, and Robert soon saw that he need not have worried about being overawed. The other guests were a curious mixture, including the supercilious young man from the Deux Arts and a couple of other faces he recognized as residents of Marlborough Court. But there was also a girl with yellow-and-green hair that stood up in spikes and another who wore a halter and shorts that showed her navel, a Chinese wearing what looked like battle fatigues, a red-haired, loud-voiced American and his equally noisy wife, and a couple of swarthy little men who talked mostly to each other. Waiters from the restaurant brought around things on toast and smoked salmon done up in rolls. Robert spoke to one of the little men, who said his name was Arminias and asked if Robert did business with Pierre. He laughed when he heard that Robert lived in the next apartment, and laughed again as he said he was a business associate.

"You deal in pictures?"

Arminias laughed again. "I am a picture framer, I choose the frame, prepare the picture. I am an important man. My friend Julio, he is important, too." He indicated the other little man.

At that moment, Pierre came over, took Arminias away, and spoke earnestly to him, perhaps rebuking him for levity. Soon afterward, Arminias spoke to Julio and they both left. Barbara was talking to the girl with spike hair. And Lucille? She had greeted him with a smile and a handshake when they arrived, but since then had not spoken to him, hardly looked at him. Yet what did he expect?

Delaporte asked if he was enjoying himself, clapped him on

the shoulder before he could reply, and said they would play chess next week. Robert joined a couple on the balcony he recognized as local residents and learned that the man was the managing director of a building firm, and had recently bought a picture from Pierre. What did Robert do? The managing director's interest diminished when he learned that Robert was no more than an accountant at Multiplex. He half turned his back and began to talk to somebody else. Would that be turning a cold shoulder, Robert wondered as he reentered the room. Most of the guests had left—it was time they, too, were gone. He tried to catch Barbara's eye, but failed. The girl with the spikes had her full attention.

Now the red-haired American and his wife were going, and Pierre left the room with them, the three deep in conversation, and Lucille came over smiling, two wineglasses in her hand. She gave him one, raised hers, and said, "Chin chin."

He drank, and had time to remark that the drink was not his usual whiskey before she took him by the hand. Then they were in the bedroom, still holding the glasses. She drained hers, gestured to him to do the same, and he did so. She took the glass from him, put it on a table, then was in his arms, shrugging off her dress, pulling at his clothes, urging him toward the bed. He tried to protest, to say this was madness, but she was murmuring something about Pierre being out for a while and they had time, and he gave way to her, gave way completely, pulling her down on the bed with an urgency equal to her own.

Now things were spinning and wheeling, he wasn't sure of place or time but was aware of himself as a different, more powerful person, so that when he felt a hand on his shoulder, rolled over and away from Lucille and saw Pierre's face purplish with anger and, as it seemed, enlarged, he was not alarmed but inclined to laugh. He was conscious of Pierre hitting him, and although the blows for some reason did not hurt he knew they should be resisted, and his strength was as the strength of ten as he got hold of Pierre and shook him to try to bring the little man to his senses.

After that, everything became out of proportion—the size of the room expanded so that the door seemed immensely distant, then as he crawled toward it along the carpet (he was on all fours, he couldn't bother to work out why) wall and door suddenly bulked up before him.

He hit his head on the wall and said, "Knock knock," hoping others would enjoy the joke. All the while there was sound, cries that seemed to come from a distance, Lucille's face alarmed and Barbara's frowning, unintelligible words coming from her. Then there was a need for air, the window and balcony a long way away, a day's crawl perhaps, but supposing you didn't run but leapt like a kangaroo, how long then?

Out of the door, along an endless passage, somebody was calling out his name and then there was a thud, a kangaroo kick at the back of his head. Unfair, he thought. It was the last thing he remembered from that scene . . .

What followed was a long nightmare, from which he constantly expected to wake and find himself in his office at Multiplex, papers round him, calculator on the desk, telephones to hand, secretary within call. But that vision was of a past reality. In the nightmare there were endless interrogations by polite, wooden-faced policemen. Then came conversations with an equally wooden-faced and equally polite solicitor who was acting for him and kept saying they must get his story straight, even though he repeatedly said he had no story.

There was a cell and then the prison hospital—there were all sorts of tests that involved metal bands put round his head and rubber ones round his arms. There was a series of talks with a pleasant, smiling psychiatrist who seemed to think there was no such thing as sanity, everybody was aberrant in one way or another. "What has all this to do with me?" he asked. "I'm simply an ordinary businessman who went to a party, was given an odd drink, and have no recollection of what happened afterward." He corrected himself. "I remember Pierre hitting me, and I shook him because he was so angry—I was trying to make him calm down."

"You shook him? You don't remember a fight or a struggle? In the bedroom? Or later in the living room?"

"I only shook him. That was in the bedroom."

The psychiatrist smiled, and made notes.

Everything was explained by his solicitor, and by Barbara, who came twice to see him and said she was doing her best.

But what they said made no sense, he didn't remember the things he was supposed to have done. He listened with wonder as he sat in the dock while the prosecuting counsel, a man as urbanely pleasant as the psychiatrist, unfolded what he said was the story of a commonplace adulterous love affair that was not connected with the police investigation of Pierre Delaporte.

"You will hear police evidence that Delaporte had a perfectly genuine business as a fine art dealer, which he used as cover for smuggling drugs into and out of this country, and that this fine art business was not only a cover but positively a means of smuggling the drugs, which were hidden in hollowed-out cavities in the specially made picture frames. The police were aware of Delaporte's activities, but delayed making arrests at the request of their European colleagues. I understand many of these arrests have now been made.

"It was necessary that you should know this background because it explains the presence of drugs at the party where Delaporte died, but I must now tell you that his drug-running activities had no connection with his death. It is the prosecution case that this is a simple matter of infatuation between an impressionable man and a beautiful young woman whose husband was away a good deal of the time. The infatuation was, as you will hear, on both sides. It was a short, stormy love affair that had a fatal ending."

That fatal ending was described by the police witnesses who had found Pierre Delaporte's body on the ground eighty feet below the balcony from which he had fallen or been pushed. The flimsy balcony rail was badly twisted, presumably by the pressure of a body. Delaporte had been dead when the ambulance arrived, and beside him was a diamond-and-ruby cuff link, which had presumably fallen from the dead man's hand.

Among the parade of witnesses that followed were faces barely remembered by Robert, faces that seemed to belong to another life. Here was the girl with yellow-and-green hair to say Pierre Delaporte had been her supplier for drugs, and that some people had taken them at the party. And there was one of the waiters who had seen Lucille and Robert go into the bedroom. When Mr. Delaporte returned, he had looked for his wife, entered the bedroom, there had been shouts and screams. The waiter had gone in.

"What did you see?"

"First Mr. Delaporte was punching Mr. Banister. Then I don't know what you'd say—Mr. Banister seemed to go crazy, he got hold of Mr. Delaporte by the throat like he was trying to strangle him. I tried to pull him off and couldn't, so I hit him on the head with some big brass ornament I picked up and he just kind of collapsed on the floor. Mr. Delaporte, he was gasping for breath and then feeling his neck. He said something about settling this here and now and she said—"

" 'She' being Mrs. Delaporte?"

"Right. Mrs. Delaporte, she said if they were going to quarrel there was no need for everybody to know about it, and Delaporte went into the living room—he was still feeling his throat and his face was a funny color—and said the party was over. There were only three or four guests still there, and they left straight away. So then Johnny, the other waiter, and me, we started to clear up, but he said we should leave it and get out. So we did."

"When you left, only Mr. and Mrs. Delaporte and Mr. and Mrs. Banister remained?"

"Right. Mr. Delaporte was still feeling his neck and wiping his face. The two ladies, they were standing in the middle of the living room."

"And Mr. Banister? Was he still in the bedroom?"

"No—just as I left, he came into the living room. Didn't do or say anything, just stood."

"What was your impression of him?"

"I'd say he was stoned out of his mind."

That was the waiter, Frank. Then there was the curly-haired porter, to tell them that Mr. Banister had asked who lived in Number 64 and that he had come in with Mrs. Delaporte, laughing and joking. There was the frock-coated wing-collared salesman to speak of the purchase of the diamond dress studs, which proved to have been extremely expensive.

And then came Lucille. There was an appreciative murmur in court when she stepped into the witness box, wearing a plain black dress with a white collar, looking very young, frail, and beautiful. The prosecuting counsel led her through her story with almost old-world gallantry, dropping his voice a little at what might be thought delicate moments.

Yes, Lucille said, she had known Pierre Delaporte for only six weeks before they married, and that was just two years ago. She knew only that he was a respected art dealer, nothing of any drug-running, although they smoked pot together sometimes, and she had once tried cocaine. And yes, it had been a happy marriage, Pierre was do dynamic—except that she did not like traveling and so usually stayed in England, which she loved. But at times she was a little lonely.

Up to this point she had spoken clearly, but she lowered her head and at times became barely audible as she told how she had met her neighbor Robert Banister and found him so charming, so considerate, all the things Pierre was not.

"I loved Pierre, but Robert was so different." She lifted her head now and said defiantly, "So English."

"You became his mistress."

The reply was whispered. "Yes."

She went on to tell the story of the lost diamong-and-ruby cuff link. "I was so devastated, so ashamed I am so careless, I feel I must make it up somehow. So we go together to this shop, I give him these studs. It is a way of saying sorry to my lover, that is all."

"This was a valuable present."

She shrugged.

"You were buying something for your lover with your husband's money, did that occur to you?"

Her head lowered again, Lucille muttered, "I did not think. It was very wrong, but I did not think."

And then Pierre had found the missing cuff link, in the bedroom, under her dressing table. He had questioned her about it. He was angry and did not believe her when she said it must have been dropped by one of the cleaners and was of no value. He could see it was valuable. This had happened an hour before the party, and so at the party she had thought she would not talk to Robert, but when Pierre had taken some guests out to say good-bye she had brought over his glass, just to say hello. Robert had said he must talk to her alone, they had gone into the bedroom, he had kissed her and started to make love, then Pierre had come in, had been furious, they fought—

"Was Robert Banister his normal self at this time?"

She shook her head violently. "Not at all. He was so strange—I had never seen him like that. I thought he would choke Pierre to death."

"And then the waiter knocked him out. What did you do after that?"

"We are in the living room. Pierre says the party is over and people go away. Pierre, he is still angry and says we will settle things, but Barbara is crying, she is hysterical. So I take her to the bathroom and say I am sorry, it is all my fault."

"When your husband said he would settle things, was Robert Banister in the room?"

"Yes, he had come in and was standing by the door. He is still strange, I do not think he knows what he is doing."

"And what do you think your husband meant by that phrase about settling things?"

Lucille shook her head. In the end her reply was a whisper. "I think he was going to fight again with Robert." Still in a voice hardly raised above a whisper, she said she had still been in the bathroom trying to comfort Barbara when she had heard shouts, a cry, then a crash. She had gone in the living room to find Robert semiconscious just beside the French window, and no sign of Pierre. Then she had gone to the balcony.

Robert's counsel was very small, superficially like Pierre in appearance, so that he felt at times disconcertingly as if he was being represented by the dead man. The little man's manner was aggressive, and in wig and gown he resembled a yapping French poodle. He was pertinacious in cross-examining Lucille, snapping away particularly at what she said and did before going into the bedroom.

"You say it was my client's glass you brought over. How do you know that?"

"I saw him put it down. I asked the waiter to refill it, then took it over to him. He drank some of it, and said he must talk to me alone."

"You know medical examination showed my client had taken LSD."

"I have been told, yes."

"And it was the first time he had taken any drug. He never took drugs with you?"

"Not with me. Whether he had taken any elsewhere, I do not know."

"I suggest you spiked the glass of wine with LSD, as a joke perhaps, to see what would happen."

She shook her head.

"And that it was not he but you who wanted to go into the bedroom. I suggest you made love to him, not he to you, because you wanted to see what would happen when your husband came back. It was a dull party and you thought you would liven it up, wasn't that the reason?"

To these questions, and others suggesting she found it amusing to have a lover, Lucille said "No" quietly, with lowered head. Robert found it unbearable that she should be so tormented and passed down a note: "Stop this line of questioning." The note was passed up to the French poodle, who ignored it, or at any rate continued with similar questions. A small quantity of some untraceable drug had been found in Pierre's body, and the poodle suggested both he and Lucille had been habitual users. This, too, she denied.

Afterward the poodle came with the solicitor to see Robert and said the cross-examination had gone well.

"Whatever happened, you knew nothing about it—you were the victim of some kind of stupid joke. And whatever happened was an accident. That's our case."

Robert said slowly and painfully, like a man learning to speak, "You shouldn't have said those things. When it's over, you see, Lucille and I will get married."

The poodle stared at him, did not comment. "I shan't be calling your wife. She was in the bathroom with Mrs. Delaporte when it happened, she couldn't say anything that would help. And I'm afraid she's bitter—I don't know what the other side might make of her."

Robert nodded, without interest.

"Now, about your own evidence—"

Robert took little interest in that, either. Carefully led by the poodle, he stumbled through his story, admitting he had fallen in love with Lucille but otherwise mentioning her as little as possible, saying he had never taken drugs, he was a peace-loving man not inclined to quarrel—when Pierre had found them in the bedroom, there had been no mention of the cuff link, and he had no recollection of what happened after being knocked unconscious.

The cross-examination that followed was no less deadly for being urbane. He talked about being "in love," prosecuting counsel said, but wasn't it a case rather of the seduction of a lonely young woman who had become infatuated with him, the extent of that infatuation being shown by the purchase of those valuable diamond studs? He had said nothing to his wife and had hidden the studs—didn't that indicate the sordidness of the affair? At the party he had been talking to two of the dead man's close collaborators, both now under arrest. Did he expect the jury to believe drugs were not mentioned? Had he perhaps said it might be fun to try something? Increasingly, as the questions flowed on, they seemed unreal, altogether unconnected with the life and personality of that Robert Banister, an accountant at Multiplex, who had unwisely moved from Quinton Close to Marlborough Court.

The judge's summing up, although equally urbane, was unfavorable to the defendant. Nobody could doubt that Pierre Delaporte's death came about as the result of a quarrel over the affections of a beautiful though perhaps rather bored young woman, the man on high said. The only question to be decided was whether it was a pure accident or the result of an attack by the defendant, in which case he would be guilty of manslaughter. The defendant had said the cuff link had not been mentioned, but the fact that it was found beside the body was proof enough that Delaporte was aware of his wife's unfaithfulness. He mentioned the respective sizes of the men and the marks on the dead man's neck caused by an apparent attempt at strangulation, and told the jury not to draw any conclusion from the fact that the accused man's wife had not been called as a witness.

Juries, however, are not slow to make the assumption that a

wife not called to give evidence in such a case can have nothing favorable to say of her husband. They took only ninety minutes to find Robert Banister guilty of manslaughter. The judge said that in view of his previously unblemished character, and some doubt about the means by which he obtained the drug he took and under whose influence he had acted, he was minded to be lenient. He passed a sentence of two years' imprisonment, of which eighteen months would be suspended. Since Robert had already been four months in prison before the trial, this meant he had only a few weeks to serve. They were the longest of his life, and during them he learned that Barbara was suing for divorce. He did not contest the case.

When he came out of prison, Robert changed his surname to Stair, moved to another part of the city, and set up as an accountant specializing in taxation matters. He wrote to Lucille at Marlborough Court, telling her he still loved her and asking if they could meet, but the letter was returned marked GONE AWAY, NO ADDRESS. A few months later, he proposed marriage to a widow who had come to him for help with her income-tax problems, and was accepted. They bought a house in Forest Gardens, a recently built estate that very much resembled Quinton Close, and settled there happily.

The two women who lived at the villa in Monaco bought with Pierre's money never talked about the past. They enjoyed, or Lucille enjoyed, the lazy life, the clothes they bought, and the trips they took together, the fact that there was never any need to worry about money or about men.

Lucille had loved Barbara from the moment that she looked up in the dentist's chair and saw that heavy, frowning face bent over her. It had begun then, when Barbara had asked abruptly whether she would like to meet again. And it was not only love she felt, but admiration for a will and intelligence much greater than her own.

For it had all been Barbara's idea and Barbara's plan, from the time Lucille learned the apartment next to theirs was vacant and said casually that it would be so much easier to spend time with each other if they were neighbors. Barbara had told her what to do, she had played her part perfectly (Barbara had said so), and now she was entirely happy. So she assured herself. Yet there were moments when she saw those heavy brows knitted and something like a scowl on the handsome face, moments when she remembered those powerful hands forcing little Pierre over the balcony while Robert lay semiconscious on the floor. In those moments she felt afraid.

DONALD E. WESTLAKE

A MIDSUMMER DAYDREAM

It's always a pleasure to encounter Donald E. Westlake's memorable rogue Dortmunder. Lately he's been turning up about once a year in a short story, and his 1989 caper "Too Many Crooks" won an Edgar award. This year we find him in an unusual rural setting, enjoying summer theater in West Urbino, New York. In addition to novels and short stories Westlake found time last year to write the screenplay for The Grifters, *one of the top crime-suspense films of the year.*

It having become advisable to leave New York City for an indefinite period, Dortmunder and Kelp found themselves in the countryside, in a barn, watching a lot of fairies dance. "I don't know about this," Dortmunder muttered.

"It's perfect cover," Kelp whispered. "Who'd look for us *here*?"

"*I* wouldn't, that's for sure."

The fairies all skipped offstage and some other people came on and went off, and then the audience stood up. "That's it?" Dortmunder asked. "We can go now?"

"First half," Kelp told him.

First half. Near the end of the first half, one of the players in bib overalls had gone out and come back in with a donkey's head on, which about summed up Dortmunder's attitude toward the whole thing. Oh, well; when in Rome, do as the Romans, and when in West Urbino, New York, go to the Saturday-afternoon summer theater. Why not? But he wouldn't come back Sunday.

Outside, the audience stood around in the sunshine and talked about everything except *A Midsummer Night's Dream*.

The women discussed other women's clothing and the men brought one another up to date on sports and the prices of automobiles, all except Kelp's cousin, a stout man named Jesse Bohker, who smelled of fertilizer because that's what he sold for a living, and who talked about the size of the audience because he was the chief investor in this barn converted to an extremely barnlike summer theater, with splintery bleachers and nonunion actors up from New York. "Good gate," Bohker said, nodding at the crowd in satisfaction, showbiz jargon as comfortable as a hay stalk in his mouth. "Shakespeare brings 'em in every time. They don't want anybody to think they don't have culture."

"Isn't that great," Kelp said, working on his enthusiasm because his cousin Bohker was putting them up until New York became a little less fraught. "Only eighty miles from the city, and you've got live theater."

"Cable kills us at night," cousin Bohker said, sharing more of his entertainment-world expertise, "but in the daytime, we do fine."

They rang a cowbell to announce the second half, and the audience obediently shuffled back in, as though they had bells round their own necks. All except Dortmunder, who said, "I don't think I can do it."

"Come *on*, John," Kelp said, not wanting to be rude to the cousin. "Don't you wanna know how it comes out?"

"I know how it comes out," Dortmunder said. "The guy with the donkey head turns into Pinocchio."

"That's OK, Andy," cousin Bohker said. He was a magnanimous host. "Some people just don't go for it," he went on, with the fat chuckle that served him so well in fertilizer sales. "Tell the truth, football season, I wouldn't go for it myself."

"I'll be out here," Dortmunder said. "In the air."

So everybody else shuffled back into the barn and Dortmunder stayed outside, like the last smoker in the world. He walked around a bit, looking at how dusty his shoes were getting, and thought about New York. It was just a little misunderstanding down there, that's all, a little question about the value of the contents of trucks that had been taken from Greenwich Street out to Long Island City one night when their regular drivers were asleep in bed. It would straighten itself out eventually, but a couple of the people involved were a little jumpy and emotional in their responses, and Dortmunder didn't want to be the cause of their having performed actions they would later regret. So it was better—more healthful, in fact—to spend a little time in the country, with the air and the trees and the sun and the fairies in the bottom of the barn.

Laughter inside the barn. Dortmunder wandered over to the main entrance, which now stood unguarded, the former ushers and cashier all away being fairies, and beyond the bleachers, he saw the guy in the donkey head and the girl dressed in curtains carrying on as before. No change. Dortmunder turned away and made a long, slow circuit of the barn, just for something to do.

This used to be a real farm a long time ago, but most of the land was sold off and a couple of outbuildings underwent insurance fires, so now the property was pretty much just the old white farmhouse, the red barn and the gravel parking lot in between. The summer-theater people were living in the farmhouse, which meant that out back, it had the most colorful clothesline in the county. Down the road that-a-way was West Urbino proper, where cousin Bohker's big house stood.

The second half took a long time, almost as long as if Dortmunder had been inside watching it. He walked around awhile, and then he chose a comfortable-looking car in the parking lot and sat in it—people didn't lock their cars or their houses or anything around here—and then he strolled around some more, and that's when the actor with the donkey's head and the bib overalls went by, maybe to make an entrance from the front of the theater. Dortmunder nodded his head at the guy, and the actor nodded his donkey head back.

Dortmunder strolled through the parked cars, wondering if there was time to take one for a little spin, and then Mr. Donkey came back again and they both did their head nod, and the donkey walked on, and that was it for excitement. Dortmunder figured he probably *didn't* have time to take a little drive around the countryside, particularly because, dollars to doughnuts, he'd get lost.

And it was a good thing he'd decided not to leave, because only about ten minutes later, a whole lot of applause sounded inside the barn and a couple of ex-fairies came trotting out to be traffic control in the parking lot. Dortmunder swam upstream through the sated culture lovers and found Kelp to one side of the flow, near the cashier's makeshift office, waiting for cousin Bohker to quit drooling over the take. "It was a lot of fun," Kelp said.

"Good."

"And it come out completely different from what you said."

Cousin Bohker emerged from the ticket office with a brand-new expression on his face, all pinched-in and pruny, as though he'd been eating his fertilizer. He said, "Andy, I guess your friend doesn't understand much about country hospitality."

This made very little sense at all; in fact, none. Kelp said, "Come again, cuz?"

"So you talk to him, Andy," cousin Bohker said. He wasn't looking at Dortmunder, but his head seemed to incline slightly in Dortmunder's direction. He seemed like a man torn between anger and fear, anger forbidding him to show the fear, fear holding the anger in check; constipated, in other words. "You talk to your *friend*," cousin Bohker said in a strangled way, "you explain about hospitality in the country, and you tell him we'll forget—"

"If you mean John," Kelp said, "he's right here. This is him here."

"That's OK," the cousin said. "You just tell him we'll forget all about it this once, and all he has to do is give it back, and we'll never say another word about it."

Kelp shook his head. "I don't get what you mean," he said. "Give *what* back?"

"The receipts!" cousin Bohker yelled, waving madly at his ticket office. "Two hundred twenty-seven paid admissions, not counting freebies and house seats like *you* fellas had, at twelve bucks a head; that's two thousand, seven hundred twenty-four dollars, and I want it *back*!"

Kelp stared at his cousin. "The *box*-office receipts? You can't—" His stare, disbelieving, doubtful, wondering, turned toward Dortmunder. "John? You didn't!" Kelp's eyes looked like hubcaps. "Did you? You didn't! Naturally, you didn't. Did you?"

The experience of being unjustly accused was so novel and

bewildering to Dortmunder that he was almost drunk from it. He had so little experience of innocence! How does an innocent person act, react, respond to the base accusation? He could barely stand up, he was concentrating so hard on this sudden in-rush of guiltlessness. His knees were wobbling. He stared at Andy Kelp and couldn't think of one solitary thing to say.

"Who else was out here?" the cousin demanded. "All alone out here while everybody else was inside with the play. 'Couldn't stand Shakespeare,' was that it? Saw his opportunity, by God, and *took* it, and the hell with his host!"

Kelp was beginning to look desperate. "John," he said, like a lawyer leading a particularly stupid witness, "you weren't just playing a little *joke*, were you? Just having a little fun, didn't mean anything serious, was that it?"

Maybe innocent people are dignified, Dortmunder thought. He tried it: "I did not take the money," he said, as dignified as a turkey on Thanksgiving eve.

Kelp turned to his cousin: "Are you *sure* it's gone?"

"Andy," said the cousin, drawing himself up—or in—becoming even more dignified than Dortmunder, topping Dortmunder's king of dignity with his own ace, "this fellow is what he is, but you're my wife's blood relative."

"Aw, cuz," Kelp protested, "you don't think I was *in* it with him, do you?"

And that was the unkindest cut of all. Forgetting dignity, Dortmunder gazed on his former friend like a betrayed beagle. "You, too, Andy?"

"Gee whiz, John," Kelp said, twisting back and forth to show how conflicted all this made him, "what're we supposed to *think*? I mean, maybe it just happened accidental-like; you were bored, you know, walking around, you just picked up this cash without even thinking about it, you could. . . ."

Wordlessly, Dortmunder frisked himself, patting his pockets and chest, then spreading his arms wide, offering himself for Kelp to search.

Which Kelp didn't want to do. "OK, John," he said, "the stuff isn't on you. But there wasn't anybody else *out* here, just you, and you know your own rep—"

"The donkey," Dortmunder said.

Kelp blinked at him. "The what?"

"The guy in the donkey head. He walked around from the back to the front, and then he walked around again from the front to the back. We nodded at each other."

Kelp turned his hopeful hubcaps in his cousin's direction. "The guy with the donkey head, that's who you—"

"What, Kelly?" demanded the cousin. "Kelly's my junior partner in this operation! He's been in it with me from the beginning, he's the director, he takes character roles, he *loves* this theater!" Glowering at Dortmunder, exuding more fertilizer essence than ever, cousin Bohker said, "So is *that* your idea, Mr. Dortmunder?" Dortmunder had been "John" before this. "Is *that* your idea? Cover up your own crime by smearing an innocent man?"

"Maybe *he* did it for a joke," Dortmunder said vengefully. "Or maybe he's absent-minded."

Kelp, it was clear, was prepared to believe absolutely anything, just so they could all get past this social pothole. "Cuz," he said, "maybe so, maybe that's it. Kelly's your partner; maybe he took the money legit, spare you the trouble, put it in the bank himself."

But Bohker wouldn't buy it. "Kelly *never* touches the money," he insisted. "*I*'m the businessman, he's the ar-tiste, he's—Kelly!" he shouted through the entranceway, toward the stage, and vigorously waved his fat arm.

Kelp and Dortmunder exchanged a glance. Kelp's look was filled with a wild surmise; Dortmunder's belonged under a halo.

Kelly came out to join them, wiping his neck with a paper towel, saying, "What's up?" He was a short and skinny man who could have been any age from nine to fourteen or from fifty-three to eighty, but nothing in between. The donkey head was gone, but that didn't make for much of an improvement. His real face wasn't so much lined as pleated, with deep crevices you could hide a nickel in. His eyes were eggy, with blue yolks, and his thin hair was unnaturally black, like work boots. Except for the head, he was still in the same dumb costume, the idea having been that the actors in bib overalls and black T-shirts were supposed to be some kind of workmen, like plumbers or whatever, and the actors dressed in curtains and beach towels were aristocrats. Kelly had been the leader of the bunch of workmen who were going to put on the play within the play—oh, it was grim, it was grim—so here he was, still in his overalls and T-shirt. And black work boots, so that he looked the same on the top and the bottom. "What's up?" he said.

"I'll tell you what's up," Bohker promised him and pointed at Kelp. "I introduced you to my wife's cousin from the city."

"Yeah, you did already." Kelly, an impatient man probably wanting to get out of his work clothes and into something a little more actorly, nodded briskly at Kelp and said, "How's it goin'?"

"Not so good," Kelp said.

"And *this*," Bohker went on, pointing without pleasure at Dortmunder, "is my wife's cousin's pal, also from the city, a fella with a reputation for being just a little light-fingered."

"Aw, well," Dortmunder said.

Kelly was still impatient: "And?"

"And he lifted the gate!"

This slice of jargon was just a bit too showbizzy for Kelly to grab on the fly like that; he looked around for a lifted gate, his facial pleats increasing so much he looked as though his nose might fall into one of the excavations. "He did *what*?"

Bohker, exasperated at having to use lay terminology, snapped, "He stole the money out of the box office."

"I did not," Dortmunder said.

Kelly looked at Dortmunder as though he'd never expected such treatment. "Gee, man," he said, "that's our eating money."

"I didn't take it," Dortmunder said. He was going for another run at dignity.

"He's got the gall, this fella," Bohker went on, braver about Dortmunder now that he had an ally with him, "to claim *you* took it!"

Kelly wrinkled up like a multicar collision: "*Me?*"

"All I said," Dortmunder told him, feeling his dignity begin to tatter, "was that you went around to the front of the theater."

"I did not," Kelly said. Being an actor, he had no trouble with dignity at all.

So he *did* do it, Dortmunder thought, and pressed what he thought of as his advantage: "Sure, you did. We nodded to each other. You were wearing your donkey head. It was about ten minutes before the show was over."

"Pal," Kelly said, "ten minutes before the show was over, I was onstage, asleep in front of everybody, including your buddy here. And without my donkey head."

"That's true, John," Kelp said. "The fairies took the donkey head away just around then."

"In that case," Dortmunder said, immediately grasping the situation, "it had to be one of the other guys in bib overalls. *They* weren't all on stage then, were they?"

But Bohker already had his mind made up. "That's right," he said. "That's what *you* saw, the big-town sharpie, when you came out of this box office right here, with the cash receipts in your pocket, and looked through that door right there in at that stage way back there, and saw Kelly was the only rustic on stage, and the donkey prop was gone, and—"

"The what?" Dortmunder had missed something there.

"The donkey prop!" Bohker cried, getting angrier, pointing at his own head. "The head! It's a prop!"

"Well, you know, Jesse," Kelly said thoughtfully, "in some union productions, you know, they'd call it a costume."

"Whatever it is," Bohker snapped, waving the gnats of show-biz cant away as though he hadn't summoned them up himself, then turning back to Dortmunder: "Whatever it is, you saw it, or *didn't* see it, when you looked right through there and saw Kelly asleep without his head, and none of the other rustics around, and right *then* you decided how you were gonna blame somebody else. And *I*'m here to tell you, it won't work!"

Well, innocence wasn't any help—overrated, as Dortmunder had long suspected—and dignity had proved to be a washout, so what was left? Dortmunder was considering violence, which usually tended at least to clear the air, when Kelp said, "Cuz, let me have a word in private with John, OK?"

"That's all I ever asked," Bohker said, with false reasonableness. "Just talk to your friend here, explain to him how we do things different in the country, how we don't take *advantage* of the kindness of people who take us *in* when we're on the *run*, how when we're away from the *city*, we behave like *decent, God-fearing*—"

"Right, cuz, right," Kelp said, taking Dortmunder by the elbow, drawing him away from the ongoing flow, nodding and nodding as though Bohker's claptrap made any sense at all, turning Dortmunder away, walking him back out toward the now nearly empty parking lot and across it to a big old tree standing there with leaves all over it, and Dortmunder promised himself, If Andy asks me even *once* did I do it, I'm gonna pop him.

Instead of which, once they'd reached the leafy privacy of the tree, Kelp turned and murmured, "John, we're in a bind here."

Dortmunder sighed, relieved and yet annoyed. "That's right."

"I dunno, the only thing I can think—How much did he say it was?"

"Two something. Something under three grand." And *that* got Dortmunder steamed in an entirely different way. "To think I'd stoop to grab such a measly amount of—"

"Sure you would, John, if the circumstances were different," Kelp said, cutting through the crap. "The question is, Can we cover it?"

"What do you mean, cover it?"

"Well, Jesse said if we give it back, he'll forget the whole thing, no questions asked."

Now Dortmunder was *really* outraged. "You mean, let the son of a bitch go on thinking I'm a thief?"

Kelp leaned closer, dropping his voice. "John, you *are* a thief."

"Not this time!"

"What does it matter, John? You're never gonna convince him, so forget it."

Dortmunder glared at the farmhouse, full now of actors, one of them with nearly three grand extra in his pocket. Probably looking out a window right now, grinning at him. "It's one of those guys," he said. "I can't let him get away with it."

"Why not? And what are you gonna do, play detective? John, we're not cops!"

"We watched cops work often enough."

"That isn't the same. John, how much money you got?"

"On me?" Dortmunder groused, reluctant even to discuss

this idea, while out of the corner of his eye, he saw Kelly heading briskly toward the farmhouse. "Why *couldn't* it be him?" he demanded. "Partners steal from partners all the time."

"He was onstage, John. How much money you got?"

"On me, a couple hundred. In the suitcase, back at your goddamn cousin's house, maybe a grand."

"I could come up with eight, nine hundred," Kelp said. "Let's go see if we can cut a deal."

"I don't like this," Dortmunder said. "I don't go along with making restitution to begin with, and this is even worse."

Running out of patience, Kelp said, "What else are we gonna do, John?"

"Search that farmhouse there. Search the theater. You think some amateur can hide a stash so *we* can't find it?"

"They wouldn't let us search," Kelp pointed out. "We aren't cops, we don't have any authority, we can't throw any weight around. That's what cops do; they don't *detect*, you know that. They throw their weight around, and when you say 'Oof,' you get five to ten in Green Haven. Come on, John, swallow your pride."

"I'm not gonna say I did it," Dortmunder insisted. "You wanna pay him off, we'll pay him off. But I'm not gonna say I did it."

"Fine. Let's go talk to the man."

They walked back to where cousin Bohker waited in the narrow trapezoid of shade beside the barn. "Cuz," said Kelp, "we'd like to offer a deal."

"Admitting nothing," Dortmunder said.

"Two thousand, seven hundred twenty-four dollars," the cousin said. "That's the only deal I know."

"We can't quite come up with that much," Kelp said, "on accounta John here didn't actually take your money. But we know how things look and we know what John's reputation is—"

"Hey," Dortmunder said. "What about *you*?"

"OK, fine. The reputations we both have. So we feel we'll try to make good on what you lost as best we can, even though we didn't do it, and we could probably come up with two thousand. In and around two thousand."

"Two thousand, seven hundred twenty-four dollars," said the cousin, "or I call the troopers."

"Troopers?" Dortmunder stared at Kelp. "He's gonna call in the *army*?"

"State troopers, he means," Kelp explained, and turned back to his cousin to say, "That wouldn't be a nice thing to do, cuz. Turn us over to the law and we're really in trouble. Can't you take the two—"

"Two thousand, seven hundred twenty-four dollars," said the cousin.

"Oh, the hell with this guy," Dortmunder abruptly said. "Why don't we just go take a hike?"

"I thought you might come up with that next," the cousin answered. He was smeared all over with smugness. "So that's why I sent Kelly for reinforcements."

Dortmunder turned, and there was Kelly back from the farmhouse, and with him were all the other rustics. Five of them, still in their bib overalls and T-shirts, standing there looking at Dortmunder and Kelp, getting a kick out of being the audience for a change.

It's one of them, Dortmunder thought. He's standing there and I'm standing here, and it's one of them. And I'm stuck.

Kelp said something, and then the cousin said something, and then Kelp said something else, and then Kelly said something; and Dortmunder tuned out. It's one of these five guys, he thought. One of these guys is a little scared to be out here, he doesn't know if he's gonna get away with it or not, he's looking at me and he doesn't know if he's in trouble or not.

Their eyes? No, they're all actors; the guy's gotta know enough to behave like everybody else. But it's one of them.

Well, not the fat one. You look at skinny Kelly there, and you see this fat one, and even with the donkey head on, you'd know it wasn't Kelly, having already seen Kelly in the first half, wearing the donkey head, and knowing what he looked like.

Hey, wait a minute. Same with the tall one. Kelly's maybe five five or five six, and here's a drink of water must be six four, and he stands all stooped, so if *he* had the donkey head on, the donkey's lips would be on his belt buckle. Not him.

Son of a gun. Two down. Three to go.

Conversation went on, quite animated at times, and Dortmunder continued to study the rustics. That one with the beard, well, the beard wouldn't show inside the donkey head, but look how hairy he is anyway; lots of bushy black hair on his head and very hairy arms below the T-shirt sleeves, all that black hair with the pale skin showing through. With the donkey head on, he'd look maybe a little *too* realistic. Would I have noticed? Would I have said, "Wow, up close, that's some hairy donkey?" Maybe, maybe.

Shoes? Black work boots, black shoes; some differences, but not enough, not so you'd notice.

Wait a minute. That guy, the one with the very graceful neck, the one who would be kept in the special block for his own protection if he were ever given five to ten at Green Haven, the one who moves like a ballet dancer; his bib overalls have a *crease*. Not him. He could cover himself in an entire donkey and I'd know.

Number five. Guy in his midtwenties, average height, average weight, nothing in particular about him except the watch. He's the guy, during the first half, while I'm waiting for it to be over, trying to find something to think about, he's the guy with the pale mark around his wrist where he usually wears a watch, so it isn't tanned. And now he's wearing the watch. Did the guy who walked by me have a pale mark on his wrist? Would I have noticed?

"John? John!"

Dortmunder looked around, startled out of his reverie. "Yeah? What is it?"

"What *is* it?" Kelp was looking frantic and he clearly wanted to know why Dortmunder wasn't frantic as well. "Do you think she could or *not*?" he demanded.

"I'm sorry," Dortmunder said, "I didn't hear the question. Who could what? Or not?" And thinking, It's either the hairy arms or the watch; hairy arms or watch.

"May," Kelp said, elaborately patient. "Do you think if you phoned May, she could send us a grand to pay off my cousin?"

Hairy arms or watch. Nothing shows on either face, nothing in the eyes.

"John? What's the *matter* with you?"

"Well," Dortmunder said, and put a big smile on his face, and even forced a little laugh, or something similar to a laugh, "well, you got us, cuz."

Kelp stared. "*What?*"

"Yeah, we took the money," Dortmunder said, shrugging. "But it was just for a joke, you know; we never meant to keep it."

"Yeah, I'm sure," Bohker said with a sarcastic smirk, while Kelp stood as though turned to stone. Limestone. In acid rain.

Kelly, cold and brisk, said, "Where is it?"

"Well, I don't know exactly," Dortmunder said. "I gave it to my partner to hide."

Kelp squawked; it sounded exactly like those chickens that a neighbor of Bohker's kept in his back yard. He squawked, and then he cried, "John! You never did!"

"Not you," Dortmunder told him. "My other partner, the actor in the cast here that's an old pal of mine. I slipped him the money and he went and hid it in the house." Hairy arms or watch; hairy arms or watch. Dortmunder turned and grinned easily at the kid with the pale band under his watch. "Didn't I?" he said.

The kid blinked. "I don't get you," he said.

"Aw, come on; the gag's over," Dortmunder told him. "If Bohker here calls his state troopers, I'll just tell them I gave you the money to hide and they'll go look in the house there and find it, and everybody *knows* I was never in that house, so it was you. So now the gag is over, right?"

The kid thought about it. Everybody standing there watched the kid thinking about it, and everybody knew what it meant that the kid had something to think about. The kid looked around and saw what it was that everybody knew, and then he laughed and clapped his hands together and said, "Well, we sure had them going there for a while, didn't we?"

"We sure did," Dortmunder said. "Why don't you and me go in the house now and get the cousin his money back?"

Bohker, sounding tough, said, "Why don't we *all* go in and get the goddamn money?"

"Now, now," Dortmunder said, mild as could be, "why don't you let us have our little secrets? We'll go in and we'll come out with the money. You'll get your money back, cousin, don't worry."

Dortmunder and the kid walked across the parking lot and up the stoop and across the porch full of gaping actors and went into the house. The kid led the way upstairs and down the hall and into the third room on the left, which contained two narrow beds and two small dressers and two wooden chairs. "Hold it a second," Dortmunder said, and looked around, and saw the one dresser drawer open about three inches. "Taped it to the back of the dresser drawer," he said.

"OK, OK, you're Sherlock Holmes," the kid said, sounding bitter. He went over and pulled the drawer out and put it on the bed. Masking tape held a bulky white envelope to the back of the drawer. The kid peeled it off and handed it to Dortmunder, who saw that it had a printed return address on the upper left corner: BOHKER & BOHKER, FERTILIZER & FEED.

"How'd you figure it out?" the kid asked.

"Your shoes," Dortmunder said. Which was a variant on the old untied-shoelace gag, because when the kid looked down at his shoes, what he saw was Dortmunder's fist coming up.

Outside again, Dortmunder crossed to the waiting rustics and held the envelop out in front of himself, flap open, so everybody could see the money wadded inside. "OK?"

Kelly said, "Where's Chuck?"

"Resting."

Bohker reached for the envelope, but Dortmunder said, "Not yet, cuz," and tucked the envelope inside his shirt.

Bohker glowered. "Not yet? What are you playing at, fella?"

"You're gonna drive Andy and me to your house," Dortmunder told him, "and we're gonna pack, and then you're gonna drive us to the bus depot, and when the bus comes in, I'll hand you this envelope. Play around, I'll make it disappear again."

"I'm not a vengeful fella," Bohker said. "All I care about is I get my money back."

"Well, that's one difference between us," Dortmunder said, which Bohker maybe didn't listen to hard enough.

Bohker's station wagon was one of the few cars left in the parking lot. Bohker got behind the wheel, his cousin Kelp beside him, and Dortmunder got in back with the old newspapers and cardboard cartons and fertilizer brochures and all the junk, and they drove off toward town. Along the way, Bohker looked in the rearview mirror and said, "I been thinking about what happened back there. You didn't take the money at all, did you?"

"Like I said."

"It *was* Chuck."

"That's right."

Kelp twisted around to look over the back of the seat and say, "John, how did you figure out it was him? That was goddamn genius."

If Kelp wanted to think what had happened was genius, it would be better for Dortmunder to keep his thought processes to himself, so he said, "It just come to me."

Bohker said, "You had to mousetrap Chuck like you did or he'd have just denied it forever."

"Uh-huh."

"Well, I owe you an apology," Bohker said, being gruff and man to man about it.

"That's OK," Dortmunder told him.

"And there's no reason you fellas have to move out."

"Oh, I think we're ready to go, anyway," Dortmunder said. "Aren't we, Andy?"

"Yeah, I think so," Kelp said.

As Bohker turned the station wagon in to the driveway at his house, Dortmunder said, "Does that glove compartment lock?"

"Yeah, it does," Bohker said. "Why?"

"I tell you what we'll do," Dortmunder told him. "We'll lock this envelope in there for safekeeping, and you give me the key off the ring, and when we get on our bus, I'll give it back to you. On account of I know you don't trust me."

"Now, that's not fair," Bohker said defensively, parking beside his house. "I apologized, didn't I?"

"Still," Dortmunder said, "we'll both be happier if we do it this way. Which key is it?"

So Bohker took the little key off his key ring, and he and Kelp watched Dortmunder solemnly lock the envelope away in the crowded, messy glove compartment, and an hour and forty-five minutes later, on the bus to Buffalo, Kelp turned in his seat and said, "You did, didn't you?"

"Sure, I did," Dortmunder agreed, taking wads of Bohker's money out of his pants pockets. "Treat me like that, threaten me with *troopers*."

"What's cousin Bohker looking at in that envelope?"

"Fertilizer brochures."

Kelp sighed, probably thinking about family complications. "Still, John," he said, "you can hardly blame the guy for jumping to conclusions."

"I can if I want," Dortmunder said. "Besides, I figured I earned this, with what he put me through. That stuff, what's-it. Anguish, you know the kind. Mental, that's it. Mental anguish, that's what I got," Dortmunder said, and stuffed the money back into his pockets.

CAROLYN WHEAT

THREE-TIME LOSER

Courtroom dramas have been especially popular on television during the past few seasons, but few convey the realism and immediacy of New York City's criminal justice system better than Carolyn Wheat's novels and stories about Brooklyn criminal lawyer Cass Jameson. The author herself has been a lawyer for the city's Legal Aid Society.

It was my own personal first day of spring. Forget the calendar, forget that forsythia was just starting to bud and the morning still held a lot of winter chill. For me, spring had sprung. I felt like a kid, when choosing red or blue Keds for summer was one of life's great decisions.

The sneakers on my feet were leather Reeboks, not red Keds (I always chose red, in spite of Mom's inevitable protest, "But Cassie, blue goes with everything.") And I wasn't back in Ohio, playing beside the creek in muddy blue jeans, I was walking across the Brooklyn Bridge, on my way to try a case in Manhattan Supreme Court.

It didn't matter. I felt like a kid, bouncy and light, ready to jump rope, play hopscotch, ride my bike across the county line. My cross-examination suit, my leather briefcase, my jury selection notes—none of these got in the way of my feeling like a frisky ten-year-old.

I mounted the steps of the walkway, taking in the full grandeur of the bridge. Gothic arches, massive as cathedral walls, ropes of cable crisscrossed in an intricate web of silver that reflected the pale sunlight. I took a deep breath of East River–scented breeze (all right, it was a strong wind), and thought of the creek back home, of the innocent child I'd been.

I know a lot more about innocence now. I just don't see much of it. I'm a criminal lawyer.

But behind my spring fever lay an uneasy feeling. First I noticed that the Lower Manhattan skyline, seen through cable webbing, looked as if it was behind bars. Then the huge granite pylons that reached deep underwater and lifted high into the sky seemed made of cold gray prison stone. The final straw was gazing out at the sweep of harbor, taking in the pewter-colored bay, Governor's Island, Lady Liberty.

Liberty. Something my client, Buckley Carlisle, wasn't likely to have much longer. He was a three-time loser, if you watched old Warner Brothers movies, a persistent felony offender if you didn't. I hate trying a case I'm going to lose.

But I had to. I was a grown-up, with no red Keds and someone else's freedom in my hands.

When I got to the courthouse, I stopped at the ladies' room, changing my Reeboks for red heels that matched my Chanel-style jacket. I untangled my windblown hair, put on crimson lipstick, and transformed myself from tomboy to trial lawyer.

Buckley was already in the hallway, as usual. Not once in our seven-month attorney-client relationship had I ever gotten there first. An uncle in Jamaica had posted bail and paid my fee; I'd frankly expected Buckley to take the next flight to Kingston.

I almost wished he had.

Buckley scared the hell out of me. The guilty ones are easy; you do your best, go home to a hot bath and a cold drink, and forget about them. The innocent you never forget.

Was Buckley innocent? I didn't know. I only knew he didn't act guilty.

Most of my criminal clients come to court—when they *do* come to court—two hours after calendar call, wearing T-shirts with obscene comments and seven earrings in each ear. All they know about the law is that they ain't did nothin' and if I'm supposed to be their lawyer, how come I can't get these charges squashed?

Buckley Carlisle showed up for every appearance, his shoes shined, his nails filed and buffed, smelling vaguely of patchouli, a scent that took me back to Indian print skirts and love beads. He dressed for court in well-cut suits, always with a touch of tropical color in the tie, the handkerchief, like a splash of paint on a cinderblock wall. He always carried the thick paperback lawyers call the "gray book"—a combination Penal Law and Criminal Procedure Law. He looked more like a lawyer than most of the members of the bar who hustled for clients in the hallways of 100 Centre Street.

If Buckley lost this case—if *I* lost this case—he'd do ten-to-twenty, minimum.

It was time for the spiel.

"Look, Mr. Carlisle," I began, "I know we've been over this before, but I want to be sure you understand what it means if you're found guilty."

"Why don't you call me Buckley today?" My client's face, dark and smooth as a buckeye, settled into a mock pout. "Have I done something to offend you, or"—the pout dissolved into a grin of immense charm—"is it that you must call me Mister Carlisle because we speak on such a momentous topic?"

We were leaning against marble walls the color of used chewing gum. Around us, lawyers, defendants, and distraught families bustled past, looking for their courtrooms in the maze of the Criminal Court Building.

"Hey," my client urged, spreading out his arms, "like the man say, 'Don' worry, be happy.' "

In spite of myself, I smiled back. "We need to talk seriously."

"And so we must be serious. All right," Buckley conceded, firming his face into a frown of concentration. "I will suppress my natural high spirits and become attentive to your every word. But first, you must let me give you a present in honor of the spring." He brought his arm from behind his back like a small boy hiding a gift from his mother and handed me a red rose in a plastic cylinder.

"Buckley, I—" It wasn't often that words failed me. Words were my medium, my tools. I owned them, the way I owned the hallways and courtrooms I spent my life in. But no client I'd ever represented had thought to give me anything. Most of the time, I didn't even get a thank you. And now I had a rose. It made what I had to say to Buckley even harder.

"I don't know what to say." To my annoyance, my voice wavered. The rose inside its plastic cage reminded me all too clearly of Buckley behind prison bars: a living thing entombed, the appearance intact, the essence embalmed.

"Say nothing," Buckley advised blithely. "Just smile."

I hate it when men order me to smile. But for Buckley, I smiled. I lifted the rose to my face, drinking in the familiar scent. It wasn't real, of course. Roses in plastic cages lose their true smell and have to be enhanced by essential oils.

I put the rose on top of my briefcase, which rested on the windowsill, "And now to business."

Buckley struck a pose. "Give it to me straight, doc. I can take it."

I hoped he could; this was my last chance to appeal to reason before the jurors were marched in.

"I just want to remind you that you've got two priors on your record, and the D.A.'s out for blood. He's offering three-and-a-half-to-seven on a plea, which is a lot better than the ten-to-twenty you'd get if we blow trial. I know you were just a kid when you took the burglar rap, but the trouble is, the judge didn't give you Youthful Offender treatment. If he had, it wouldn't count against you now. But he didn't, and it does. As to the second crime—"

"As to the second conviction," my client interrupted, "that was a misunderstanding. I'm an 'ardworkin' man with a respectable occupation. I accept the plea of guilty because I am new in this country and am afraid to litigate."

"Even so," I continued, feeling more desperate with every minute that passed, "those prior convictions make you a three-time loser."

"But Cass," Buckley said, his voice pleading, "I done this lady no wrong. I was in jail once, for t'ree long years, and it was like a curse on me. I was like a wild bird lock up in a cage, wings clipped. Are you tellin' me to go back to that?"

"I'm telling you that the D.A.'s got a witness who made a positive ID, who says she saw you in good light for at least fifteen minutes. You say you were home alone, reading a book. I believe you, but that means you have no alibi. Even a Manhattan jury"—Manhattan juries are notoriously liberal, thank God—"may find it hard to acquit."

"Now don't be underestimating my intellingence, Miss Jameson." Carlisle held up a cat-black hand with long, bony fingers. "I am very well aware of the precarious position in which I find myself. But I 'ave no choice. I must go all the way, and I 'ave every confidence in you as my barrister."

"I'm not a barrister—"

"Court's in session," a friendly court officer warned. I stepped into the courtroom in time to hear the bailiff open the court day with the time-honored words: "All rise." While my client and I had been talking, the courtroom filled with the necessary personnel: judge, assistant district attorney, clerk, and court officers.

The jurors were black, white, Hispanic, Chinese. They were teachers, housewives, one accountant, two postal workers, and a host of other occupations.

In an odd way, they were enjoying the performance of their civic duty, like kids on a field trip to the museum.

If I'd been the one on trial, I'd have done anything to keep from putting my fate in their hands. But then the lawyer was never born who truly trusts a jury.

Why did Buckley Carlisle trust them? Why hadn't he flown to Jamaica and hidden out in a cane field? Wasn't that the real reason the rich uncle had posted his bail—to give him a chance to escape?

Buckley had to be innocent—or stupid in the first degree.

"Mrs. Mildred Eldridge," the clerk called out, and a wizened old black women, leaning on the arm of the court officer, hobbled into the room. Her legs were thin as pipe cleaners; she could hardly have weighed a hundred pounds.

On the one hand, she was one hell of a sympathetic witness. On the other hand, she looked around the courtroom, blinking like a mole. Around her neck, she wore a black cord attached to thick glasses.

The state's chief witness took her oath in a voice that shook as badly as her palsied hand. Her fingers were bent from arthritis; she hunched like a crone.

I glanced at Buckley. A small smile lifted his lips. "Mrs. Eldridge is one very old lady," he whispered. "Her sight is none too good, you know. I expect you will make a point of this in your cross-examination."

My spirits rose. There was hope after all.

Direct and short and sweet. Just what I'd have done if I'd been the D.A. Put the witness on, let her tell the story, and hope to hell she didn't have to endure too much cross.

The story was sad but simple. Mrs. Eldridge had been at home—she was always at home, tending her twin brother, who was dying of cancer in the only bedroom. In fact, he had died since the crime, making her the only witness the People had.

Her doorbell rang. She ignored it. In her Harlem neighborhood, ignoring the doorbell was the best policy. It rang again, persistently. She went to answer, knowing how her brother hated noise.

There was a man at the door. A black man. A young man, well dressed and well spoken, in a singsong Jamaican accent. He told her he had a delivery for an upstairs neighbor. She didn't know what neighbor he was talking about, and she didn't want to let him in, but the next thing she knew, he was in.

He was in, standing at the door, showing her the beautiful quilt that had been delivered to Mrs. Jacquard on the fifth floor. Mrs. Eldridge didn't know Mrs. Jacquard well; how could she talk to someone who only spoke Creole French? But she knew the name and said, yes, she'd hold the delivery for her neighbor. The young man was so friendly, so willing to hold the quilt open for her to see, that she almost considered buying it herself. The young man said she could, said the quilt was cash on delivery, and if Mrs. Jacquard wasn't interested enough to be home when it came, why it could be sold to anyone who'd pay the fifty dollars.

Fifty dollars. That was the rub. She finally told the young man she couldn't spend that kind of money, not possibly, and saw him fold the colorful quilt back into a thick square, then step out of her doorway. He'd decided not to leave it after all, but to give Mrs. Jacquard another try.

When she went into the bedroom to give her brother his medicine, she noticed the missing jewelry box. The little TV she'd bought him with her Social Security money was gone too, and so was the silver frame with her parents' pictures.

"I felt like the biggest fool in the U-nited States of America,"

Mrs. Eldridge said. "Gawking at that there quilt while all the time he was holding it up so's some thief could crawl behind it into the bedroom and steal me blind."

The blanket scam. One of the oldest cons in the world.

The climax of her testimony was A.D.A. Bernstein's asking her if she recognized anyone in the courtroom. Mildred Eldridge stood up, grasped the railing of the witness box with one hand, and pointed her twisted finger at Buckley Carlisle.

"That's him," she said, her voice stronger than at any other point. "That's the man who done kep' me at the door, talking that West Indian trash, while the other one rob me. Took the onliest treasures I had left in this world. My opal ring my Mama give me when I wasn't but fifteen years of age. My pearls from Aunt Ruby, she died after I come up North."

I objected. It wasn't a popular move. Juror number five glared as though I'd slapped the old woman. It wasn't even a legal objection; I just wanted to detour the witness's trip down memory lane.

Not only was I overruled, but the witness kept on going as though I hadn't said a word.

"How could you take them pictures?" She asked Buckley directly, as though they were the only two people in the room. He stared back blandly, his face an ebony moon. "They *my* folks, not your'n. I expect you pawned the frame, which don't make no never-mind to me. But if you could see your way clear to letting me have my pictures back, I'd be very much obliged, thank you kindly." Her voice had taken on a feisty edge that had juror number seven, a black postal worker, giving her a surreptitious grin.

I glanced at the A.D.A. Whatever Saul Bernstein's original intention, he wasn't about to stop his witness while she was winning over the jury.

"Your honor," I pointed out, "this witness isn't answering questions, she's giving a speech."

"Sustained." A technical victory. Bernstein immediately put another question to his witness.

"Were those the only photographs of your parents in your

possession?" he asked. It was leading as hell, but I didn't dare object. I'd asked for a question; I'd gotten a question.

"Yessir, they was. Since my albums that I brought all the way from Alabama was stole in a burglary, I disremember how long ago. All my family was in them albums, people been dead fifty years and more. Gone now, all gone."

At another time, in another place, I'd have felt sorry for Mildred Eldridge. There was no doubt that somebody—and in her long, hard life, maybe more than one somebody—had taken from her things she loved. But it wasn't Buckley. That was what I had to keep my eye on. It wasn't Buckley.

"And how much did you say you paid for the television set you bought your brother?"

She'd already said it once, but Bernstein was on a streak and he knew it; the jurors were eating it up.

"I done told you that already, mister. Ain't I said I bought it from Honest Kareem's House of Appliances on Hundred Twenty-Fifth Street? Ain't I said he give me the special senior citizen discount, so's it only come to a hundred eighty-nine dollars and sixty-four cents? And that was two Social Securities, which I didn't mind giving up on account of I had my late husband's benefits and I knew how much poor Amos would enjoy that little set. Wasn't no bigger than a picture postcard, but he could see all his stories and the Hour of Power on Sunday."

Finally, the words I'd been dying to hear: "No further questions."

I rose, thinking fast as I walked past the prosecution table to about the middle of the jury box. The direct had been interesting for what *hadn't* been said: no description of the man beyond the fact that he was tall and spoke with a West Indian accent. How much had the nearsighted old lady really seen of the man who kept her talking at the door?

One of the choices a defense lawyer makes is how long the witness stays on the stand. Given this one's ability to win points with the jury, I decided to hit Mrs. Eldridge with a few questions, hardball her about her eyesight, question her ability to observe and remember, and sit down.

"Mrs. Eldridge, did you call the police after the robbery?"

She nodded. "I did. And it took them a whole hour and fifteen minutes to come. I could have been dead on my kitchen floor all that time for all they cared."

"And when the police came, did they ask you what happened?"

"Course they did. They wasn't stupid."

"And what did you tell them?"

"Told them what I told this here court. Told them the truth, as God is my witness."

I preferred to leave God out of this, so I stopped warming up and threw the pitch.

"Did you describe the man to the police?"

She nodded. It was the first time she hadn't given an answer in words, usually more than the question called for.

"Did you tell them how tall he was?"

Another nod.

"And didn't you say he could have been anywhere from five feet seven to six feet tall?"

This time the judge ordered her to stop nodding and give her answer in words. She grunted a grudging "yes."

"And you told the police he spoke with a West Indian accent, is that right?"

"Yes."

"Isn't it true, Mrs. Eldridge, that those details were the only ones you were able to give the police?" I'd seen the police reports, so I knew how meager her descriptions had been.

A.D.A. Bernstein's objection was sustained. Good. That meant I could mention one by one all the details that should have been in a good description and show the jury they'd been missing in Mrs. Eldridge's.

"Did you tell them how old the man was?"

"I said he was maybe twenty, maybe thirty. Hard to tell with young peoples."

"Maybe twenty, maybe thirty. That's a big difference, Mrs. Eldridge."

Bernstein's objection was drowned out by his witness' answer: "To you, maybe. You still a young girl. When you gets to my age—"

"And how old is that, Mrs. Eldridge?"

"Be seventy-six next birthday, if the Lord spares me."

"Did you tell the police how long the man's hair was?"

She stared at Buckley. "Short, just like now."

"But you didn't tell that to the detectives, did you, Mrs. Eldridge? You said you didn't remember how long his hair was, isn't that right?"

"I only know he didn't have them dirty dreadlocks, like most of them has."

"When you say *them,* Mrs. Eldridge, who do you mean?"

"You all know who I mean. Them peoples from the Islands what comes up here to New York and lay around all day smokin' reefer."

I looked over at Buckley, ready to stop any outburst he might make. He sat calmly, his neatly manicured hand resting on the gray book as though it were a Bible.

Juror number ten, a thirtyish woman who'd answered my *voir dire* questions with a marked West Indian accent, frowned.

I decided the point had been made, and moved on. "I notice you wear glasses, ma'am. Do you need them all the time, or just for reading?"

"I needs them all the time." The answer was so low the judge asked her to repeat it. "They bifocals. For faraway and close-up both."

"And just how far away was this man you say spent fifteen minutes talking to you?"

"He closer than you is now."

I started walking slowly toward the witness box. "Stop me," I told the witness, "when I get to where he stood."

One giant step. Mother, may I? Two giant steps.

"Stop," the witness ordered. I was three feet away. I said so to the court reporter, and the distance was stipulated into evidence.

"Three feet away. And yet he could be twenty or thirty? Five feet tall or six feet?" Before Bernstein could object to my giving my summation during cross, I asked, "Mrs. Eldridge, you said you wear your glasses all the time, is that right?"

She nodded vigorously, on solid ground again. "All the time."

I went in for the kill. "Then why are they on a cord, ma'am? Isn't that so you can take them off, the way you have now?"

Bernstein was on his feet, objecting, but I had the jury hanging out of the box, so I kept talking.

"What kind of light do you have in your kitchen, Mrs. Eldridge?"

"One of them fluorescent lights. Like a ring."

"And was the light on?"

"It was on." Her old eyes shifted away from mine, hiding something. I didn't know what, but I knew it could be important. Dangerous, too. Rule Number One in cross is never ask a question you don't know the answer to.

I decided to break it. "Do you know how many watts that fluorescent bulb is, Mrs. Eldridge?"

"How'm I supposed to know something like that?"

"Is there a window in the kitchen, or was the bulb the only light?"

"There's a window on the airshaft."

She was still hiding something. Her mumbled answers and averted eyes told me as much. But what?

I glanced at Buckley. He leaned forward in his seat, eyes firmly fixed on Mrs. Eldridge. When he saw me looking, he began to blink, slowly at first, then faster. Nerves, I decided. No wonder, the time he was facing.

I'd had a fluorescent light in my kitchen in Greenwich Village, before I moved to Brooklyn. I remembered how annoying it was when it started to burn out, the way the light blinked brightly, then darkened.

"Mrs. Eldridge," I said, my voice sounding more confident than I felt, "that fluorescent light was burning out, wasn't it?"

She hung her head and mumbled an answer I couldn't hear.

"May I remind the court that the witness is under oath." I said it softly, but it got the desired result.

Mildred Eldridge raised her head, looked me in the eye, and said, "It's the truth. That light was flickering something awful. Like the oil lamps down South when I was a child. Nobody to fix it, what with Amos laid up and that super no damn good."

Bingo-bad description, bad eyesight, bad lighting. All I needed were a couple more questions to nail it home to the jury, and Buckley was as good as free.

"Mrs. Eldridge, when you first opened the door to the man, he said he had a delivery for your neighbor, is that right?"

"Yes, and I knew right off he was trouble, on account of it ain't the kind of building where peoples get deliveries. The elevator usually broke, so nobody want to come all the way up the stairs to the fifth floor."

"But this man did?"

"He say he took the steps on account of the lift was busted. He meant the elevator, I suppose."

A tiny bell went off somewhere in my head. *Lift*, not *elevator*. Just as Buckley had called me a barrister instead of a lawyer. I brushed the thought aside. Didn't most West Indians use some British expressions?

Mrs. Eldridge continued. "He asked me to take the quilt for the lady. Not that I didn't want to be neighborly, but you don't never know who be coming into your house. But there wasn't nothing I could do," she said with a sigh. Her eyes filled. "It wasn't the first time they got in on me. Last year some mens come, said they from the in-surance. They wasn't from no insurance, they just got in to rob an old lady. Year before that, I was broke into, they got my wedding ring and everything."

"Move to strike, Your Honor." Desperation play, but what else could I do? "Not responsive to the question."

"Your Honor," Bernstein protested, "counsel opened the door. She just doesn't like what walked in."

"Overruled," the judge said with a smile. The smile was for me: that was *my* line Bernstein had used.

"You don't know how it is," Mildred Eldridge went on. "How it is to live in that house with a dying man—and before that, it was my second husband Prescott lying in that selfsame bed, coughing his lungs out—and knowing that any time they wants to peoples can come and push they way in and take anything because you ain't got the strength to stop them."

"Your Honor!" I was practically shouting. "Move to strike. There's no question before this witness."

His Honor granted the motion. Big victory. The jury had heard every word and weren't about to forget the image of old Mrs. Eldridge alone in her apartment, waiting to be ripped off.

The trouble was, neither would I. Who was the three-time loser in this case—Buckley Carlisle or Mildred Eldridge?

I went back to my strong point. "Mrs. Eldridge, isn't it true that the only things you remember for sure about the man in the doorway is that he was tall and spoke with a West Indian accent?"

"I don't appreciate nobody coming into my house and taking what's rightly mine, especially when they ought to have stayed where they belond, not come up from the Islands to rob decent folk. Ain't they enough crooks in this city without we bring in more?"

"Mrs. Eldridge, that's no answer to the question." I spoke loudly wondering whether the old woman's hearing was as bad as her sight.

"And he smelled funny, too." Juror number ten didn't like that at all. A.D.A. Bernstein looked as though he couldn't wait for the one o'clock lunch break. Knowing Judge Rodriguez, it would come any minute now. He'd been known to break for lunch in midsentence if the clock struck one.

"He smelled like that sweet oil the Muslims sell in the subway," Mrs. Eldridge went on. "Like incense."

Like patchouli. Like Buckley Carlisle.

It suddenly struck me that the blinking eyes he'd shown me during my questions about Mrs. Eldridge's fluorescent light had nothing at all to do with nerves. He'd blinked to lead me into asking the very questions that had set the seal on my successful cross. He'd known that bulb was flickering, and he'd known it because he'd been the man in the doorway, holding the quilt.

I was still dazed, my mind unable to form another question, when the judge called the lunch recess.

Don't get me wrong. I've represented guilty clients before. It's part of the job I've learned to accept. But not this time. Not with the picture of Mildred Eldridge opening her door to men she knew would take from her, yet having no choice but to let them in.

I had no choice either. I had to win this case for Buckley Carlisle. I had to continue grinding Mildred Eldridge into tomato paste, destroying her credibility with the jury, so Buckley could go free. It was my job. My grown-up job.

I walked back to the defense table, taking my place next to Buckley without looking at him, staring straight ahead as the young A.D.A. helped Mildred Eldridge off the stand, as the bailiff led the jurors to the jury room, as the judge left the bench.

The smell of patchouli that clung to my client's clothes sickened me; it no longer reminded me of innocent flower children.

There was a lot I wanted to say to Buckley. I said none of it.

My client had no such reticence. "Cass, your cross-examination was most satisfactory," he said, his smile wide and welcoming. "I especially liked the way you asked her about the glasses."

Sure he did. Buckley had chanced the trial not because he was innocent, but because he'd known Mildred Eldridge was an old lady who couldn't make her identification stick any more than she could keep thieves out of her house. Even worse, there was no rich uncle in Jamaica; Buckley Carlisle's bail had been posted out of the proceeds of his ripoffs. Mildred Eldridge was paying my fee.

I'll see you after lunch," was all I answered.

Lunch was a walk to City Hall Park, where I tossed the plastic-caged rose into the first garbage can I saw.

I knew how Mildred Eldridge felt—like the biggest fool in the U-nited States of America. Buckley Carlisle's charm, his smile, his plastic rose had flimflammed me into thinking him an exotic tropical fish instead of a killer shark.

I sat on a bench next to an old man feeding pigeons, watched a group of pro-day-care demonstrators march around City Hall, and thought long and hard. Long and hard and without result. All I got was cold—it still wasn't spring—and hungry. No brilliant ideas came to me.

I didn't want to win this case. I had to win this case. Not only was it my job, but Buckley's familiarity with the gray book meant he'd know if I fudged. He'd have grounds for appeal if his lawyer didn't defend him with all the vigor he was entitled to under the Constitution.

I believe in the Constitution. It's what keeps me going through all the guilty pleas, all the suppression hearings, all the sentencing of my work life. But I also believed in Mildred Eldridge.

Back in the courtroom, it took a while to round up stray jurors, and get all the players back into position. While we waited, Buckley showed me some notes he'd made.

"I want you to ask this woman how it is she can be so certain I am the man who robbed her," he said. His tone was firm; there was none of the jokiness of our morning talk.

His skeleton hand rested on the gray book. I wondered how I could have seen its presence as a token of innocence. If I hadn't been snowed by his charming smile and smooth British talk, I'd have known it for what it was: the sign of a jailhouse lawyer.

"Buckley," I began patiently, "that's the kind of question a freshman in law school knows better than to ask. It's too open-ended. The witness could say anything."

"I want you to ask her. She's an ignorant old woman. She picks on me because I am Jamaican, don't you know? She say all Jamaicans lay about smokin' ganja day and night. She is rotten with hate, like a mango in the sun. Ask her why she thinks it is me. Ask her."

There's a story every law student learns in evidence class. Two men had a fight. One bit off the other's nose. A witness was asked several questions about the event, all of which he answered by admitting he hadn't seen the nose bitten off. The defense lawyer made the fatal mistake of asking One Too Many Questions: "If you didn't see him bite the nose off, how do you know he did it?"

The classic answer: "I saw him spit it out."

Buckley Carlisle was begging me to ask One Too Many Questions.

If I held firm, refused his request, we'd win the case. If I did as he asked, I ran the risk of snatching defeat from the jaws of victory.

I did it. I rose to my feet, approached the witness box, and asked Mildred Eldridge how it was she could be so certain Buckley Carlisle was the man who kept her in the doorway.

"It was his hands, Miss. You can always tell by they hands. See, I used to be a manicurist before my own hands done twisted up so bad." She looked down at her fingers, gnarled as roots, then back up at me.

"I notices hands. How long the fingers is, how well they be kept, how big the half-moons in the nails are. In the old days, when I worked at Bethea's Beauty Shop in Harlem, I used to put polish on the girl's fingers and leave the half-moons white. That's the way they liked it in them days. So maybe I couldn't tell you about his hair or nothing, but I could tell you them hands right down to the fingernails."

She proceeded to do so. I objected, of course, telling the judge the answer wasn't responsive. Once again, Saul Bernstein, grinning broadly, reminded me that I'd opened the door.

The jurors got to inspect Buckley's hands. They probably also smelled patchouli. Anyway, they were out less than two hours before they came in with a conviction.

It was tough hearing the click of the handcuffs on Buckley's wrists.

That's when you know it's final, when you hear that click.

He asked me to slip the gray book between his hands as they led him away. I had no doubt he'd be boning up on appellate practice very soon, and that the first point he'd raise was incompetence of trial counsel. The record would show I'd asked Mildred Eldrige a monumentally dumb question; it wouldn't show my client begged me to ask it.

Some days it's hard being a grown-up.

APPENDIX

THE YEARBOOK OF THE MYSTERY AND SUSPENSE STORY

THE YEAR'S BEST MYSTERY AND SUSPENSE NOVELS

Lawrence Block, *A Ticket to the Boneyard* (Morrow)
Robert Daley, *A Faint Cold Fear* (Little, Brown)
Nelson DeMille, *The Gold Coast* (Warner Books)
Colin Dexter, *The Wench Is Dead* (St. Martin's Press)
Elizabeth George, *Well-Schooled in Murder* (Bantam)
Reginald Hill, *Bones and Silence* (Delacorte)
P. D. James, *Devices and Desires* (Knopf)
John LeCarré, *The Secret Pilgrim* (Knopf)
Elmore Leonard, *Get Shorty* (Delacorte)
Ed McBain, *Widows* (Morrow)
Sharyn McCrumb, *If Ever I Return, Pretty Peggy-O* (Scribners)
Brian Moore, *Lies of Silence* (Doubleday)
Walter Mosley, *Devil in a Blue Dress* (Norton)
Marcia Muller, *Trophies and Dead Things* (Mysterious Press)
Bill Pronzini, *Jackpot* (Delacorte)
Rosamond Smith, *Nemesis* (Dutton)
Julian Symons, *Death's Darkest Face* (Viking)
Paco Ignacio Taibo II, *An Easy Thing* (Viking)
Scott Turow, *The Burden of Proof* (Farrar, Straus & Giroux)
Barbara Vine, *Gallowglass* (Harmony Books)

BIBLIOGRAPHY

I. Collections

1. Allbeury, Ted. *Other Kinds of Treason.* London: New English Library. Sixteen espionage and crime stories, four of them new.
2. Ambler, Eric. *The Army of the Shadows and Other Stories.* Helsinki: Eurographica. The first collection of Ambler's short fiction, in signed limited edition containing the title story and two mysteries solved by Dr. Jan Czissar. (1986)
3. Bova, Ben. *Future Crime.* New York: Tor Books. Two novellas and six stories, 1965–88, about crime in the future.
4. Brennan, Joseph Payne. *The Adventures of Lucius Leffing.* Hampton Falls, NH: Donald M. Grant. Thirteen stories, nine new, in the third collection about the occult sleuth.
5. Brown, Fredric. *Happy Ending.* Missoula, MT: Dennis McMillan Publications. The sixteenth volume of Brown's uncollected pulp writing, containing science fiction, poetry, and some letters, as well as a lengthy memoir by his wife, Elizabeth.
6. ______. *The Water-Walker.* Missoula, MT: Dennis McMillan Publications. The seventeenth volume in the series, containing three stories, short versions of two novels, and eighteen short-short "Feedum & Weap" puzzle tales with rural settings.
7. Chesbro, George C. *In the House of Secret Enemies.* New York: Mysterious Press. Ten stories, 1971–88, about dwarf private eye Mongo, mainly from *AHMM* and *Mike Shayne Mystery Magazine.*
8. Dahl, Roald. *Ah, Sweet Mystery of Life.* New York: Knopf. Seven stories, six from previous collections, some criminous.
9. Fish, Robert L. *Schlock Homes: The Complete Bagel Street Saga.* Bloomington, IN: Gaslight Publications. All thirty-two of Fish's Sherlockian Parodies from *EQMM*, 1960–81, including nine previously uncollected.
10. Gardner, Erle Stanley. *The Adventures of Paul Pry.* New

York: Mysterious Press. Nine stories from the pulps, 1930–33, with an introduction by Robert Weinberg.

11. ______. *The Blonde in Lower Six.* New York: Carroll & Graf. A short novel and three stories, 1927–61, about crook-detective Ed Jenkins, from *Argosy* and *Black Mask.*
12. ______. *Dead Men's Letters.* New York: Carroll & Graf. Six novelettes from *Black Mask*, 1926–27, about Ed Jenkins.
13. Gilbert, Michael. *Anything for a Quiet Life.* New York: Carroll & Graf. Nine stories about semiretired solicitor Jonas Pickett, all from *EQMM.*
14. Greeley, Andrew M. *All About Women.* New York: Tor Books. Twenty-three stories, seven new, some criminous.
15. Greene, Graham. *The Last Word and Other Stories.* London and New York: Reinhardt/Viking. Twelve stories, one new, 1923–89. Several are criminous, including a detective story published in 1929.
16. Greenwald, Ken. *The Lost Adventures of Sherlock Holmes.* New York: Mallard Press. Thirteen new stories based upon the original radio plays by Denis Green and Anthony Boucher, broadcast during 1945–46.
17. Hamilton, Charles. *The Complete Casebook of Herlock Sholmes.* London: Hawk Books. Ninety-five stories, 1915–52, in the longest series of Sherlock Holmes parodies. Introduction by Norman Wright. (1989)
18. Henderson, C. J. *What You Pay For: The Jack Hagee Collection.* Brooklyn: Gryphon Publications. Eleven private eye stories from *Hardboiled, Espionage,* and other publications. Introduction by Wayne Dundee.
19. Highsmith, Patricia. *Tales of Natural and Unnatural Catastrophies.* Boston: Atlantic Monthly Press. Ten stories of crime and horror, published in England in 1987.
20. Jacobi, Carl. *East of Samarinda.* Bowling Green, OH: Bowling Green State University Popular Press. Twenty-one adventure and mystery stories from the pulps, 1934–44, almost all criminous. Edited by Jacobi and R. Dixon Smith.
21. Lansdale, Joe R. *By Bizarre Hands.* Shingletown, CA: Mark V. Ziesing. Sixteen crime and horror stories, two new. (1989)

22. Mortimer, John. *Rumpole à la Carte.* New York: Viking. Six new stories about the English barrister.
23. Powell, James. *A Murder Coming.* Toronto: Yonge & Bloor. Fourteen stories, 1966–86, all but three from *EQMM.* Introduction by Peter Sellers.
24. Pronzini, Bill. *The Best Western Stories of Bill Pronzini.* Athens, OH: Swallow Press/Ohio University Press. Thirteen stories, two new, mainly criminous. Introduction by Robert E. Briney.
25. Skvorecky, Josef. *The End of Lieutenant Boruvka.* New York: Norton. Five novelettes set in Czechoslovakia in the late 1960s.
26. Whitechurch, Victor L. *The Chronicles of Humphrey Judd.* London: Ferret Fantasy. Six stories about an amateur detective, from *Pearson's Weekly*, 1899.

II. Anthologies

1. Adams Round Table. *A Body Is Found.* New York: Wynwood. Nine new stories and one reprint from *Woman's Day*, by a group of New York area mystery writers.
2. Adrian, Jack, and Robert Adey, eds. *The Art of the Impossible.* London: Xanadu. Nineteen stories, one new, plus a playlet and a novella, all dealing with locked rooms and impossible crimes. U.S. edition: *Murder Impossible* (Carroll & Graf).
3. Ardai, Charles, ed. *Great Tales of Madness and the Macabre.* New York: Galahad Books. Twenty-nine mystery and fantasy stories, twelve from *EQMM* and *AHMM*, the rest from *Isaac Asimov's Science Fiction Magazine* and other sources. Introduction by Lawrence Block.
4. Beals, Stephen, ed. *Mysteries from the Finger Lakes: Short Stories from Six Lakes ARTS Magazine* (formerly *In-Between)* Seneca Falls, NY: Six Lakes ARTS. Seven stories from a regional publication, 1987–89.
5. Burns, Rex, and Mary Rose Sullivan, eds. *Crime Classics: The Mystery Story from Poe to the Present.* New York: Viking. Seventeen stories in a selection designed for the

general reader as well as for use in college mystery fiction courses.

6. (Collins Crime Club) *A Suit of Diamonds.* London: Collins. Thirteen new stories commissioned for the sixtieth anniversary of Collins Crime Club. No editor credited.
7. Craig, Patricia, ed. *The Oxford Book of English Detective Stories.* Oxford and New York: Oxford University Press. Thirty-three stories, from Sherlock Holmes to the present.
8. Estleman, Loren D., and Martin H. Greenberg, eds. *P. I. Files.* New York: Ivy Books/Ballantine. Fourteen private eye stories, 1948–88, in the first of a planned series.
9. Gorman, Ed, and Martin H. Greenberg, eds. *Stalkers.* New York: Roc Books/New American Library. Reprint of a 1989 limited edition of eighteen new crime-suspense stories, mainly horror, with the addition of a nineteenth story by Barry N. Malzberg.
10. Gorman, Ed, Bob Randisi, and Martin H. Greenberg, eds. *Under the Gun.* New York: Plume Books. Twenty-one of the best mystery and horror stories of 1988.
11. Greenberg, Martin H., ed. *The New Edgar Winners.* New York: Wynwood. Ten Edgar-winning stories from the past decade, in the annual anthology from Mystery Writers of America. Introduction by Donald E. Westlake.
12. Greenberg, Martin H., and Charles G. Waugh, eds. *Devil Worshippers.* New York: DAW Books. Fifteen stories, mainly fantasy, a few criminous.
13. Hale, Hilary, ed. *Winter's Crimes 22.* London: Macmillan. Seven new stories by British writers.
14. Harris, Herbert, ed. *John Creasey's Crime Collection 1990.* London: Gollancz. Sixteen stories, three new, in the annual anthology from the Crime Writers' Association. (U.S. edition: Trafalgar Square/David & Charles)
15. Heald, Tim, ed. *A Classic English Crime.* London: Pavilion. Thirteen new stories for the Agatha Christie Centenary, by members of the Crime Writers' Association. (U.S. edition: Mysterious Press)
16. Hoch, Edward D., ed. *The Year's Best Mystery and Suspense Stories 1990.* New York: Walker. Fourteen of the best stories of 1989.

17. Hutton, Don, ed. *The Super Feds: A Facsimile Selection of Dynamic G-Man Stories from the 1930s.* Mercer Island, WA: Starmont House. Stories from the pulps. (1989)
18. Jakubowski, Maxim, ed. *New Crimes 2.* London: Robinson. Nineteen new stories, two reprints and two articles. (U.S. editions of *New Crimes* series: Carroll & Graf)
19. Kaye, Marvin, ed. *Haunted America.* Garden City, NY: Doubleday/Guild America Books. Forty-seven stories, mainly fantasy, a few criminous.
20. Knight, Stephen, ed. *Dead Witness: Best Australian Mystery Stories.* New York: Penguin. Sixteen stories by Australian and British writers, 1866–1987.
21. (Mallard Press) *The Best Crime Stories.* New York: Mallard Press/Octopus. Twenty-four stories from various sources.
22. Manson, Cynthia. *Mystery for Christmas and Other Stories.* New York: Signet. Twelve Christmas mysteries from *EQMM* and *AHMM.*
23. (No Exit Press) *Match Me Sidney! The No Exit Press Crime Anthology.* Harpenden, England: No Exit Press. A British edition of the 1988 Private Eye Writers of America anthology *An Eye for Justice,* augmented by four additional stories plus Cornell Woolrich's 1942 novel *Phantom Lady.* (1989)
24. Pronzini, Bill, and Martin H. Greenberg, eds. *Christmas Out West.* New York: Doubleday. Thirteen Christmas stories with western settings, four new, some criminous.
25. Randisi, Robert J., ed. *Justice for Hire.* New York: Mysterious Press. Fifteen new stories in the fourth anthology from the Private Eye Writers of America.
26. Roberts, Garyn G., Gary Hoppenstand, and Ray B. Browne, eds. *Old Sleuth's Freaky Female Detectives (from the Dime Novels).* Bowling Green, OH: Bowling Green State University Popular Press. Three dime novels from *Old Sleuth Weekly,* 1886–1911, featuring early examples of women detectives.
27. Sellers, Peter, ed. *Cold Blood III.* Oakville, Ontario, Canada: Mosaic Press. Sixteen new stories by Canadian writers.
28. Sullivan, Eleanor, ed. *Ellery Queen Presents Readers' Choice.* New York: Davis Publications. Three winners and a

runner-up for *EQMM*'s annual Readers' Award, in a booklet published for promotional purposes.

29. Wallace, Marilyn, ed. *Sisters in Crime 2.* New York: Berkley. Twenty-one new stories by women writers, in a continuing anthology series.
30. ______. *Sisters in Crime 3.* New York: Berkley. Twenty-one stories, seventeen new.
31. Zahava, Irene, ed. *The Third WomanSleuth Anthology: Contemporary Mystery Stories by Women.* Freedom, CA: The Crossing Press. Seventeen stories, all but two new, in the third of an annual series.

III. Nonfiction

1. Breen, Jon L., and Martin H. Greenberg, eds. *Synod of Sleuths: Essays on Judeo-Christian Detective Fiction.* Metuchen, NJ: Scarecrow. Six essays.
2. Cannaday, Marilyn. *Bigger Than Life: The Creator of Doc Savage.* Bowling Green, OH: Bowling Green State University Popular Press. A critical biography of pulp writer and mystery novelist Lester Dent.
3. Conquest, John. *Trouble Is Their Business: Private Eyes in Fiction, Film, and Television, 1927–1988.* New York: Garland. A detailed listing by author, with cross-references by character name.
4. Coren, Michael. *Gilbert: The Man Who Was G. K. Chesterton.* New York: Paragon House. A new biography of Father Brown's creator.
5. Depkin, F. *Sherlock Holmes, Raffles and Their Prototypes.* New York: Magico. A translation and digest, by Jay F. Christ, of a book first published in Germany in 1914.
6. Drew, Bernard A. *Lawmen in Scarlet: An Annotated Guide to the Royal Canadian Mounted Police in Print and Performance.* Metuchen, NJ: Scarecrow Press. Annotated listings for some 500 works of fiction and 225 films in the mystery, western, adventure, and romance genres.
7. Eskin, Stanley G. *Simenon: A Critical Biography.* Jefferson,

NC: McFarland. A detailed biography of Maigret's creator, with bibliography and filmography. (1987)

8. Falk, Quentin. *Travels in Greeneland: The Cinema of Graham Greene*. London: Quartet Books. Updated version of a 1984 book.
9. Gibbs, Rowen, and Richard Williams. *Ngaio Marsh, a Bibliography of English Language Publications*. Scunthorpe, England: Dragonby Press. A booklet that includes valuations of first editions.
10. Gill, Gillian. *Agatha Christie: The Woman and Her Mysteries*. New York: The Free Press. A study of her life and writing.
11. Haining, Peter. *Agatha Christie: Murder in Four Acts*. London: Virgin/W. H. Allen. Illustrated survey of Christie's work on stage, film, radio, and television.
12. Hart, Anne. *The Life and Times of Hercule Poirot*. New York: Putnam. A "biography" of Agatha Christie's famed sleuth.
13. Hieb, Louis A. *Tony Hillerman—A Bibliography*. Tucson: Press of the Gigantic Hound. A bibliography of the creator of Navajo detectives Joe Leaphorn and Jim Chee.
14. Huang, Jim, ed. *The Drood Review's 1990 Mystery Yearbook*. Boston: Crum Creek Press. Second of an annual series listing books published during the previous year, together with awards, periodicals, bookshops, organizations, and conventions.
15. Joshi, S. T. *John Dickson Carr: A Critical Study*. Bowling Green, OH: Bowling Green State University Popular Press. A study of Carr's various detective characters, together with an analysis of his philosophy and writing techniques, and a bibliography of his work.
16. Kenney, Catherine. *The Remarkable Case of Dorothy L. Sayers*. Kent, OH: Kent State University Press. A new biography of Lord Peter Wimsey's creator.
17. Lellenberg, Jon L. *Nova 57 Minor: The Waxing and Waning of the Sixty-First Adventure of Sherlock Holmes*. Bloomington, IN: Gaslight Publications. How a pastiche was mistaken for a genuine Holmes story after Doyle's death, complete with the story itself, by Arthur Whitaker.

18. Lewis, Peter. *Eric Ambler*. New York: Continuum. Ambler's life and work, with a detailed study of his eighteen novels.
19. Lovisi, Gary. *Sherlock Holmes: The Great Detective in Paperback*. Brooklyn, NY: Gryphon Publications. A bibliography of American and British paperback editions of the Holmes books.
20. Malloy, William. *The Mystery Book of Days*. New York: Mysterious Press. A datebook of important events linked to mystery fiction.
21. McCormick, Donald, and Katy Fletcher. *Spy Fiction: A Connoisseur's Guide*. New York: Facts on File. A greatly expanded version of the 1977 volume *Who's Who in Spy Fiction*.
22. McLeish, Kenneth, and Valerie McLeish. *Bloomsbury Good Reading Guide to Murder, Crime Fiction & Thrillers*. London: Bloomsbury. Alphabetical guide to leading mystery writers and subject areas.
23. Menendez, Albert J. *The Subject Is Murder: A Selective Guide to Mystery Fiction, Volume 2*. New York: Garland. A supplement to the 1986 guide, covering mysteries published since 1985.
24. Moody, Susan, ed. *The Hatchards Crime Companion: 100 Top Crime Novels Selected by the Crime Writers' Association*. London: Hatchards. Results of a poll of CWA members, with a brief comment on each book.
25. Morris, Virginia. *Double Jeopardy: Women Who Kill in Victorian Fiction*. Ithaca, NY: University Press of Kentucky. A study of violent women in Victorian literature.
26. Newton, Michael. *Armed and Dangerous: A Writer's Guide to Weapons*. Cincinnati: Writer's Digest Books. A comprehensive history, description, and glossary of firearms, with common mistakes the writer should avoid.
27. Panek, Leroy Lad. *Probable Cause: Crime Fiction in America*. Bowling Green, OH: Bowling Green State University Popular Press. A study of how and why American crime fiction has developed differently from its British cousin.
28. Roth, Martin. *The Writer's Complete Crime Reference Book*. Cincinnati: Writer's Digest Books. A handbook of police procedure for the crime writer.

29. Sampson, Robert. *Deadly Excitements: Shadows & Phantoms*. Bowling Green, OH: Bowling Green State University Popular Press. Twenty-nine articles on the pulp magazines, twenty-four reprinted from various fan publications, 1972–89.
30. ______. *Yesterday's Faces: Volume 5, Dangerous Horizons*. Bowling Green, OH: Bowling Green State University Popular Press. A continuing study of pulp magazine characters, with this volume devoted to adventure heroes.
31. Schleh, Eugene, ed. *Mysteries of Africa*. Bowling Green, OH: Bowling Green State University Popular Press. Seven essays by various hands examining mystery writers like Elspeth Huxley, James McClure, and Matthew Head who frequently used African settings. Native African mystery writers are included.
32. Schopen, Bernard A. *Ross Macdonald*. Boston: Twayne. A study of his work.
33. Stevens, Serita Deborah, and Anne Klarner. *Deadly Doses: A Writer's Guide to Poisons*. Cincinnati: Writer's Digest Books. Detailed information, including symptoms and antidotes, for household, medical, industrial, and other poisons, including poisonous snakes and spiders.
34. Underwood, Lynn, ed. *Agatha Christie*. Glasgow: HarperCollins. The official Christie Centenary Celebration book, profusely illustrated, containing brief articles and reminiscences, lists of her books, plays and films, and an early uncollected short story, "Trap for the Unwary." Published for the Agatha Christie Centenary Trust by Belgrave Publishing, Ltd., distributed by HarperCollins.

AWARDS

Mystery Writers of America "Edgar" Awards

Best Novel: Julie Smith, *New Orleans Mourning* (St. Martin's Press)

Best First Novel: Patricia Daniels Cornwell, *Postmortem* (Scribners)

Best Original Paperback: David Handler, *The Man Who Would Be F. Scott Fitzgerald* (Bantam)

Best Fact Crime: Peter Maas, *In a Child's Name* (Simon & Schuster)

Best Critical/Biographical: John Conquest, *Trouble Is Their Business: Private Eyes in Fiction, Film and Television, 1927–1988* (Garland)

Best Short Story: Lynne Barrett, "Elvis Lives" (*EQMM*, September)

Best Young Adult: Chap Reaver, *Mote* (Delacorte)

Best Juvenile: Pam Conrad, *Stonewords* (Harper & Row)

Best Episode in a Television Series: Paul Brown, "Goodnight, Dear Heart" (*Quantum Leap*, NBC)

Best Television Feature: Cynthia Cidre, *Killing in a Small Town*, based on the book *Evidence of Love* by John Bloom and Jim Arkinson (CBS)

Best Motion Picture: Donald E. Westlake, *The Grifters*, based on the novel by Jom Thompson (Miramax)

Grandmaster: Tony Hillerman

Special Edgar: Jay Robert Nash, *The Encyclopedia of World Crime*

Robert L. Fish Award: Jerry F. Skarky, "Willie's Story" (*AHMM*, June)

Best Play: Rupert Holmes, *Accomplice*

Crime Writers Association (Britain)

Gold Dagger: Reginald Hill, *Bones and Silence* (Collins; U.S. edition: Delacorte)

Silver Dagger: Mike Phillips, *The Late Candidate* (Michael Joseph)

Gold Dagger for Nonfiction: Jonathan Goodman, *The Passing of Starr Faithfull* (Piatkus)
John Creasey Memorial Award for First Novel: Patricia Daniels Cornwell, *Postmortem* (Macdonald; U.S. edition: Scribners)
Last Laugh Award: Simon Shaw, *Killer Cinderella* (Gollancz)
CWA '92 Award: Michael Dibdin, *Vendetta* (Faber)
Rumpole Award: Frances Fyfield, *Trial by Fire* (Heinemann)
Diamond Dagger Award: Julian Symons

Crime Writers of Canada "Arthur Ellis" Awards (for 1989)

Best Novel: Laurence Gough, *Hot Shots* (Gollancz)
Best First Novel: John Lawrence Reynolds, *The Man Who Murdered God* (Viking)
Best Nonfiction: Lisa Priest, *Conspiracy of Silence* (McClelland & Stewart)
Best Short Fiction: Josef Skvorecky, "Humbug" (*The End of Lieutenant Boruvka*, Lester & Orpen Dennys; U.S. edition: Norton)
Special Award: Eric Wilson

Private Eye Writers of America "Shamus" Awards (for 1989)

Best Novel: Jonathan Valin, *Extenuating Circumstances* (Delacorte)
Best First Novel: Karen Kijewski, *Katwalk* (St. Martin's Press)
Best Paperback Original: Rob Kantner, *Hell's Only Half Full* (Bantam)
Best Short Story: Mickey Spillane, "The Killing Man" (*Playboy*)

Bouchercon "Anthony" Awards (for 1989)

Best Novel: Sarah Caudwell, *The Sirens Sang of Murder* (Delacorte)
Best First Novel: Karen Kijewski, *Katwalk* (St. Martin's Press)
Best Paperback Original: Carolyn Hart, *Honeymoon with Murder* (Bantam)
Best Short Story: Nancy Pickard, "Afraid All the Time" (*Sisters in Crime*, Berkley)
Best Film: *Crimes and Misdemeanors*
Best Television Series: *Inspector Morse* (*Mystery*, PBS)

Malice Domestic "Agatha" Awards (for 1989)

Best "Domestic" Novel: Elizabeth Peters, *Naked Once More* (Warner)

Best "Domestic" First Novel: Jill Churchill, *Grime and Punishment* (Bantam)

Best "Domestic" Short Story: Sharyn McCrumb, "A Wee Doch and Doris" (*Mistletoe Mysteries*)

Lifetime Achievement: Phyllis A. Whitney

NECROLOGY

1. Joseph Payne Brennan (1918–90). Author of mystery and fantasy fiction, including three collections of stories about psychic sleuth Lucius Leffing, as well as a detective novel, *Evil Always Ends* (1982).
2. Robert D. Brown (1924–90). Author of three mystery novels as "R. D. Brown," including the paperback Edgar nominee *Hazzard* (1986).
3. Bernice Carey (1910–90). Author of nine mystery novels, 1949–55, notably *The Beautiful Stranger* (1951) and *The Three Widows* (1952).
4. T. E. B. Clarke (1907–89). British author of seven mystery novels, including *Murder at Buckingham Palace* (1982). Thomas Ernest Bennett Clarke won an Academy Award for his 1951 screenplay *The Lavender Hill Mob*.
5. Roald Dahl (1916–90). Popular British author of children's books and macabre crime stories, including his Edgar-winning collection *Someone Like You* (1953) and *Kiss Kiss* (1960).
6. Robert George Dean (1904?–89). Author of fifteen mystery novels, 1936–53, plus four spy novels as "George Griswold," 1952–55.
7. Rex Dolphin (1915–90). British author of ten mystery novels, 1959–69, all but one about Sexton Blake, a popular series sleuth whose cases were recorded by many authors.
8. Friedrich Duerrenmatt (1921–90). Swiss playwright and novelist, best known for his drama *The Visit* (1958) and his five suspense novels beginning with *The Judge and His Hangman* (1954).
9. Stephen Frances (1917–90). British author of two mystery thrillers under his own name and several under "house names" like "Hank Janson" and "Peter Saxon."

10. Leo Giroux (1934?–90). Author of three horror-suspense novels starting with *The Rishi* (1985).
11. Jeanne Hart (?–1990). Author of two novels, including *Fetish.* (1987)
12. Dan Herr (1917?–90). Coeditor with Joel Wells of two anthologies of Catholic mysteries, *Bodies and Souls* (1961) and *Bodies and Spirits* (1964).
13. Jack Iams (1910–90). Author of eight mystery novels, 1947–55, notably *Girl Meets Body* (1947) and *Death Draws the Line* (1949).
14. Jean Johnson (1897?–1989). Short-story writer, contributor to *Mystery Digest, Detective Story Magazine*, and other publications.
15. Laurence Meynell (1899–1989). British author of more than seventy mystery novels and thrillers beginning with *Bluefeather* (1928).
16. Joyce Porter (1924–90). British author of some nineteen novels and fifteen short stories, many about Inspector Dover.
17. Manuel Puig (1932–90). Mainstream Argentine writer who authored a single detective novel, *The Buenos Aires Affair* (1976).
18. Peter Rabe (1921–90). Author of some twenty-five novels, mainly paperback, 1955–74, notably *Murder Me For Nickels* (1960).
19. Dorothy James Roberts (1903–90). Historical novelist; probable author, as "Peter Mortimer," of a single mystery novel, *If a Body Kill a Body* (1946).
20. Elliot Roosevelt (1910–90). Son of President Franklin D. Roosevelt and author of six novels with his mother, Eleanor, as detective.
21. Belle Spewack (1899–1990). Coauthor, with husband Samuel, of two mystery novels and a mystery play, 1928–34.
22. Nedra Tyre (1921–90). Author of six mystery novels, 1952–71, starting with *Mouse in Eternity*.
23. Charles Spain Verral (?–1990). Adventure pulp writer who contributed occasional mysteries to *Clues, Thrilling Detective*, and other pulps.

24. Charles Marquis Warren (1912–90). Historical novelist who published a single mystery, *Deadhead* (1949).
25. Dr. Julian Wolff (1904?–90). Noted Sherlockian, editor of *The Baker Street Journal*, and head of the Baker Street Irregulars, 1960–86.
26. Hazel Wynn-Jones (?–1990). British author of three books, including *Death and the Trumpets of Tuscany*.

HONOR ROLL

Abbreviations:
AHMM—Alfred Hitchcock's Mystery Magazine
EQMM—Ellery Queen's Mystery Magazine
(*Starred stories are included in this volume. All dates are 1990.*)

Adcock, Thomas, "Straight Down the Middle," *AHMM*, July
Ardai, Charles, "The Balancing Man," *AHMM*, May
Bankier, William, "The Locked Roomette," *EQMM*, November
———, "A One-Man Dog," *EQMM*, December
Barnard, Robert, "An Exceptional Night," *EQMM*, March
*Barrett, Lynne, "Elvis Lives," *EQMM*, September
Block, Lawrence, "The Burglar Who Dropped in on Elvis," *Playboy*, April
*———, "Answers to Soldier," *Playboy*, June
Bullard, Barbara C., "Are You Done?" *EQMM*, October
Carroll, William J., Jr., "Silent Warning," *AHMM*, September
Caudwell, Sarah, "An Acquaintance with Mr. Collins," *A Suit of Diamonds*
*Cohen, Stanley, "Hello! My Name Is Irving Wasserman," *A Body Is Found*
Crawford, Dan, "Cargo," *AHMM*, August
Crenshaw, Bill, "Passing for Love," *AHMM*, March
D'Ath, Justin, "Whatever Happened to Crocodile Jarvis?" *AHMM*, August
Davis, Dorothy Salisbury, "A Silver Thimble," *A Body Is Found*
Dundee, Wayne D., "Naughty, Naughty," *Justice for Hire*
Fredericks, W. W., "Paid in Full," *AHMM*, February
Friedman, Mickey, "Night in the Lonesome October," *A Body Is Found*
———, "Lucky Numbers," *Sisters in Crime 2*
Geraghty, Margaret, "Ten Brown Bottles," *EQMM*, September
*Gorman, Ed, "Prisoners," *New Crimes*
*Grafton, Sue, "A Poison That Leaves No Trace," *Sisters in Crime 2*

Hardwicke, Glyn, "The Elixer," *EQMM*, April
*Harrington, Joyce, "Andrew, My Son," *Sisters in Crime 2*
______, "The Makeover," *Cosmopolitan*, September
Healy, Jeremiah, "Someone Turn Out the Lights," *Justice for Hire*
Hess, Joan, "Another Room," *EQMM*, October
Hoch, Edward D., "Captain Leopold's Birthday," *EQMM*, February
______, "The Crypt of the Gypsy Saint," *EQMM*, April
*______, "The Detective's Wife," *Crosscurrents*, October
______, "The Problem of the Haunted Tepee," *EQMM*, December
Hodgkinson, Debbie, "Part Time," *AHMM*, March
Howard, Clark, "Return to the River Kwai," *EQMM*, April
*______, "Challenge the Widow-Maker," *EQMM*, August
______, "Deeds of Valor," *EQMM*, November
Ison, Graham, "At Last, You Bitch," *Winter's Crimes 22*
Jarrett, Flip, "The Game," *EQMM*, November
Kantner, Rob, "Tall Boys," *AHMM*, March
Kraft, Gabrielle, "Wow Finish," *Sisters in Crime 3*
Limon, Martin, "A Coffin of Rice," *AHMM*, June
Lovesey, Peter, "The Valuation," *EQMM*, February
Malzberg, Barry N., "Darwinian Facts," *Stalkers*
Maron, Margaret, "My Mother, My Daughter, Me," *AHMM*, March
Massarelli, Peter, "Once Upon a Time," *EQMM*, December
McCrumb, Sharyn, "The Luncheon," *Sisters in Crime 2*
Moody, Susan, "Freedom," *New Crimes 2*
Muller, Marcia, "Somewhere in the City," *The Armchair Detective*, Spring
Murphy, Warren, "And One for the Little Girl," *A Body Is Found*
O'Brien, Meg, "Kill the Woman and Child," *Sisters in Crime 3*
Olson, Donald, "No Hard Feelings," *EQMM*, January
______, "The Jumbo Ivories," *EQMM*, March
______, "Incident in Termite Park," *EQMM*, May
______, "By Night Disguised," *AHMM*, October
Owens, Barbara, "A Marty Kind of Guy," *EQMM*, September
*Pronzini, Bill, "Stakeout," *Justice for Hire*
*Rendell, Ruth, "An Unwanted Woman," *EQMM*, December
Savage, Ernest, "Shannon's Way," *EQMM*, January

———, "A Hell of a Couple of Days," *EQMM*, March
Skvorecky, Josef, "Humbug," *The End of Lieutenant Boruvka*
Slesar, Henry, "Hanged for a Sheep," *EQMM*, June
Stodghill, Dick, "Pictures in a Book," *AHMM*, February
*Symons, Julian, "The Conjuring Trick," *EQMM*, March
Thomson, June, "Wrong Number," *EQMM*, April
Turnbull, Peter, "Perverse Judgement," *EQMM*, July
Wasylyk, Stephen, "Collision," *AHMM*, November
*Westlake, Donald E., "A Midsummer Daydream," *Playboy*, May
Wheat, Carolyn, "Cousin Cora," *Sisters in Crime 2*
*———, "Three-Time Loser," *The Armchair Detective*, Fall
White, Teri, "Outlaw Blues," *Sisters in Crime 3*
Whitehead, J. W., "The Right Thing," *EQMM*, June